RUNAWAY TIDE

A SEA GLASS INN NOVEL

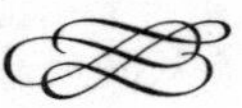

JULIE CAROBINI

Dolphin Gate Books

Cover photos from Shutterstock.com and Depositphotos.com

Cover design by Roseanna White Designs

JULIE CAROBINI writes inspirational beach romances and cozy mysteries … with a twist. Visit her at www.juliecarobini.com

ALSO BY JULIE CAROBINI

Sea Glass Inn Novels

Walking on Sea Glass

Runaway Tide

Otter Bay Novels

Sweet Waters

A Shore Thing

Fade to Blue

The Chocolate Series

Chocolate Beach

Truffles by the Sea

Mocha Sunrise

Available in ebook (print coming soon):

Cottage Grove Mysteries

The Christmas Thief

All Was Calm

"We can nowhere evade the presence of God … He walks everywhere incognito."

— C.S. LEWIS

CHAPTER 1

Regret slid through Meg like the cold wash of the morning tide. Still, she ran. Wet sand flying. Salt-saturated air on her skin. No matter that she wore her favorite suit, the one with the Gucci calfskin belt that made her long to stroll a piazza in Milan. Earlier this morning after she and Jackson Riley, her new boss, clashed over an agreement he'd made behind her back with one of *her* clients, she kicked off her ALDOs and took off for the beach. Anything to get away from ... *him*.

Maybe she should have quit the moment her ex became her boss. Surely she would have been able to find another sales position, maybe even set down roots in some other beautiful place. She had both the education and real-world experience to find such a position. Jackson's father, William, had seen to that—something for which she would be eternally grateful.

Jackson, a.k.a. "the enemy," ran behind her now, gaining on her. She pictured the contours of the enemy's face, the cleft of his chin ... those rich browns that blended to form the waves in his hair—and hated herself for it. What might have been between them ... could never be. He had made that clear years before. Meg accelerated, kicking up wet sand behind her, frustration and old hurts building. What a spectacle they must have made running down the beach!

Jackson closed the gap between them. Though no match for his strength, she believed she could outrun him. He had surprised her with his speed, but she doubled her efforts, pumping her arms like a triathlete racing toward the next leg of her event.

Her lungs constricted. Liddy, her best friend, chose running as a sport, something she did to stay in shape, maybe even de-stress after a long day, but Meg? Not so much. Pain jarred her right knee, which threatened to collapse, but pride kept moving her forward, the heels of her feet digging into wet sand, the bounce of labored breaths in her chest. Oh! She would give Liddy so much grief about this later.

"Meg—slow down." The words flew from Jackson's mouth like darts.

She did not want to talk to him. She wouldn't! Not after what he had done …

Jackson chased after her, skirting the ocean's edge, the enemy who would not give up. Neither would she.

What was wrong with her? Meg prided herself on being calm. She was the doer, the poker face when times called for it. An inkling in her brain said she should slow down long enough to hear him out—it was the right thing to do, the mature choice. The last place she ever thought she would find herself was on the beach butting heads with her boss. If William were alive, that would still be the case. William had always been like a patient father to her, teaching her how to navigate the hotel business, and sometimes life in general.

Though Jackson had been slow to surface after his father's death, that all changed recently when his sister Pepper decided to bring her accounting skills to the company. Since then Jackson appeared to have something to prove—that he was no longer the restless wanderer, the man who seemed to have no regard for the family business. He looked the part, too. Now whenever he strolled through the inn's entry doors, a ripple skittered through the staff. The women swooned. The fabric of European-cut suits hugged his body, showing off his efforts at the gym. His once-lean frame had morphed into cut edges embraced by tanned skin.

Was it her imagination or did she really feel the heat of Jackson's breath on her neck as she ran from him? A chill traversed down her arm. She could almost sense his hot grip on her forearm, the strength of his tug, pulling her closer to his body. She was not his possession. Not now, not ever again.

She gulped muggy air, pulling it deeper into her lungs.

"Meg!"

She slowed, turned, and glared at him, a low buzz circling her head. "Leave. Me. Alone."

"I can't."

His eyes were hooded, as if she had caused him some kind of pain, but she knew it was all an act. "You won't."

She kept her eyes trained on him. His shoulders rose and fell, his breathing matching their rhythm. His cheeks burned red and he moistened his lips. He did not, however, look away from her. "Are you willing to talk now?"

Meg crossed her arms in front of her ribcage, coaxing her body not to show any sign of stress, certainly nothing to match Jackson's level of fatigue. As far as she was concerned, the mile-long run they had both meted out—in business wear, no less—took nothing more from her than a turn down the first-floor interior hall of Sea Glass Inn might have.

Jackson exhaled. "Adele is the mother of a college buddy. Just a chance meeting and I jumped on it. For the good of the hotel, of course."

Inhale. Exhale. Look at him, she thought, standing there trying to sound rational, as if he had not just swooped in and caught the big fish that she had been baiting for months. If Jackson had not wrangled …

"You said yourself she had been waffling about whether to

bring her company to us. The opportunity to end that indecision presented itself to me without any warning."

She considered how he looked at her, his stare unwavering, as if imploring her to hear him out, to realize that *she* was being unreasonable. Maybe even selfish.

He took a step toward her, the naughty puppy that had run away. Inches from her now, the hardness of his chest pressed against his dress shirt, perspiration seeping through. "Can't we both admit that I did you a favor?"

Meg gasped. "A favor? Who asked you to?"

He bit down on his bottom lip, as if to shut himself up. Surely he knew that his reasoning was about to implode—and that she would do nothing to stop it. "You ... you gave away too much, Jackson. And right when I was about to close a great deal all around. How was that doing me—or the hotel—any favors?"

His eyes flashed as if she had dared to do the unthinkable: challenge Jackson Riley, hotel owner ... her boss.

Her heart squeezed in her chest. "I think you figured out that you had a connection to my client and you made a meeting happen so you could be the hero. Did you have a copy of a contract in your back pocket too? And a pen for her to sign it right then and there?"

"You're being ridiculous now."

Maybe, but she didn't care. The realization that life at the inn had forever changed brought a lump to her throat. "Your father would never have said something like that to me."

"My father ... my father did a lot of things that I question."

"Like promote me to sales director?"

He didn't answer. Didn't have to. William was gone and Jackson called the shots now. Who was she to question him? She had made a promise to William that she would stay on at Sea Glass Inn and help make it, and the other inns in the chain, successful. Did anyone other than her care about that now? She dropped her arms to her sides, pursed her lips, and turned to run again. But he took hold of her upper arm and drew her back toward him. "That's not what I meant."

"Forget it. It's obvious we aren't meant to have this conversation."

"And what conversation is that?"

She looked dead into his eyes "The one about why you have been trying to get rid of me ever since your father died and you became head of the hotel chain."

"Nothing about that sentence is true."

"No?"

He stepped closer, both hands on her upper arms now. His touch both warmed her and caused goosebumps to alight on her skin. A talent, for sure. A sea breeze tousled his hair, mesmerizing her. Looking away would break the spell … but did she really want to be the one to break it?

"I do not have it out for you, Meg," he said quietly, drawing her attention back to his mouth. "My father valued your work ethic and so do I."

Sweet talker.

He frowned, his eyes penetrating. "Did I say something wrong … again?"

This time, she looked away. If this were any other employer … any other situation … she could make sense of it. But there was nothing normal about this situation. Rational people did not get into sparring matches with their bosses on the beach. Not without litigation of some sort.

Jackson stepped closer, his voice so low she had to strain to hear it over the sound of coursing waves. "When we get back to the hotel, let's pull out the contract and go over it together."

Was he really extending a peace offering? After these many months of switching between the cold shoulder or the perfunctory comment? He gave her a fraction of a smile, reminding her, albeit briefly, of when they had spent time alone together. Before he left the state …

"Meg?"

She couldn't take her eyes from his, except to let her gaze drop to his mouth. Why did he leave her when he did? Didn't he realize that she had done what she thought best. He cut off her thoughts with the brush of his lips, followed by a kiss that tasted wild and unprovoked. One hand tangled with her hair as the other found the small of her back. Her knees weakened as she pressed herself into him.

Slowly, he pulled his mouth away, eliciting a gasp from her. He smiled more widely this time, his voice thick. "My father was right about you," he whispered. "You are stubborn ... but you always come around."

Her stomach tumbled sharply. Hot tears pushed toward the corners of her eyes. The kiss ... this show of affection had nothing to do with her, with their past, and everything to do with him. She looked up, ignoring the wide-eyed look of surprise on his face. That was all an act, too. "Never again, Jackson."

She stumbled backward then recovered, vaguely aware of that same low buzz overhead. She began to run again, harder this time, her feet somehow aware of the importance of getting far away from Jackson as fast as possible.

"Meg—hold up!"

Tears fell from her eyes in angry bursts. She had allowed herself to weaken, but it would not happen again. She vowed to avoid any such ache in her chest ever again.

"Duck!"

Meg jerked a look back, as if by reflex. Despite the shadow that passed over her, she did not slow—until her foot collided with something buried in the sand. Without warning, she fell to the sand, the sickening snap of bone the only sound that lingered. With a searing start, she realized that the throbbing, unrelenting pain coursing through her body emanated from her foot.

So much for thinking Meg would be pleased with his help. Jackson sat back, leaning with force against the leather loveseat in his condo, chin up toward the ceiling, picturing Meg as she confronted him on the beach. Those butterfly lashes reawakened something in him that, up until now, he had chosen to forget.

Jackson picked up his drink from the glass coffee table and took a swig, remembering the way his day had started. He had casually mentioned to Meg that he'd signed a client she had sent a proposal to, but with one look, she had set him ablaze. Her scrutiny had rocked him, so much that he had to remind himself that *he* was the head of Riley Holdings—not Meg.

He should not have been surprised by her reaction. Though they were about the same age, Meg had been a part of the family hotel chain for … well, longer than he had—though Jackson's absence had not been his idea. His father had sent him away and that was that.

Over the years, Meg had become known around the hotel for her quick wit and business acumen, her ability to catch a plane on a phone call's notice, all wrapped up in a quiet and strikingly professional woman. Well, except for the tirade she had directed his way this afternoon.

Meg had wandered into his father's office one foggy afternoon in late winter. Not long after that day, his father took Meg on as his assistant, well before she had any business answering phones for the likes of William Riley, president of Riley Holdings. His father had taken a liking to her unlike anyone else he had ever known. "The best way to find out if you trust someone," his father had once said, quoting Hemingway, "is to trust them."

Trust. Now there's a loaded word. Had his father ever trusted him? Would he even be in this position now if his father had not died so suddenly?

He shut his eyes, reliving the years that he barely remembered. When his father hired Meg, Jackson had been too busy attending classes and chasing late-night ragers to care much about the petite brunette who had turned William Riley's office into a virtual command center for his burgeoning company.

But even through all the repeated studying and partying, Jackson noticed the new life Meg had given a simple admin position. His father had apparently been impressed because he promoted Meg first to sales assistant, then sales manager, and finally, to sales director for the entire chain of boutique hotels—small and fledgling as it may have been. Of course, it had grown substantially since then.

What happened between Jackson and Meg during the years in between was … complicated. And until today, over. Or so he thought. Jittery, he set down his glass and stood, looking into the black night through his living room window. Though he searched for stars, nothing remarkable stood out to him.

Admittedly, she had made him angry with her accusations—and with her taunts du jour about his father. He rubbed the back of his neck, his muscles taut and unforgiving. How could he stay angry with her when she had no idea of the shortfall the company was facing?

He had not set out to pull the rug out from under her by signing Adele's group to the hotel. It had been Pepper's idea, really. A good one from her, for once. "Didn't you say you once knew the son of the owner of CartCo?" she had said.

Though he had mentioned that fact in a moment of bravado, it was partially true. He had once lived in the same residence hall as the woman's son, Todd. So when he had found the opportunity to bump into Todd at a college game, he asked if his mother still headed up CartCo. And when he'd said yes? Well. The rest was history.

When Meg found out that CartCo had signed with him and not with her, he might as well have told her that he was burning down the hotel and building a sports bar in its place. Her reaction stunned him at first. Meg had always kept her emotions in check around the staff. His father appreciated this about her—the ability to stay calm amidst the dizzying speed of hotel work, including the often-intense volley of negotiations. It had taken time—and distance—for Jackson to cultivate that ability for himself, something he surely would have perfected if his father had not died so suddenly.

After telling him what she thought of him, Meg marched off to the beach, an unreasonable jut to her chin. He should have left her there to cool off, but something about her actions dared him to follow her. By the time he reached the sand, she was already far ahead of him. He had a second chance to stop himself—and should have—but she had already burned so far under his skin that he blistered. First, she laid into him about the contract, then she taunted him about his father—an off-limits subject if he had ever heard one.

Jackson tried to shake off the memory. He sat down, took up his glass again, and gulped down the rest of his drink. But he could not stop thinking about Meg and the way she had taken him on. Her warm skin had flushed, fire intensifying those almond-shaped eyes until a yearning tugged at him. He should have been incensed by her harsh tone, but his body had been taken over by aliens. Yeah, that was it. Aliens had shot him up with some sort of magic and paralyzed all threads of common sense.

By the time he had caught up to her, he was panting like a jackass, his mind unable to provide reason or to suffocate his yearning to spin her toward him and kiss her. Hard. If he were honest, he had dreamed of that moment ever since he had left California, long before his father passed away. When the fantasy presented itself for the taking, he stepped into it with full force, and for a brief few seconds, the fantasy had nothing on that kiss: comfort and sizzle in one. She had kissed him back, no doubt. But when he whispered something … what was it he had said, exactly? That she was stubborn? Her expression had fallen into a torturously flat line. She wrenched herself away from him and began to run again, and he just watched, rooted to the spot. It was as if he had become hyper focused on her movement away from him, as if his one chance to right the wrongs were charging away forever.

Something, though, caught his eye briefly. What kind of bird was that? He still wasn't sure. All he could remember was staring after her, his mind in a state of physical and emotional confusion, before catching sight of her being dive-bombed. He called out to her. She spun back around and took off again, her feet catching on a pair of flip-flops buried in the sand. His heart dropped to his gut when she went down, and he took off, skidding into the sand next to her. Agony marred her face, the sound of her pained cry stabbing at him, and any frustration over her accusations had fled.

CHAPTER 2

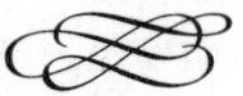

"What were you running from, anyway?" Her friend Liddy sat curled up on the end of the couch after driving Meg home from the emergency room.

Meg twisted her mouth and looked away. "You mean *who*."

"Wait ... you were running from a who?"

Meg had managed to dodge this detail—and any mention of "the kiss"—on the ride home. Nor had she told Liddy about the onlookers on the beach who had gathered around her, the ones Jackson had shooed away as the lifeguard and his stretcher showed up. Jackson had driven her to the emergency room, but as soon as she had been safely deposited inside, Meg asked him to leave. She shifted and winced, as much from the pain as from all memory of the incident.

Liddy leapt up. "What can I get for you? Water? Coffee? Glass of wine?"

Meg nestled against the mountain of pillows Liddy had piled behind her head. The doctor said she was lucky—though her foot sustained a fracture, the bones did not appear to be displaced. In other words, she might not have to have surgery.

"Probably shouldn't mix wine with the meds—tempting as

that is."

Liddy nodded, her hand migrating to the bump at her abdomen.

"Let's talk about something else," Meg said, weary. "Tell me about my little nephew or niece."

"Baby is doing great … and nice try, by the way. I still want to know who you were running from. Though I have my suspicions."

"My behavior was horrifying, Lid. I don't know what happened—no, wait. I do. I snapped. He knew how hard I had been working to nail down a contract with CartCo, so when I heard that he signed them for a better deal and without even consulting me, I lost it."

"So, you were running from Jackson … as in, physically running?"

Meg slid a look at Liddy, whose mouth hung open. She groaned. "You look as incredulous as I feel. Yes! I physically ran from Jackson."

"But you … you don't like running. You're a yoga girl."

"Somehow pulling a star pose didn't seem like it would be as effective."

"Wow. Who knew you had that in you?" Liddy said, lying back as if trying to take it all in. "At least you're done now with the chef's world tour."

Last year the hotel's head chef won a spot on the show *Celebrity Chef,* and Meg had spun that adventure into a marketing gold mine for the small chain by traveling around the country with him as he gave cooking demos at their other properties. Alas, Chef left the company to open his own restaurant, a move that Pepper blamed on Meg. "You made him too popular—too valuable!"

Meg could never win with that woman.

"Don't remind me about all the travel I did." A flush of something uncomfortable rolled through her. Her mind spun and Meg held back a sob, unsure of whether it was the meds talking or the sobering realization that she might be grounded for a while. "I'm supposed to go to Florida tomorrow."

"Well, that's not happening."

"I can't believe it. Instead of watching amazing sunsets on Siesta Key, I'm stuck on this couch. It fries me that Pepper is going in my place."

Liddy's expression perked. "Really?"

Pepper's presence around the inn was relatively new, and most assuredly unwelcome. After William died and it became clear that Pepper would co-lead the company with Jackson, the inn went through some growing pains—a.k.a. disputes between the siblings. Mostly, though, these spats were handled off-site and the staff was blissfully unaware. That is, until both Jackson and Pepper decided to make Sea Glass Inn their home base—and Pepper's overbearing attitude toward the staff began to surface. "Fine, fine. I know the team will be happy to see Pepper gone. I just wish it were me."

"Maybe this is a sign that you should slow down a little. I am horrified that you got hurt—you know I am—but you're always darting off to faraway places. Maybe all this head time you're going to have will be good for you. You'll be able to reflect and pray, and you'll finally get some much-needed rest so you can heal."

Healing. There was a novel thought. Maybe she should jet off to Europe. Whenever William seemed to be having a tough day he would say, "Meg, book me a trip to Italy!"

She'd laugh and say, "You're not going to Italy. Too much to do here."

He would always shake his head then, a sad little smile on his face. "Ah, but Italy … Italy will always heal!"

Liddy watched her. "You okay?"

"Yes, sorry. Lost in thought from all the … medication. If you're thinking that I plan to sit on this couch all day, though, well, I have no intention of doing that."

"I just meant I hope that you cancel some of your trips for a while. I mean, I need my friend here to lie to me when my chin doubles and my varicose veins start showing!"

"You have Beau for that!"

"Good thing my husband's a terrible liar." She paused. "Things are really going to change. I always thought I'd have children someday but rarely ever thought seriously about what that would be like in the day-to-day."

"Aw, you'll be a great mother."

"I know we don't talk about this very often, but what can I say? I have baby brain these days. What about you, Meggy? Do you want to have kids someday?"

She turned an answer over in her mind. "That's not something I've thought about much. For me, life is more about seeing the world and booking the next big juicy event." She glanced at Liddy, who subconsciously rubbed her belly. "Guess that sounds rather shallow, doesn't it?"

"Of course not. You do a great job for Sea Glass Inns—I had no idea how good you were until I moved out here and started working with you. Honestly, if you weren't my best friend I might've been a little intimidated by you."

Meg winced, but this time not from physical pain.

"Don't take that the wrong way. I just meant that you are focused and professional ... and have I mentioned sexy?"

Meg coughed out a laugh. "Stop it! Laughing makes my foot hurt!"

Liddy put three of her fingers to her mouth, feigning an apology. "Oops. Sorry, hon. I call it like I see it." She giggled and rested a hand on Meg's blanketed legs. "Listen, how about I take you and my little peanut to Disneyland after he's born. Kind of a way to tap into your maternal side."

Meg laughed, harder this time. "Or make me never, ever want to have children."

"Yeah, I guess the happiest place on earth may not apply to

worn-out parents."

"Oh, I don't know. I guess it could be fun ... "

"Meg?"

"Hmm?"

"You have actually been to Disneyland, right?"

Those tears that had threatened to form earlier sprang into action again. "Once. When I was very young. I hardly remember it, though."

"With your mom?"

Meg caught eyes with Liddy. "My dad was there, too."

Liddy gave her friend a sobering look. "You never mention him. What was he like?"

"I-I don't really know. I was so young when he died. It's just that when you mentioned Disneyland, I had this strange flashback."

"You mean from when you were a kid? What do you remember?"

She scooched herself up into a seated position, her back still resting against the pillows. "I think we shared pineapple ice cream or something. I remember how cold it was, and how my dad laughed every time I took a bite and jumped up and down so I wouldn't freeze. Then I'd lean in for more."

"That's a sweet memory. Pineapple froyo is a thing at Disneyland, so ... you have a good memory."

"Yes, well, it's one of the few I have," Meg said. She did not remember much else about her father, and her mother rarely mentioned him—nor did she have pictures of him plastered everywhere. That was fine with her. He must have been a pretty bad guy for her mother to stay silent all these years.

Liddy slid from the couch and stood. "I'm going to go. You look tired and should get some rest."

"Okay, Mom."

Her friend smiled and leaned her head to one side. "Seriously, promise me you'll rest. Don't be too quick to pick up that phone—

unless, of course, it's your best friend calling. Oh—and don't let me see you at work anytime soon!"

"Thanks for being here." She watched her friend leave and lock the door behind her. A yawn slipped out. Then another. When she first arrived home from the hospital, her pain level had made it difficult to think about sleep. But her fatigue had grown, proving to be stronger than the pain—a not unwelcome thought. Her mind and body began to drift from the present, interrupted only once by a call from her mother checking up on her. She took the call and felt herself drifting again. Yet though she longed to wrap herself in slumber and to plant herself deeply into the comforts of home, she knew she would not be able to stay put for too long.

TWO DAYS LATER, Meg smoothed her hand down the side of the pink maxi skirt she had slipped into, which with a heavy, clumsy cast on her foot wasn't easy. Using one crutch to stabilize her, she buttoned her white blouse and straightened up as much as possible. She glanced in the mirror, taking in the fresh and feminine outfit, and carefully avoided staring at the circles that had formed under her eyes. Faint worry lines marred her forehead, too, likely from the constant presence of residual pain.

Her phone dinged, announcing that Uber had arrived. Slowly she made her way outside, waving to the driver to wait for her. As it turned out, it took longer to hobble to the car, toss her briefcase on the seat, and lower herself inside than it did to ride over to her office at the inn.

Hannah, the hotel's stalwart bell captain, spotted her and motioned for one of the valets to grab a wheelchair, but she waved him off. Hannah came out from behind her desk near the front entrance, frowning. "You sure you don't want some help, Meg? One of my guys can take you all the way to your office, no problem." She lowered her voice. "Especially if you want to get in there fast so you won't be, uh, seen."

Meg shook her head, barely pausing. "No. Thank you. I'm good." Hannah, she decided, had too much time on her hands. The front entry slid open and she swung her foot forward for momentum, careful not to make eye contact with anyone at the front desk. If she could make it past the concierge desk that sat in the center of the hotel's lobby, she'd be golden.

"Meg! You're here!" Too late. Trace scrambled out from behind the desk, gave her a hug, then pulled back, scrutinizing her. "You look peaked."

"I am a little tired."

"Did you really have to come in?"

"Duty calls."

"That's for sure." She paused. "Pepper is taking over your travels for you, right?" Trace's voice held a hint of hopefulness in it.

"Yes, Pepper has gone to Florida."

Trace blew out a relieved breath.

"It's just one trip, Trace."

"That all? I'd heard it would be more. Hmm, well, I guess we'll just count our blessings right now that she's gone away at all." Trace took another look at Meg's cast-bound foot, then caught eyes with her again. "Not that your accident was a blessing or anything."

Meg smirked. Her armpits hurt and a shot of pain darted through her leg, reminding her that she was no longer in the comforts of her own home. Maybe she should have given it another day. It was one thing to get bored at home, and quite another to have to be "on" at the office. For the first time since she wrestled herself out of bed this morning, Meg wondered how long she would last.

Trace reached for the briefcase dangling from Meg's fingers. "I'll grab this and walk with you. Where's your purse?"

Meg nodded toward the briefcase. "Wallet's inside."

"Smart woman. No sense carrying around two heavy bags

when you're injured." Trace said they headed for the sales office—Meg's office would be at the far end of the hall—"What's your prognosis?"

"My doctor says that the bones in my foot do not appear to be out of place, so if I can make it for six weeks without putting a lot of pressure on it, I will hopefully be able to avoid surgery."

"Thank goodness for that! And how did it happen anyway? Hope it's a good story—I need a good story right now."

Meg gave her head a shake and smiled, grateful for Trace's upbeat attitude and for the fact that, apparently—and unlike Hannah—she had no idea how she broke her foot. "I tripped over a pair of flip-flops. How's that for a good story?"

"Depends. Were they bejeweled or just boring old rubber flip-flops?"

"Does it matter?"

"Kind of, if you want to imagine who they belonged to." Trace clucked her tongue. "Will make the whole ugly mess with Jackson so much more fun to re-tell if the flip-flops belonged to a celebrity of some type."

Meg stopped. "You already know what happened, don't you?" she said, looking Trace squarely in the eyes.

"Only what Thomas told me—he was on his break at the time. Said he saw you go down like a Jenga tower."

"Ah." Thomas worked days as a valet. She remembered him as the one who Liddy dated briefly, before she met Beau. "I'm fodder for the staff now, I take it."

Trace put her hand on Meg's shoulder. They had just arrived at her office door. "If it helps any, he thought about running over there and saving you himself, but then Jackson dove into that sand right next to you. Said the boss looked pretty freaked so he backed away ... you were in good hands already."

Meg glanced at her door, then at Trace. She raised her brows. "Would you mind?"

"Of course!" Trace threw open the office door and waited for

Meg to enter.

Meg gasped, her eyes taking in the plethora of pillows, woolen throws—and a wheelchair!—all stuffed into her average-sized office. She peeked at Trace, hoping she would tell her that Liddy had come in early to outfit her workspace, but sensed, with a sinking in the pit of her stomach, that Jackson had likely been the one to do some rearranging. It made her nervous.

She gave Trace an inquiring glance, just in case. Trace shrugged. "Don't ask me. All this stuff looks new and I only shop at thrift stores." Trace flopped onto the couch and snuggled into one of the throws. "Well, come on. Might as well get comfy."

"That's not nec—"

Sally Myers, Jackson's admin, stepped into Meg's office from the adjacent sales department. She had been working for Sea Glass Inn for years, first assisting in the engineering department and later moving to sales. She still dressed from a bygone era in lined knee-length suits, no-frills pumps, and a daily string of pearls. "Lovely to see you, Meghan," she said, sending a slightly assessing look at Trace who was nearly prone and had wrapped herself in a blanket. "May I help you to the couch?"

"Sally, do you happen to know where these things came from? The blankets, the pillows"—she swept a hand toward the wheelchair— "the chair?"

Sally smiled warmly. "Mr. Riley asked me to get them for you. Do you like them? Is there anything else I can add to help you be more comfortable at work?"

"No, nothing. Thank you, Sally." She did not plan on staying around one second longer than necessary, but why burden Sally with that information?

"Oh by the way," Sally said, stopping short of exiting Meg's office, "I've sent your travel schedule to Ms. Riley, but she is going to need more detail. I know that you prefer to make your own arrangements, so I did my best to give her a rough draft of your agenda. She will, of course, need names and contact numbers so she will be able to reach out to clients as soon as she arrives in each city."

"Ms. Riley? Oh, no, no. Pepper will not be meeting with any of my clients on this trip. She will be attending a few trade shows in Florida on my behalf, and maybe checking in on the staff at Sea Castle Inn, but that's it."

"Oh, dear. She asked for your schedule, saying she would be extending her trip to seek out some of your clients since you are, you know, 'under the weather.' I assumed you and she had talked." She fiddled with her pearls. "I am not quite sure what to do now, Meghan. She is our boss, after all."

Meg closed her eyes, dizzy. Yes, Pepper was technically one of the bosses, but Meg had a hard time accepting her. Except for her apparent financial expertise, she was nothing like her kindhearted father. From the day she stepped on-site at Sea Glass Inn, Meg had sensed a deeper disruption where Pepper was concerned. She was a numbers woman and seemed to guide her every decision by the bottom line, ignoring the needs of the staff, and often, those of the guests too. Whereas Meg felt like a resident of Venus to Jackson's home planet of Mars—Pepper always seemed to be from another galaxy altogether.

Meg hobbled toward the couch and sat down on the end opposite Trace.

Jackson poked his head in through the doorway as if it were completely natural for him, a daily occurrence. "There a problem in here?"

Meg eyed him. "There is. Pepper asked Sally for my travel schedule—"

"And her list of clients," Trace chimed in from her cradled position.

Sally rattled those pearls of hers one final time. "Well, if you will all excuse me, I will leave you to sort all this out." She closed the door behind her.

"I'm not giving your sister my client list," Meg muttered,

hoisting her cast onto the coffee table. Heat and sweat broke out on her skin. Why had she not stayed in bed this morning?

Jackson looked from her to Trace and back again. Trace must have taken that as a sign to leave and stood up, dropping her blanket to the couch. "My break is over, so I'll be heading back." She turned to Meg. "If you need me to come wheel you out of here later, all you have to do is text me."

Meg nodded at Trace, but barely. She was still too horrified at the thought of Pepper meeting privately with her clients. Jackson sat down across from her in an oversized chair that had seen better days. He wore no tie today, and the top button of his shirt was open, exposing sun-kissed skin. Meg looked away.

"Pepper's harmless, you know. Said she just wants to help you out while you're grounded."

"And you believe her?"

He scowled. "Why wouldn't I?"

Something flashed in Jackson's eyes. She was frustrating him and she knew it. Sometimes she had to remind herself that he was her boss and she just a lowly peon. Part of her wanted to brush up on her Italian—she'd taken a year of it in high school—and book a flight to Rome. She glanced again at her oversized leg, the one that ached with a ferocity whenever she moved it. Italy wouldn't be happening anytime soon.

"Listen, I didn't come here to talk about my sister. She's probably too busy booking sightseeing tours to bother with your clients." He leaned forward, his hands clasped, his eyes prying. "And I didn't come here to talk about the kiss either."

"Could we not?"

"Talk about it? Sure. Done."

As usual, she noticed, Jackson could turn off his emotions as if they were powered by a switch.

He continued, "As you know, Judy, our CSM, is going on maternity leave. I think you'd be the perfect person to step in for her, with help from the rest of the team, of course."

"You want me to take the conference services manager job?"

"Temporarily. You can still make sales calls by phone and follow up with current clients." He looked at her elevated leg, a grim line to his mouth. "That hurting a lot?"

"Not really," she lied.

"I will help you with the CSM thing and with your calls—especially if you have any site tours coming up."

An arrow of pain sliced through her. She stilled her breath, hoping he would not notice the sheen of perspiration breaking out across the bridge of her nose. "You're going to help me? The head of Riley Holdings?"

"I have decided to stay on-site for the time being. What better place to run the company from than my father's flagship operation?"

This news should have thrilled her because Meg knew how much this place had meant to Jackson's father. Up until now, though, Jackson's interest in it seemed to be more about talking big and then running off to another site. Case in point: He had asked for her opinion about updating the property and even putting in a spa, but dropped the subject after the chef debacle. It was as if he had grown tired of the subject and moved on.

"Are we on the same page?"

"I could help out temporarily, but I just don't think I will be around long enough to fully service the CSM position. It might be good to bring in someone else and let me help them."

"Meg, you need to stay put for a while." He paused. "I saw your fall … your reaction … and … just give yourself a chance to heal, okay?"

He didn't owe her an olive branch, and yet it appeared that this was exactly what he was offering. If she were not in such excruciating pain—pain that was growing by the minute—she might have protested more. Instead, Meg nodded her head, agreeing to work with Conference Services, all the while wondering what Jackson was up to.

CHAPTER 3

Jackson pulled his Mercedes to a stop in front of Meg's home in midtown. She turned to him. "Thank you again for the ride. It wasn't nec—"

She didn't finish her sentence because he had already hopped out of the car and opened the trunk to retrieve her crutches. She had tried to beg off when he insisted on driving her home tonight, but by the time she had made it out to the valet stand, he was waiting there, engine running. In front of her home now, he came around and opened the passenger side door, extending his hand to her.

She slipped her hand into his. He steadied her and she avoided his eyes. "I'll take my crutches now," she said, and slipped each one of them beneath her arms.

Jackson followed behind her carrying her briefcase. She wanted to see him leave quickly and was about to turn to him and offer her thanks again when she noticed her front door ajar. She stopped.

Jackson must have noticed too, because he moved on ahead of her. "Wait here," he called back over his shoulder.

Had she left her door open this morning? Maybe so. Pain,

mingled with a hurried meeting with an Uber driver in front her home, may have distracted her. Disheartening as it was to think of her house being open to the world all day long, the explanation made so much sense.

Jackson pushed open her door, an annoying creak greeting them, like something out of a B-rated horror flick. Confident that he would find nothing other than her living room in its normal disarray, she leaned forward and whispered, "Johnny, don't go down into the basement."

He flicked her a brief look of concern, followed by a mischievous wink. "I'll be sure not to."

Behind him, she hopped up the solitary step, nearly losing her balance. She let out a yelp and grabbed a handful of his shirt before he had made it all the way into the house. He turned partway and reached out to steady her, his eyes gleaming. "Let me save us from the killer first, and then I'll carry you over the threshold."

His voice was soft, like butter, giving her an unexpected thrill despite the odd predicament they found themselves in.

He opened the door wider and stepped fully inside while she waited on the stoop. Within seconds, she became acutely aware of the aroma of … what was it? Sautéed garlic … maybe even some tomatoes. She frowned. *The crook cooked?*

Meg pushed her way in. A woman hustled out of the kitchen holding a wooden spoon and wearing a tomato-splattered apron. At least she hoped the bloody mess was tomato … "Mom?"

"Of course, it's me! Who else would be cooking your dinner?"

"Wait … what?" She searched her brain, trying to recall her mother saying anything about coming for a visit. She leaned her head to one side. "Did I know you were coming?"

"I assumed you would know. After you told me you broke your leg, I couldn't leave you here all alone to fend for yourself. What kind of mother would I be?"

"When did I tell you I—actually, it's my foot, Mom. When did I tell you?"

Her mother furrowed her brows, staring at her. She always did that when she was annoyed. A light went on in Meg's head. "Oh right. You called me the night of the accident ... but I was sleepy from all the meds."

Her mother shut her mouth and nodded once. "That explains it. I forgive you for forgetting. Good thing I had a key."

Meg slid a glance at Jackson as if to offer a silent apology, but Jackson stepped toward her mom and held out his hand. Her mother grasped it with her free one. "I'm Deena."

"Hello, ma'am," he said. "I'm Jackson Riley."

"Very polite! So, you're the son of the famous William Riley."

"You knew my father?"

Her mother seemed to startle at his question, but she recovered. "No, not really." She smiled and glanced at Meg. "Just from what my daughter has told me."

Surprising. Meg and her mother did not speak all that often. They weren't at odds, exactly, but different in about every way imaginable. Meg had decided long ago that her mother spoke in code, while she tended to hit topics head on—most of the time anyway. While it was true that Meg usually spoke in positive terms about her former boss, she never, until now, realized that her mother was listening. The thought brought her some comfort.

A sudden onset of pain and confusion rocked Meg and she tossed her crutches onto the couch and plopped onto it. "I'm so sorry to have scared you, Jackson. Thanks for bringing me home." She waved a weary hand toward her mother. "As you can see, everything's under control here, so you can go now." *Was that too pointed?*

"Absolutely not. I won't hear of it." Her mother jabbed a fist into her side. The wooden spoon dripped sauce all over the floor. "Jackson, you are staying for dinner."

Meg let out a gasp in protest. "Mother, he does not want to—"

"Dinner smells delicious. I will be glad to stay." He turned to Meg, a smile so devilish she thought she saw tips of horns. "I'll help your mother. Can I get you something to drink?"

Her mother spun away and headed into the kitchen, calling out, "I'll get the wine!"

Would it be too much if she were to call out for her mother to hurry?

MEG'S MOTHER did not look a thing like her. Instead of Meg's petite frame and blunt-cut brown hair, Deena was pleasantly shapeless, like an old-fashioned grandmother, though her unlined face made him think she could not be much older than mid-fifties. She wore her straw-colored hair pulled tightly into a ponytail and drank her wine with a hearty fervor.

He sat across from Meg, allowing his attention to pass over the dining room décor. Decidedly modern, but not stuffy. No harsh lines anywhere. Solid wood table with elegant legs that met dark wood floors. Faint blue walls and crown molding painted white. A purple orchid rose from a blue-and-white cloisonné vase. He reminded himself to reignite their discussion about adding a spa to Sea Glass Inn.

Deena popped up from the table and, without asking, piled a second helping of spaghetti onto his plate and added more Cabernet to his glass. She was as sure of herself in the kitchen as one of the cooks at the hotel's restaurant. From his brief relationship with Meg, he knew she only made salads at home; otherwise, she ate out. He wondered if her eating preferences had changed.

He slid his gaze to Meg, whose eyes had lowered to slits. Was his presence boring her? Though he regretted her injury more than he dared think about, he held out hope that the trauma of the past few days played a factor in her inability to stay conscious—rather than his acceptance of her mother's dinner invitation.

"Have another helping, Meghan," her mother said, reaching for her daughter's plate.

Meg wagged her head no.

Deena halted. "How will you get better if you don't eat?"

"By not stuffing myself with gluten."

"Don't tell me you are gluten free now!"

Meg shrugged. "Would that be so surprising? Plenty of people have discovered gluten to be at the root of their problems."

"And that's why you broke your leg? Because of all the gluten you eat?" Her mother's faint brows rose.

Meg sent him an almost imperceptible look before shaking her head and releasing an exasperated laugh. "My foot, Mom. I broke my foot—not my leg."

Deena picked up the ceramic serving bowl from the table. "So, I can dish you up more spaghetti then?"

"Argh!" Meg handed her plate to her mother. "Fine! Make me fat ..."

Jackson's chin followed the action. Left, right, left ... he felt like he was at Wimbledon.

"Good. Save room for dessert," she said, setting down the bowl and taking her own seat again. "I brought us some frozen yogurt —eating that won't hurt your weight at all."

Meg's countenance fell. She caught him watching her and abruptly looked away. They were funny together, she and her mother, lovable even. But in the short hour or so that they had been together, he had noticed a strange tautness that showed up on occasion. This wasn't the first time during the evening that he had noticed tears forming in Meg's eyes.

Maybe he should go. He scooted his chair back, intending to offer his thanks and leave the two to sort out whatever needed sorting. Deena waved him to stop. "Don't leave before dessert." He looked to Meg for some kind of incentive to stay. She held his gaze for several seconds but did not join her mother in the invitation.

He stood. "I believe I'm going to have to take a raincheck." He bowed his head to Deena. "Thank you for a delicious dinner, Mrs. — "

"Please call me Deena."

"Thank you for feeding me tonight, Deena." He turned to Meg. "Sleep well."

CHAPTER 4

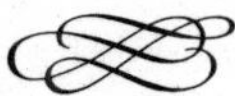

The pain in her foot had lessened overnight. If she kept her weight off of it, maybe she would heal more quickly. She certainly would not need surgery. Meg sighed and rubbed her eyes, the thought of staying home all day the equivalent of impending doom.

It was still dark and she couldn't sleep, so she picked up her iPhone from the nightstand and checked the time. 4:45. No doubt her mother would be in a deep sleep for at least a few more hours. A conflict waged in her mind over her mother's presence. One part of her wanted to assure her mother that she was fine and encourage her to go back home to her house and her chickens and her stepfather. The other part of her experienced a strange sort of peace about her mother being so close. Meg had moved from the middle of California out here to the coast when she was 17 and never looked back. Ever since last evening, she found her mind wandering back … just a little.

Gingerly, she slipped out of bed, reached for one of the crutches leaning up against the wall, and limped over to the bathroom. She promised herself to be careful. Less than an hour later, Uber dropped her off at the hotel. Rudy was out front, washing heron droppings from the bricked driveway. He offered her a kindly smile, and she longed for New York City, where Times Square was scrubbed shiny clean every morning. She made her way past the valet station, noting a lone male attendant looking bored and a little sleepy. She then slipped into the hotel, gave a nod to the night auditor shuffling through paperwork at the front desk, then slowly made her way down the long hall to her office. Once inside, she shucked the crutches and made herself comfortable on the couch. She had rarely sat on it before the accident, choosing more often to sit at her desk by the window, but its softness welcomed her aching body.

One by one, she called the tiny sales office of each property in Oregon, Washington, and Florida. She checked in with each sales manager, casually mentioning her injured foot so as not to alarm anyone, and assured each office that she would be in touch with clients by phone. She asked each of them to forward any calls that needed immediate follow-up.

Meg then made a list of clients to call, grouping them by how far away they were located. Being on California time, she knew she had a better chance of catching most of them in the office, maybe even before Pepper did any damage. At least she hoped so. She wanted to believe Jackson that Pepper was all talk. Maybe, she thought, he had already warned her not to involve herself in the client base that Meg had already built.

She started with those three hours away, then two, then one for those closest. One by one, Meg called her clients—and potential clients. Some had booked events with her at Sea Glass Inn or one of their sister properties in the Pacific Northwest or Florida. Some had considered one of her proposals, but not actually signed. All had been contacted by Pepper, but thankfully, not one had agreed to meet with her.

Loyalty was one of her favorite attributes.

Still, after each call she found herself seething a little more.

Jackson poked his head in through the doorway. "You're here early. Am I allowed to enter?"

"You are the boss."

"This is true." He stepped inside, his slacks tan, his dark denim shirt unbuttoned at the top. "You look—how shall I say this?—peeved. Did you and your mother have a falling out after I left?"

"Pepper told my clients that she is now their main contact."

Jackson didn't react to her sudden change in subject except to say, "I see. Did she tell you that?"

"No." She glared at him, noting the amount of energy anger was pulling from her. It was too early to be this upset, and out of character for her, but nothing was normal these days. "They did. I called every single one of them, and thankfully, reached everybody. Well, at least those on my hot list and a few others. I also contacted each on-site sales assistant." She didn't mention that she asked them all to run interference, though she suspected he understood.

"You've been busy."

"That's all you have to say to me?"

His thick grin faltered. "What do you mean by that?"

"What was last night all about anyway?"

He gave his head a quick shake, a look of incredulity growing in his eyes. "Last night? You mean dinner?"

"Why would you take my mother up on her offer of dinner when you knew what was going on behind my back?"

"Hold on a second." He paused. "This isn't like you, Meg."

She blinked back emotion. Oh, she needed a pain pill. She grabbed her purse and rummaged around inside of it until she found the bottle of ibuprofen. Two max. She wouldn't take anything stronger.

Silently, Jackson retrieved a bottle of water from the mini-fridge in the office. He untwisted the cap and handed the bottle to her.

She took it, swallowed down the pills, and put the bottle back on the table. Her heart pounded against the wall of her chest. She didn't feel like herself anymore.

Jackson stood to leave, but Meg continued. "I know how some salespeople act, always undermining each other, one-upping … after all the trade shows I have attended, I've pretty much seen it all. But I've never experienced the same kind of treatment from my boss. It's surreal."

Jackson crossed his arms and leaned against the wall near the door. "I understand that this is not a normal situation. My sister and I are working through the logistics of how to split up the duties of Riley Holdings—"

"I think you are behind this," she blurted, "behind your sister undermining everything I have worked for."

He straightened. "Me? Are you serious?"

Anger swelled within her at dizzying speed. Where was all this coming from? She glanced at the monstrosity of her foot, then at Jackson. "I have no plans to leave."

"No one is asking you to."

She couldn't look at him, her voice dropping. "You have wanted me out of here ever since …"

A beat of silence enveloped the space between them.

"Ever since what?" he said. All evidence of a lingering smile had evaporated.

She would not go there. Part of her wanted to hash it all out … once and for all. If only she had never dated him, had never succumbed to his charm, his wit, his … good looks. She was young and dumb and would never forgive herself because now look what's happened? William died suddenly and she was about to have her carefully planned world pulled from under her. Panic squeezed her lungs. What would she do? Where would she go?

"Well?"

She shook her head. He had always blamed her for the breakup, but she was not the one who, while they were growing close, suddenly announced that he would be leaving for another job far across the country. She should not have been surprised. Men leave—that's what they do. His father had just promoted her, so it was not as if she could pick up and follow him off to wherever he landed. Not like he had asked her to anyway. She hadn't wanted him to dump her first, so she took care of that for the both of them.

Jackson put one hand on the door, but turned to her first. "My father promised you a job here as long as you want it. I'm not about to violate that promise, and my sister is aware of this too. But it's up to you how you will handle that job."

She shrugged, keeping her face a mask. "I hear you, Jackson. And though I have had no plans to leave up until now, that doesn't mean I haven't had offers."

He yanked open the door, a hard edge to his jaw. "I'll be unavailable the rest of the day."

He left without looking back, delivering a punch to her insides as the door slammed shut. She was over him, but she'd learned that lingering grief often showed up without warning. And sometimes that kind of grief caused people to do things they might not ordinarily do, like throw out a threat that was not entirely true.

She sniffed, fending off rising emotion. Sure, she had participated in the usual chamber-mixer banter, "Hey, Meg, what can we do to lure you away from Riley's dilapidated hotel?" or "You'd make a great addition to our team—sure we can't pull you away from ol' William?" Of course, when William passed away so suddenly, those same people were nothing but kind, offering her condolences and encouragement. "It's a good thing you're there to keep steering the ship," they'd said. "Keep up the good work."

How would it look if she showed up at their doors now with her resume in hand?

A part of her felt that abruptly leaving the inn would somehow dishonor William. She would never understand how Jackson could so easily leave the family business the way he had—leave his father without an heir to train, to come beside him and step in when the time was right.

Maybe that was the reason William decided to leave shares of Riley Holdings to a daughter he barely knew. And look how that turned out? Pepper was brash, overbearing, and unkind to the staff. And she wasn't going anywhere.

If William did not trust his son enough to leave him alone in charge, how could she herself ever trust Jackson either?

JACKSON LOOSENED his tie on his second lap around the inn, thankful that the property's length provided him with enough time to work off some steam. If he heated up anymore he'd have to remove his shirt, too, and how would that go over with the staff? He nearly laughed. Sure would give Meg more ammunition against him.

She drove him nuts. How could he continue to allow this?

"Nice day for a walk."

His heart leapt. He turned his chin to find Rudy, the head of maintenance, looking up from a kneeling position next to a yellowing hedge. "Rudy. Didn't see you there."

"Didn't think so. But since this is your second time around, thought I might give you a shout out. Wouldn't want to startle you."

"I see. Yes, well, it is a nice day. Sunny, warm … some of the many reasons for the inn's popularity."

"Your father always said so, too."

"He owned a lot of hotels, but I think this was his favorite."

"True statement, if I ever heard one. I've been to every one of the sites, you know, but this one seemed to be the one he always gravitated too. Miss him a lot around here. One of a kind, your dad. How you farin'?"

"Can't complain." Sweat rolled down his back and he tried not to think about the wet drip forming on his dress shirt. He had forgotten all about Rudy's long-term employment with the chain. He would have to do better at remembering things like that. "What are you working on?"

"Oh, this here? Drip system is clogged so I'm pokin' another hole in the tubing and affixing a new spigot." He pulled himself up, grunting as he did. "Should work like a charm now. Small fixes like that can save the hotel lots of money in replantings."

"I see." He didn't really. In fact, he rarely walked out here much and found it enlightening that Rudy would notice something so small.

"If you don't mind me sayin', you looked awfully downcast on your first go-round, and downright troubled on your next. I don't want to overstep, of course. But I can be a good listener, if you need one."

I need one. Jackson stuck a hand in his pocket, his mind a volley of conflict. Even if he cared to divulge his thoughts to Rudy, he would have to tame them first. "Thank you for the offer, Rudy. I can see why my father thought so highly of you." He paused. "If you don't mind, I think I will head back to my office now."

Rudy smiled and nodded. "Sure thing. Have a blessed day now."

Jackson made a U-turn along the path toward his office. He had only intended to blow off some steam, but had not considered that he could have been noticed. Rudy had been a constant presence at the inn, not that Jackson had thought about that much. For the first time in the many years that he had been aware of Rudy's work, this is the first time he had ever had a one-on-one conversation with the man. As Jackson entered his palatial office, he could not get the older man's imploring expression out of his head. He'd had to shake him off—he couldn't be divulging his unrest to a stranger. Well, a stranger to him, anyway.

Jackson sat behind his desk and picked up an envelope. Sally had left him the daily mail, each envelope slit open with the top of its contents pulled out slightly, just as his dad had always requested. His assistant insisted on keeping things as they were, as if doing so would somehow honor his father.

Sally.

Rudy.

Meg.

Each of them seemed to know more about his father than he did—and he'd grown up around him. Meg, especially, had gained his ear more than most. It took one summer of work at the inn for him to see that Meg was his dad's confidant and that he trusted her implicitly. Once Jackson was far away, working for another company entirely, his father promoted Meg again and again. *It should have been me.*

"Son, don't be jealous of someone else's success," his father once said to him. He tossed the envelope onto the pile on his desk.

Time had passed and it *was* he who was running the company now. Well, he and Pepper, a truth he chose not to dwell on much. He noticed a trickle of relief running through each staff member whenever he or she learned that Pepper would be off-site for a time. Seemed he wasn't the only one to tire of her quickly.

Meg was another matter altogether. The staff loved her. During his first visit to the inn after his father had passed away, he found her up playing poker with the night auditor. She was manager on duty that night—or MOD—and could have been resting in one of the hotel's suites until she was needed. Instead, she had decided to keep watch with one of the staff members. Jackson discovered this when, unable to sleep, he had decided to drive over to the hotel to look over the contents of his father's office without constant interruptions of condolences or questions. He strolled through the double doors that night expecting to see the night auditor's head down and the lobby empty when he spotted her behind the front desk, still wearing one of those well-fitted suits of hers. The red one that reminded him of a shiny new Porsche. He knew right then and there that she was different from any top manager he had met, that she had not forgotten where she had started.

He clenched his jaw, sending pain through his mouth. Meg thought he wanted her out, or at least to make her life miserable … and maybe there was some truth to that. It was well known that whenever a new management company stepped into a chain of hotels, they swept house. The current salespeople would be given the boot, and those with a fresher presence—and new contacts —brought in.

He didn't know what to believe about Meg ... his father … or even himself anymore. Things had changed. His father was a good man, this was widely known. But he could be a pushover sometimes. The inn showed signs of wear throughout the interior, for instance. The staff had become complacent, too, something he had changed simply by updating his wardrobe and showing up unannounced over the past few months. His father thought too small. This place—the entire chain of inns—could be, no, they *should* be bigger and better and more.

He thought Meg understood this. Wasn't that why she ran with the idea of promoting the inns with the chef's newfound celebrity? She showed brilliance in the face of a challenge—pushing their brazen chef to fulfill his contract by traveling the country to give interviews and demonstrations at the company's other less imposing properties. Such acumen!

Jackson exhaled, the sound of a sigh filling his ears. He spun his chair and stared through the windows behind his desk. This place could be grand, he thought. It *should* be grand. And the other properties would fall in line. He knew it. Meg knew it, too.

The realization of Meg's part in the inn's success rose through him as if someone had tugged on the shade of his mind. She drove him crazy—had firmly planted herself under his skin—but what would happen if she suddenly left Sea Glass Inn and began working for one of the competitors? Rock. Hard place.

CHAPTER 5

When Parker, one of the valets, showed up at her office unannounced to drive her home, Meg could have kissed him. Who knew sitting on a couch all day could be so exhausting?

"The boss sent me," he said. "I'm to use the wheelchair." He nodded to the chair that had been banished to the corner of her office. For once, she didn't complain. She had planned on calling a ride service to bring her home, but Parker's arrival saved her the trouble.

Liddy called Meg's cell as she was being wheeled down the hall. "I have something for you," she said. "Need a ride?"

"Parker has ride detail," Meg told her. "But meet me at home—you can run interference with my mother. Hahaha."

"'K. Be there in a sec."

Meg arrived home to find Liddy's car already parked in the drive. She sent Parker a brief wave, unlocked the door, and stepped in to find her mother steaming the drapes. Liddy lounged on the couch, a comical smile on her face. "Hey, you. Your mom and I were talking about old times."

"You mean when we were delightful children?"

Her mom clucked. "You two were a handful. Remember that time you decided you wanted to go to a concert—what was that band's name again? Anyway, you had to be 16 years old or something to get into that venue, so what did you do?"

Liddy feigned concentration, tapping her mouth with her forefinger. "I believe we waited until we were the appropriate age, isn't that right, Meggy?"

Meg lowered herself onto the loveseat opposite Liddy, grateful for the comforts of home, but slightly on edge over having to keep up the banter.

Her mother turned toward Liddy. "Wrong," she said, shaking the nozzle of the steamer at them both. "You girls dressed up in skirts and high heels—who knows where you found them—and you put on more makeup than a clown act. You two looked like a couple of hoochie mamas!"

Meg rolled her eyes. "Please don't ever say that word again."

"What? Hoochie?"

Liddy laughed. "Your mom always did have a great vocabulary," she said to Meg. "And come to think of it, I believe that was the very incident that turned you into a fashion queen."

Meg glanced at the plain black maxi skirt she had pulled out of her closet this morning. A far cry from her usual tailored suits. She had not thought about it until now, but she missed her wardrobe. And her routine.

Her mother bustled in with a bottle of wine and three glasses.

She missed her quiet, too.

"None for me," Liddy said, hand on her belly. "Give Meg my share."

"Of course," Deena said. "What in the world was I thinking?" She poured two glasses and held one out to her daughter. "Looks like you need this. Lots of lines on your face tonight."

When had her mother become so direct? "Thanks. I think."

Liddy stood. "This baby, happy as I am to be growing him, is aging me. That's for sure. But for someone who broke a bone only a few days ago, you look mahvelous dahling."

Meg held up her glass. "You are too kind."

"Okay, now, I hope you don't think this strange, but I was out shopping today, strolling around the village, and saw something I thought you'd like." She bent to pull something out of her bag. "It's not practical at all, unless of course you consider something that will keep you anchored to the couch practical."

Meg craned her neck to see. "What is it?"

Liddy pulled out a thick, hard-bound book, the colors on its jacketed cover vibrant. "Here. It's a book about northern Italy. You're always talking about seeing it someday, so I thought maybe, since you're, you know, grounded for a while, that you might have time to dream a little."

Unexpected tears filled her eyes. *Must be the wine.* "Liddy, it's gorgeous."

Her mother stepped across the room. "That is a beautiful book all right. And expensive too, I bet. I knew you liked to travel but didn't know you were interested in Italy!"

Meg nodded. "So much of my travel is work related. Italy will be where I will go someday when I have time to explore."

Her mother got up and headed toward the kitchen, wagging her head. "Will wonders never cease. Coming here was a stretch for me." She continued to chatter while rummaging around in the kitchen. "I've never really cared to leave California. Don't know how the travel bug bit you so hard."

Meg didn't either because her mother was right. She never traveled as a child, never even went on a plane until the time William sent her to a trade show in Phoenix. The biggest move she had made prior to that was when she left the middle of the state to drive to the coast. She packed a bag and a year's worth of savings and headed west, stopping when she found the inn. She had never seen anywhere so beautiful in her life and knew she had come home.

Meg looked at Liddy. “It’s perfect. Thank you so much.”

Liddy watched her thoughtfully. “Can I get you anything else? You look more relaxed now than you did when you got home, but I’m guessing you’re still in some pain. Am I right?”

She sighed and glanced toward the kitchen. “I’m fine. It was a long day,” she said, carefully avoiding any mention of her conversation with Jackson, “but it’s good to be home now. I’m sure my mom will fulfill her maternal fussing quota tonight.”

Liddy laughed. “With that, then, I think I’ll get going. Beau will be home soon.” She leaned down and hugged her friend. “Enjoy the book … dream a little, my friend.”

Meg’s mother peeked through the kitchen doorway. “You leaving, Liddy?”

“Yes, I’m out of here, Deena. Going to feed my husband and”— she glanced down at her stomach— “the little peanut, too.”

“It was lovely to see you. Take care of that baby—and that husband of yours.” She took in the sight of her daughter resting on the couch. “I think I will be in town for a while.”

Liddy smiled, and as she left, sent Meg a knowing look.

Meg ran her hand over the hardbound book on her lap, the jumble of colors calming her more than anything she could recall. “Hey, Mom,” she called out.

Her mother came to the doorway.

“I’m thinking of just having something light and then curling up with this book tonight. Is that okay with you?”

Her mother joined her in the living room. “I think that is a wonderful idea. Let me bring you a salad—I know you like them —and I will bring you your pain meds too.” She glanced at Meg’s nearly untouched glass of wine. “Done with this?”

Meg nodded. “Sounds great, Mom.”

Her mother downed the glass of wine and headed off to the kitchen. As promised, she brought over a salad—an artful plate of greens, beets, and goat cheese—along with a pill to take the edge off Meg’s residual pain and a glass of water to wash it down.

Shower and sleep were calling, but she could not resist another few minutes with the book Liddy had brought her. The last thing she remembered was being mesmerized by the juxtaposition of effervescent color, water, and an Italian hillside.

Sleeping Beauty ... except for the drool. Jackson had not thought of the fairytale in years—or ever—but for some reason this moment brought the story to mind. Meg snored softly on the couch, still wearing the clothes he had seen her in at work the day before.

He glanced up at Deena, who stood in the darkened room in a robe that looked like an old housecoat that his grandmother liked to wear. She looked as groggy as Meg. "She going to be okay?" he whispered.

"Maybe I shouldn't have slipped her that muscle relaxer."

He felt the stretch of his forehead as his brows rose. "She was in a lot of pain, I take it?"

"Oh, she was, but she wouldn't admit it. So when she asked for a pain pill I gave her something stronger."

He bit his lip and nodded. No doubt this would not go over well with Meg when she found out. She might not be too crazy about finding him hovering over her either. A glimpse of purple caught his eye. Meg's black suitcase stood in the corner, a purple ribbon tied around the handle. *Probably her bag still packed for the trip she was supposed to take to Florida.*

He sighed, regret expanding within him, and stood. "Guess I'll leave her here to sleep it off," he said.

Her mother nodded. "I think that would be best."

"What are you two talking about?"

Jackson jerked a look toward the couch. Meg's saucer-sized eyes peered back at him. He squatted down. "I tried calling you several times, and when you didn't answer, I decided to drive over."

She wrinkled her brow, never taking her eyes off of him. "I don't understand," she said, her voice thick. "You came to drag me to work?"

"No, no … not at all. I was … I was …"

"He was worried about you, Meghan. You never sleep this late."

Meg slid a look at her mother, then back at Jackson. She rubbed her temple. "What time is it?"

Jackson held his phone out for her to see. "10:30."

She sat up with a start, tossing aside the woolen throw. "What? How can that be? Oh, oh ..." Meg's hand found her mouth. "I think I'm going to be sick."

Her mother took off for the kitchen and returned with a paper bag. She thrust it into Jackson's hands. "Here."

He put it on the floor in front of Meg and rubbed her back. "You'll be okay."

Meg sat quietly for a few minutes, her hand moving from her mouth to her stomach. "I think it may have passed." Her face knotted with confusion. "I-I don't understand what happened, but it looks like I may have fallen asleep here."

Jackson gave Deena a pointed look.

Deena huffed a sigh. "Oh, all right. Meghan, I gave you one of my muscle relaxers last night and I think it made you fall asleep."

"Mother!"

Deena chuckled. "You must have needed it, is all I can say. I think I'll just wander back to bed for a while—my daughter's not the only one who appreciates sleeping in."

Meg shook her head as her mother hightailed it out of the living room. "I can't believe this … I can't believe it's so late." She flipped her legs off the couch, her cast thudding onto the floor. She flashed a look at Jackson. "What are you doing here anyway?"

There's my angry sales director ... "I had left a couple of messages for you and when you didn't pick up …"

"You decided to drive over here and stare at me until I woke up?"

It sounded ludicrous to him too. What had he expected to accomplish by driving over here? What if she had wanted a day off? She was entitled to that—though protocol would have called for her to let someone at the inn know she would not be coming in. He swallowed, thinking. "Not exactly. I have set up a meeting with Maritime Tour & Travel and they specifically requested that you attend."

She let out a sigh and closed her eyes. "Well, of course they did. I've been after them for months to include us on their weekly tour stops." She opened her eyes again and stared at him. "I had to eat a lot of rubberized chicken at the chamber meetings to get them to notice Sea Glass Inn."

He smiled, hoping her attempt at humor meant he was forgiven.

"So, what time is the meeting?"

"One o'clock."

She nodded once, then slowly stood. "I'll be ready in twenty minutes, if you want to wait."

"I'll be here." Jackson sat in the silence. He hated that he had been the one to wake her—at least, in this way. But when she didn't answer her phone this morning, well, his imagination got to him. A twist in his gut had caused him to wonder just how serious she had been about those offers. The more he had thought about her running off to work for the competition, the more he questioned his sense. Especially with his sister being such a wild card in the whole operation. If Sea Glass Inn and her sister properties were to grow into the world-class operations he dreamed they would be, he would need someone on his side that shared that vision. Besides, Meg knew more about the operational side of running events at the hotel the way his father had directed—not that Jackson would ever admit this publicly.

A text lit up his phone and he swiped it away with his thumb. Who was he kidding? It took a lot more than the threat of losing Meg to the competition to cause him to violate all kinds of human resources laws to drive over here and stand over a sleeping employee. Jackson ran a hand through his hair and bit back an expletive. Old feelings had surfaced the moment his mouth had found hers out on that beach, and he feared that he had been making one mistake after another ever since.

IF SHE HAD to keep her eyes open another five minutes, Meg feared she would die on the spot, or possibly pass out. Marcie from the tour company sat next to her in one of the chairs across from Jackson who sat at his desk listening intently.

"I want to make sure that my guests are offered foods and experiences that they cannot find anywhere else," Marcie was saying. "Otherwise, there really is no reason to make a change to our current schedule."

Jackson gave Meg an imploring look. He had already offered her a customized menu that included local organic fare and two vegetarian options. He had also suggested a wine or craft beer tasting especially for the tour guests.

"How about some outside options for your guests, Marcie? Now that the foods and beverage events have been settled, I suggest we offer your tour and travel clients a sea glass hunting expedition—our staff knows some of the best and most secretive collection sites."

"Oh, I love that idea!"

"There is also an estuary a short distance from here where they can view rare birds in their natural habitat."

She clapped her hands together. "A choice! We can give them a choice ... between those two excursions. I love it!"

Jackson winked at Meg when Marcie wasn't looking. He leaned forward then, all business. "And, of course, our valets are available to provide rides to those who would like to golf."

Marcie nodded. "Yes, yes, that's always popular with our clientele, but I do have to say, you have provided some wonderful alternatives to the standard golf fare." She stood, reached across Jackson's desk, and shook his hand. Then she turned toward Meg and enveloped her in a hug. "All your hard work has paid off, dear one. I'm very excited and pleased to put together a new tour option for our clients. I will be in touch soon—take care of that foot of yours!"

With Marcie gone from Jackson's office, Meg sat back down and closed her eyes. She willed herself not to drift off to sleep sitting up—how embarrassing would that be?

"Coffee?"

Her eyes snapped open. Jackson stood near his credenza, a full pot of coffee by his side. "You look like you could use another cup."

"I'll take it to go." She stifled a yawn. "I want to draft Marcie's contract before she changes her mind."

He grinned. "Good idea." Sally's voice through the intercom interrupted the coffee pouring. "Jackson, Pepper is on line one. Are you able to talk?"

He glanced at Meg. "This should only be a minute."

He picked up the phone. "Pepper, it's Jackson."

The unmistakable screech of Pepper's voice came through the line. Meg did not hear what Jackson's sister said—not that she cared to know—but she could tell this was no friendly phone call.

Wearily, Meg stood, sticking a crutch under each arm. She wondered for the umpteenth time if armpits could bruise.

Jackson scowled and put his hand over the receiver. "Tell you what," he whispered, "you hobble on down to your office and I will bring it to you."

With a nod, she left him to deal with whatever crisis Pepper had conjured up. As an only child, Meg had often wondered what it would have been like to have a sibling to talk to, especially during the years after her father's death. She knew her mother had tried her best, but there had always been a strange distance between them. Why, she could never quite nail down.

Liddy sidled up beside here. "Hi, there."

"Hey, yourself."

"You really should use that wheelchair, you know."

Meg sighed. "Might have to. My pits are killing me."

"Well, then, that's it. It's a chair on wheels for you, missy! And I'll be the one to push you around."

"Ha. As usual."

"Oh please. If I had the ability to push you around, you know I would have done so long ago—but you're too tough for that."

"What I am not about to do is allow a prego woman to push me in a wheelchair. I should be the one pushing you. I'm sick of thinking about myself. How are you feeling, anyway?"

"Great. Still jogging some, though not with the energy I had before."

Meg's heart surged. Her friend had gone through brain surgery the year before, then married her dreamboat, and now was pregnant with their child. Their remarkable year had introduced Meg to the idea that miracles still existed.

"You amaze me."

Liddy followed Meg into her office. "Speaking of amazing, you and Jackson seem to be making quite a team after all."

"I think we have an understanding," Meg said, carefully.

"Understanding? You mean after the infamous beach chase incident?" Liddy's voice shook, clearly unable to make eye contact with Meg. "I know it wasn't his fault that you fell, but he must feel some responsibility … since he was chasing you and all."

"Are you laughing?"

Her friend let loose a peal of laughter. "I'm … I'm so sorry. I hate that you got hurt—hate it!—but I just wish I had seen him running after you in his British-cut suit."

Meg sat and rubbed her eyes, stifling back a laugh of her own, though the incident seemed anything but funny to her. "You are such an idiot."

Liddy plopped down next to her, still smiling. "Yeah, I know. Let's blame it on baby brain."

"I have to tell you something."

Liddy squinted. "What is it?"

Meg sighed and looked up to the ceiling. "I am only telling you this because I'm sure someone saw it and will be gossiping about it soon." She flicked a look at Liddy. "Jackson kissed me."

"Wait. Are you and he back together? Why did I not see this?"

She shook her head. "No, no, not at all. It was all ... all a mistake. Another dumb misunderstanding. If I could take it back, I would."

"When did *said* kiss happen, exactly?"

"On the beach. He kissed me when he caught up with me."

"Oh!"

"But he didn't mean it. It was obvious that it was one of those in-the-moment things. I became so upset with myself that I turned and ran—and that's when I fell."

"Oh, Meg. I'm sorry for laughing. This explains why Jackson's been so attentive lately."

"Attentive ... I guess that's one way to look at it. Has nothing to do with anything between us, though."

"Other than a lawsuit," Liddy said.

Meg gave her a grim laugh. "Yes, other than that."

"Knock, knock." Jackson entered the room holding a mug of coffee. "I've brought you your coffee, Sleeping Beauty." He handed Meg the cup, his face a mask.

Liddy slid Meg a questioning look. Meg ignored her.

"Thanks." She took a sip. "Everything okay with Pepper?" It had crossed her mind more than once that Pepper's call may have been a direct result of all the phone calls Meg had made, warning her clients.

Jackson hesitated. "She was checking in. You know, the usual Pepper." He was evading her question, but not very well. Something in his tone had changed since she had left his office a short while ago, and he might as well have been speaking to a client. Maybe it had to do with Liddy being in the room.

He shoved a hand in his pocket, a distracted gaze flitting about the room but landing nowhere.

Sally stepped into the office. "Oh, you *are* here," she said to Jackson. Her eyes flickered onto Meg briefly before looking away. "Pepper asked me to find you. She sent an email over for you to review."

"Thank you, Sally. I will get to it later today." He turned to Meg. "Enjoy that coffee." Then he slipped out of the room.

CHAPTER 6

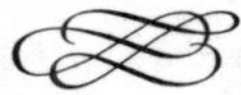

"You need to stop meddling, Mom."

"If you define meddling as taking care of my only child, then I won't be complying with that order anytime soon."

"For one thing, you drugged me. Isn't there some law against slipping a mickey in someone's water glass?"

"In 1940s gangster movies, maybe. What has gotten into you, Meghan? You have been on edge since the moment you got home. I'm worried about you."

"I know you meant well, but I can't take anything stronger than one pain pill. Don't you remember that about me?"

Her mother wrinkled her forehead as if straining to recall this tidbit from her daughter's childhood. "I don't remember that. Does it make you sick?"

Meg shook her head, not relishing the thought of getting into this subject now—not like there was ever a good time to discuss their family's underbelly. "You know what I mean … Uncle Greg told me once that his addiction to pain pills came about from his accident. I've had an aversion to medicine ever since."

Her mother's mouth fell open. "I've never heard you say that."

Maybe you never listened.

"You broke a bone in your body. You would rather live with that pain than take something to help you sleep?"

She wanted to say, *If it meant that I could avoid a lifetime of addiction like Uncle Greg, then yes.* But she dared not belabor this talk. For as long as Meg could remember, the subject of her mother's brother and his problem with addiction brought more angst than constructive dialog. She set down her fork. "Bottom line is that you put me in a terrible predicament at work. I was late and tired and unable to think straight for most of the day."

"And you think Jackson would have fired you?"

"Anything is possible."

"Oh please! There is not one smidge of possibility of that, for heaven's sake. William Riley practically worshiped you, and his offspring would not want to dishonor their father by firing the most loyal employee they have ever had!"

Meg pulled back. "And you know this how?

Her mother's eyes widened before her expression quickly collapsed again. She shrugged. "You said it a time or two."

"I don't recall saying much of anything to you about William."

Silence.

Her mother swallowed a bite of chicken. "Well, all I know is that you hurt yourself very badly ... just look at that foot of yours. And here you are, working so hard despite that pain. If there was any thought of firing, you could sue."

"For what?"

"Firing a disabled woman!"

Meg laughed at that. Hard. She considered the look on Pepper's face if she were to be served a lawsuit like that. The woman's characteristic screech, the one being served a subpoena would certainly ignite, reverberated in her head, and she laughed some more. Come to think of it, this entire day—waking up to her boss peering at her, her mother in her bathrobe, *the muscle relaxer in her bloodstream*—all of it melted Meg into a pathetic, laughing mess. She laughed until tears fell, the thought of hyperventilation not far from mind.

Her mother shot up from the table. "My word, get onto the couch," she said, attempting to lift her daughter from the dining chair. "You're delirious."

This only brought more laughter. Meg lifted her hands into surrender. "Okay, okay. I'll get up by myself." She continued to crack up, her mother holding her by the elbow as if this would offer her support. Still smiling at the ridiculousness of it all, Meg sank onto the couch.

Her mother sat on the coffee table and examined her, her mouth pursed. Meg noted the lines around her mother's eyes deepening as she reached out and felt Meg's forehead with the back of her hand. The simple action hearkened back to when she was a child and calmed her uncontrollable laughter.

Meg reached up and touched her mother's hand, the feel of her skin precious. She could not recall the last time she had felt her mother's touch and the tears returned, this time in a slow drip. She sobered considerably. "Are you happy, Mama?"

Her mother shut her eyes momentarily then allowed them to flash open again. "Happy as can be."

"I know that Uncle Greg's situation makes it hard on you sometimes."

Her mother shook her head like she was dislodging an unwelcome thought. "Oh, don't you worry about that. He's just … he's just confused."

"Confused? He has been in and out of rehab or jail most of my life."

"Now, I said I don't want you to worry about that."

"Well, I worry about what it is doing to you … what it's done."

"What do you mean?"

"I think his life makes you worry. I have seen a far-off look in your eyes for as long as I can remember. It's not your fault, you know, his addiction."

Her mother extricated herself from Meg's touch and patted her daughter's hand. "Meghan, there is no need to point fingers any which way. I think we need to change this subject right now."

Meg bit the inside of her lower lip. She had seen this kind of reaction from her mother before, a strange sort of agitation. Rather than push an issue that she had been wanting to explore for most of her life, once again, Meg let the subject go.

THE NEXT MORNING a quote popped into Meg's mind. "Hard times prepare ordinary people for the extraordinary." She sat at her desk, tired of the cast that hung on her leg like a soggy sling of cardboard. At least, that's what she pictured the insides of the cast to look like now. She hated to think about what her leg looked like—probably an overcooked sausage.

The quote was something William said often, though she had not realized until now that she had memorized it. She was feeling quite ordinary at the moment, which was likely why this particular quote speared her.

She glanced around her office, aware that the upgraded furniture and reading material had been brought in as a sort of peace offering. The bookcase held classics, such as books written by Jane Austen, Charlotte Bronte, and Frances Hodgson Burnett, and her coffee table was strewn with back issues of *Forbes*. She could not imagine having the time to enjoy any of it, but if she found herself suddenly homeless, her office at the inn would make a comfortable studio apartment.

Sally appeared in her doorway. "Jackson has requested that you join him for a staff meeting in his office in ten minutes."

Meg checked the time and glanced at the blinking light of voicemail on her phone. She had planned on answering email and phone messages and then meeting with the catering department to review incoming conferences. But she had to remind herself that life had changed for her at the inn, and like it or not, her calendar was no longer her own. "Hard times … ordinary people." Maybe she was on the right track. She was feeling far less than extraordinary now.

Ten minutes later, Meg wheeled into Jackson's office. He had not yet arrived, so she parked herself next to Trace, who sat in front of Jackson's desk.

Trace stifled a yawn. "Hey, Meg. Obviously, I'm a team player and all, but I still don't understand why I am needed in this meeting."

Same here. "I guess we'll soon find out."

Jackson strode into the room, his expression brooding. He brushed by them both without saying a word, taking a seat at his desk where he began to scribble on a notepad. *Just like his father.* The familiar sight caught Meg off guard and she swallowed a sudden lump in her throat.

He tapped his pen on his desk and looked up. "Liddy coming?"

"Hello, everyone," Liddy said as she rushed into the room. She took a seat next to the others.

Jackson cleared his throat. "I called you all here for a pre-con meeting. Actually, this is more of a *pre*-pre-con meeting for CartCo.

Meg stiffened at the name of the company that Jackson had so brazenly courted right from under her. She avoided eye contact, forcing herself not to care.

"Adele will be stopping by in a few minutes," he added before zeroing in on Liddy. "We will need you to create a way for the group's guests to reserve rooms online." He swung his chin toward Trace. "I would like you to assist Meg with some logistics of the breakout space—there will be a general session and many smaller meetings throughout the weekend."

Meg sat there, silent.

"You're our best with these types of events," he said to Meg, interrupting her thoughts. "What do you have to add to this conversation?"

You mean, like, what in the world was the head of Riley Holdings doing acting like a meeting planner?

Sally arrived at the door before Meg could betray herself. "Excuse me, but is there anything more you need for today's meeting?"

Jackson rocked in his chair like he was thinking, and the rest of the room fell silent. Sally caught Meg's eye. "Anything you can think of?"

"Yes, there are a few things I can think of. Please bring us copies of CartCo's working agenda and the map of the space they would like to use. And if you could ask catering to bring in waters and coffee for our meeting with the client, I think we would all appreciate that."

Sally nodded. "Absolutely."

Meg turned back to Jackson. "What was it you were asking?"

He stared at her for a beat. Before he could answer, Adele Grant strolled into the office wearing acorn-gold athleisure, her icy blonde hair pulled back into a sleek ponytail. "Jackson," she drawled, "how lovely to see you again." From the top of her shiny head down to her white Y-3 sneakers, the woman appeared ready to play hard.

Jackson came out from behind his desk and offered Adele his hand, but she pulled him into a hug instead. Trace leaned toward Meg and whispered, "Pretty cougar-licious, if you ask me."

Liddy reacted to Trace's observation with a squeak and a slap of a file folder on her knee.

Sally hurried into the room and handed Meg a file labeled "CartCo Event." Behind her a black-vested server named Jorge slipped in with a pitcher of water and a tray of glasses.

One-Mississippi-two-Mississippi-three ... That's how long it took until Jackson could extricate himself from Adele Grant's embrace. Huh. Though Meg had been in contact with Adele for months with calls and proposals regarding her company's event, something told her that Jackson's "magic" touch was less about the magic and more about the … touch.

THE REMAINDER of the meeting was spent watching Adele bat eyes at Jackson while the rest of the women in the room—dubbed "the forgotten three"—tapped away on their phones, ostensibly taking notes. It was an exhausting experience watching her boss try to finesse his way through negotiations with a woman who knew what she wanted and how to get it.

After the meeting ended and Meg had returned to her office for more follow-up calls and a drive-by meeting with catering staff members who happened to be on-site that afternoon, fatigue set in. She could either succumb to an afternoon nap—probably not the best option if she expected to conquer her to-do list today—or take a stroll outside. "Stroll" being the operative words since using the wheelchair would likely be the most efficient, painless way to make her way around the property.

The air had cooled some and whatever day's heat remained was tempered by a soft breeze. She loved this view—light dappled waves, cloud-white sails hoisted in the distance, a canopy of blue above her. She cranked both rims of her chair forward.

Jackson's familiar voice interrupted her thoughts. "May I help?" He didn't wait for her answer, but instead began to push her chair gently forward along the winding path.

She kept her eyes focused ahead and attempted to relax. A squirrel skittered out of the way, lightening the mood.

"You were quiet in the meeting," he said.

"Mm-hm."

"Reason?"

She thought about this. "Well, I could have done a tree pose in a corner wearing a bikini and that woman would not have noticed me."

"I would have."

She sucked in a breath and forced herself to exhale. Goosebumps alighted on her skin so she crossed her arms, rubbing them with both her palms.

"Did the others have any input I should know about?"

"Other than Trace's 'cougar-licious' comment, you mean?"

Jackson let out a sarcastic laugh. "She did not."

Meg smiled at Trace's bravado. "She did."

They continued on the undulating path, mostly in silence. Meg shaded her face with one hand, keeping her gaze on the horizon. It would be easier to ignore the struggle between them—at least, she thought he struggled too.

Finally, Jackson spoke again. "Give it to me straight, Meg. What did you think of my performance in there?"

Did it matter what I thought? "Was that before or after your client jumped you?"

He swore softly. "You're being ridiculous."

"Ridiculous ... crazy ... *hysterical.* That's me, I guess."

"Not fair. I'm not a mansplainer ... if that's what you're not so subtly hinting at."

She laughed. "Fine ... though I did not accuse you of that."

"I asked you to give it to me straight."

"Right. Okay. Here it is: You gave away the store."

He scoffed. "I did not."

She groaned. "You asked what I thought."

"I asked what you thought of my performance, my ability to land the big fish, so to speak."

"Or shark."

"Whatever."

She crossed her arms again, noting that though the sea was within reach, her mind had decidedly gone elsewhere. "Jackson, you are a professional. I assure you that you looked the part and said what you needed to say."

"I appreciate that."

She should have stopped there, but her mouth kept working.

"In the end, CartCo has signed a large contract with Sea Glass Inn and, I guess, that's all that matters."

"And you don't sound very sure about that. Why?"

He had slowed now. She turned and said what had been percolating in her mind all afternoon. "The promises you made her will stretch our staff to their limits. They will be running around relentlessly—and you cut their gratuity by a third. You gave them every spare bit of space in the hotel without setting industry-acceptable food and beverage minimums." She paused. "Should I go on?"

"No. You've said enough." An edge returned to his voice and he picked up the pace, causing her to look forward again. She momentarily feared she would end up in the cold waters of the Pacific.

"You said you wanted my opinion. If it helps any, your father asked me for mine on occasion, too." Her windpipe tightened. She missed William Riley, more than she had ever told a soul. Everywhere she looked she saw his mark upon this inn—and all the others in this family-run chain. She just wished ...

"That's funny," Jackson said, a flatness to his voice. "He never asked mine."

"Maybe it's because you chose to leave him." *And me.*

He stopped the wheelchair and stepped out in front of her. "You don't understand a thing about those days, Meg."

Carefully, she stood.

"You should stay put."

She shook her head and used the back of the chair to keep herself balanced. He rooted himself in place, a scowl marring his mouth. His eyes flitted to her face, but he crossed his arms as if to give a "hands off" stance.

"What don't I understand? That you and your father were constantly at odds?"

She searched those hardened eyes of his, his set jaw.

"You think I didn't hear you and your father arguing? About money? About Pepper? About how to run inns?

"Stop it."

"You were kind of a pain in the butt back then, but ..."

"May I remind you? William Riley was my father—not yours."

She was going to finish by saying that she had seen changes in him, changes she thought his father would have appreciated. But he had drawn blood with his remark. She fought the torrent building behind her eyes. Though she might not be able to physically run, she could certainly walk away—or sit back down in that darn chair.

She wobbled and his hand darted out to steady her. She leaned into his strength while alternately fighting it. Beneath heavy lids, his eyes searched her face, his breath upon her cheek like a magnet, holding her in place. He brushed a strand of flyaway hair from her forehead and hooked it behind her ear. The touch of his skin on hers stirred up turmoil she didn't care to revisit.

"You have no right to criticize my relationship with my father."

"Maybe not," she said, her voice hushed, "but I can't stand by and let you criticize him either."

"On the contrary, as an employee, you have no jurisdiction over who I can or cannot criticize—and you certainly have no license to criticize your boss."

He jerked his hand from her cheek, the jolt affecting her like a physical shove. Once he had disappeared, Meg lowered herself into her wheelchair and waited for her heart to still before making her way back to the inn.

CHAPTER 7

"Did you really just use the term 'gold digger'?" Jackson sat at his desk tapping the tip of his pen on its surface and watching the sun slip into the sea. His sister had been barking at him over the phone for the past fifteen minutes.

"You need to stop trusting her so much with our company's information," she said. "Wherever I go, it's Meg this and Meg that. That should not be! She is just an employee, Jackson."

As an employee, you have no jurisdiction ... He winced, recalling how he had thrown similar words into Meg's face earlier today. Jackson shifted in his chair. "Let's keep the derogatory terms out of this conversation, Pepper."

"Fine, fine. You go ahead and protect Daddy's little protégé all you want. I don't trust her at all."

"Why not?"

Pepper sighed dramatically, like his question was a waste of her precious time. "I think she took advantage of Daddy ..."

He hated when she called their father that. William Riley was Father—not Pops, Dad, or Daddy—just Father. *Always.* Jackson rifled a hand through his hair, trying to shake away some of the frustration this call was causing him. Pepper had known their father how long? A few months before he died suddenly? What did she know about him anyway? Silently, he chastised himself. It was easy to write off a person he never knew … never cared to know. As trying as Pepper's behavior was—and "trying" was putting it mildly—it was not her fault that she had only known William Riley for a short time. Perhaps if their father had lived, Jackson and Pepper would not have been thrown together like strange ingredients in an unusual recipe.

"And what is this?" she said as her voice dug back into his thoughts, a pitch higher this time. "This expense account you have given her? She flies here and there, staying in our hotels, drinking our wine, gobbling up our food—"

Jackson threw the pen, like a dart, at the wall across from his desk. "That's enough, Pepper. You are making this something bigger than it is. You are only angry that none of her clients were available to talk to you."

"Exactly. So tell me! Tell me why it is that each and every client of hers that I have tried to speak with on my travels has been unavailable. Doesn't that strike you as odd?"

That Meg would have warned them of his meddlesome sister's impending arrival? Not at all.

Technically, he could see Pepper's point. It would not be unusual for the general manager or other executive of a hotel to reach out to a client before the onset of an event. Some might say it would be expected and welcomed. Yet he understood why Meg would become concerned about his sister's sudden interest in her clients' affairs. His sister was a miser when it came to hotel spending. She wanted the moon—but only if she could wrap one of those fancy scarves of hers around its surface and pull it down without spending a penny. Meg's plans were derailed when she tripped and fell at the beach, and she no doubt worried that Pepper's overbearing interest in her clients' agreements with the hotel would further hinder her efforts to close a deal or finalize plans, whatever the case may be.

After ending his call with his belligerent sibling, Jackson sat in the silence. Had Meg really told him to his face that he had been a pain in the butt? He scoffed and leaned his head against his chair, remembering the first time he had seen her, way back when, for someone other than his father's assistant.

He'd been lounging by the pool when he noticed her striding by, head down, eyes on a document. "Must be something urgent for you not to notice the view today."

She looked up, her brow puckered. "I'm sorry?"

He stood, slipped bare feet in flip-flops, and approached her. She wore a skirt, a blazer, and pointy-toed shoes despite the mid-July weather. "It's a beautiful day. Where are you headed in such a rush?"

"To talk to Chef."

"Forget about that. Come paddle boarding with me." He flashed her the smile that had netted him more dates in college than he could count.

"Chef is waiting."

"Let him. He'll be here until, what, eleven? Later? There's a whole ocean out there and you're missing it with all these—" he grabbed the stack of files from her arms and hid them behind his back— "papers."

"Jackson."

"Call me Jack."

"Okay ... Jack. Your offer is tempting, but I really do have to get these banquet orders over to the chef."

He lifted the files over his head and searched the perimeter of the pool area until his eyes landed on one of the servers. He motioned her over.

Meg shook her head and reached for the files, but he dodged her, grinning.

"Sir?" the young woman asked when she walked up to them. Her gaze stroked his bare chest.

He reveled in the title that he neither deserved nor embodied and handed the woman Meg's stack of files. "I'd like you to take these to the restaurant. Chef is waiting for them."

"Absolutely. I would be happy to."

She sidled off and he turned to Meg. "So, you'll come with me?"

She had crossed her arms by now. "I really can't."

"And the reason is ...?"

She peered toward the ocean beyond the inn. A longing mixed with something else softened her face. It was as if something troubling had crossed her mind.

He reached for her hand. "One drink then. My father won't mind. Trust me."

She hesitated and he could tell by the way her eyes lit slightly that she did not want to turn him down. "And you will clear this with your father?"

"Promise."

THE MEMORY FADED, and he found himself whispering into the night, *What happened?* The night refused to answer him, but his conscience did. He had put her in her place tonight with his declaration that she was nothing more than an employee here at the inn. While that may have been true in HR's eyes, Jackson knew that her connection to this place ran deeper—deeper than even he understood.

But his pride had gotten the better of him today.

His father once said that he thought of Meg as his daughter. Thought that was strange since he had a daughter—well, not one that he knew very well, but he had one. But William Riley treated Meg like an extension of himself. "She has my drive, a spirit similar to my own, but she carries a sadness with her," he recalled his father saying. "It would behoove you to speak to that sadness." He never knew—or cared—what that meant.

That was a lie ... he did care, but what did his attempt to show his concern get him? A door shut in his face—by both Meg and his father. He glanced around the well-appointed room. He sank deeper into his father's leather chair, taking in the expanse of sky that shadowed the water. Everything about the office—the furnishings, the framed photos on the wall with his father and heads of corporations—screamed professional. So why did he feel more like a high school junior without a ticket—or a date—to the prom?

MEG RETURNED HOME BY LYFT, exhausted and longing for silence. A full day on the phone or in meetings used to invigorate her, but lately she'd found herself spent before sundown. Even her attempt at a few minutes of solitude overlooking the sea had been torpedoed by Jackson's interruption. She tried not to think of how poorly that had ended.

She stood on the front stoop of her home, about to insert the key into the lock when she stopped at the sound of crying. Mom's tears. Quickly, she unlocked the door and limped inside, tossing her crutches to one side.

"Mom?"

Sobs. More sobs. Mom's arms were folded in front of her on the dining room table, her face buried, her shoulders bouncing, a napkin crushed in one hand.

Meg made her way across the room and gently rubbed her back. Deena sat up with a start, her face splotched red and swollen.

"Tell me what happened."

Her mother attempted to sop her face with the thin, wet napkin. "Oh, it is nothing for you to worry about. I've had a bad day, that's all."

Meg eyed her. She doubted that something as ordinary as a bad day could produce this amount of emotion, yet she knew that treading lightly with her would go a long way toward uncovering the truth. Meg grabbed a stack of napkins from the table and set them in front of her mother. "You know, you really don't need to stay here any longer. I appreciate you stepping in to help me after the, um, accident, but you really should be getting back to your own life now."

Her mother grabbed both of Meg's hands, nearly causing her to stumble. "You are my own life!"

Meg lowered herself into a chair. "I-I didn't mean … of course, I understand. I just meant that it can be hard to live out of a suitcase. No one understands that better than me!" She smiled and patted her mother's hand. "And I'm sure Adam is missing you something fiercely."

A couple of fresh tears seeped from her mother's eye, but Meg held her tongue. Of course, this outburst had little to do with the doldrums, but if she were to force the issue, her mother might clam up—something she had done her entire life whenever a crisis occurred. By the time Meg usually learned the truth behind a crisis, such as her uncle's drug addiction, the problem had grown to mammoth proportions. Part of her wanted to scream: *Just tell me what really happened!*

That's when she noticed the notepad beneath her mother's other hand. Reading upside down was not her forte, especially when trying to do so nonchalantly, but the words "county jail" came across as clear as the day's blue sky.

Her mother tore off the top sheet of the pad and crushed it in her hand.

Meg took a careful breath. "Who?"

"Nothing for you to worry about in your condition."

"I'm not pregnant."

Deena pushed away from the table, and her chair leg screeched against the wood floor.

Meg put her hand over her mother's to stop her. "No, Mama. Not this time."

Her mother's chest rose and fell and her eyes flitted around with nowhere to land until they found her daughter's. "It's Greg ... he's in jail." She looked away as if her brother's shame was her own.

"I am so sorry." And she was. As far as Meg knew, her Uncle Greg had been doing well. After a lifetime of addiction and spates in rehab, he had found a girlfriend and together they had started a gardening business.

"He was caught selling marijuana."

Meg leaned her head to one side. "While it may not be advisable, that's not exactly illegal these days in California, is it?"

"It is if you don't have a license, which you cannot get if you have a record." She sighed, a hiccup rattling her chest. "His lawyer is saying he might lose his business license now—he was growing the plants in with the azaleas."

Oh brother.

Her mother continued to work over the sopping napkin in her hand. "If only he could afford to go back to rehab ... he had to leave so abruptly last time."

"Really? Why?"

Her mother didn't answer right away. "Was getting too costly," she finally said. "Let's change the subject. How was work?"

Clamming up had begun. The abrupt change of subject had always been disorienting to Meg, but she sighed knowing there was little she could do for her mother when it came to Uncle Greg. Maybe she would give her some space.

"I used to love going to work each day, but less so these days," she finally said, dragging herself from the table. She needed a bath and maybe a glass of wine.

"Your foot hurting you?"

"Not as much anymore, although it is tiring lugging it around."

"Then why don't you love your job anymore?"

Meg paused. *Where do I begin?* "Well, I miss traveling, for one.

Hopefully my doctor will give me clearance so I can get back in the air again."

"But it's more than that?"

"I'm not used to so much competition." There, she said it. "The only person I used to compete with was myself, but now Jackson and even his sister, Pepper, have been breathing down my neck. It's unsettling."

"Be careful, Meghan. It never looks good to bite the hand that feeds you."

Meg grimaced. "I would never—"

"Oh no?" Her mother's right brow pulled upward. "You bit mine when you decided to leave at 17. I could have tried to stop you, but you were so pig-headed."

Stunned. That's the only word that came to mind. Hadn't her mother helped her pack her car and handed her two twenties for the road? "You … never said that before. You had just gotten married … I thought you were fine with my dream of living by the coast."

Her mother pursed her lips, puffing out her cheeks. "You are my only child. What was I to do, hog tie you to a post rail? No. You wanted to leave so I did not protest, but if you want to know, yes, it made me sad."

Meg swallowed. Her mother suddenly looked frail to her, weary. She had never meant to cause her sadness, but had she thought much about how her leaving might affect her? Not really. Instead, Meg had taken the money she had earned at the mall, loaded up her car, and headed west. Liddy had already married the first time and left the area, so without her best friend to keep her around, she had decided to follow her own dream.

"I'm sorry, Mom. I had never considered you felt anything but as excited as me about my new adventure. If it helps any, I missed you a ton. Almost turned the car around twice."

Her mother appeared to brighten. "I'm so glad you didn't—my daughter is not a quitter!"

Meg laughed.

"So, don't put it into your head that you need to quit your job, young lady. The competition will only make you stronger. You need to figure out a way to get along with the son of the best boss you have ever had!"

Finally, something she and her mother could agree on.

CHAPTER 8

One of the best inventions ever: drive-thru espresso. Fortunately, Meg's Uber driver willingly made the detour before work. She ordered a double-shot cappuccino, wanting something strong before she set foot into the inn today. She had turned over a new leaf. Despite her misgivings and issues with Jackson, she had a job to do. One that William had trained her to flourish in, and to honor him, she would continue to move forward and be the best sales director she could be. She glanced down at her foot, which was now fastened into a boot with Velcro. During her doctor appointment earlier in the morning, she had learned that she had safely avoided surgery—halleluiah!—and had transitioned from that wretched cast into a boot that could be removed for baths.

At the inn, she nestled into her desk chair and picked up the phone. Before she could punch in a few numbers, Jackson ducked into her office.

"Hey," he said.

"Hello, Jackson."

"I deserved that."

She scrunched her brow. "Deserved a hello?"

"A formal one," he said, a scowl on his face. "Listen, you and I need to call a truce starting today."

She didn't see a white flag anywhere so she waited.

He took in the sight of her foot in its black-booted glory. "Good news, I see."

"Right. I won't be suing you."

He hesitated, then grinned. "My prayers have been answered."

"Did you want something, Jack?"

His eyebrows pulled upward. "Yes. Lunch. I have some—some *things* I'd like to discuss with you before a meeting I have tonight."

"With one of my clients?"

"Funny. No. With potential investors."

It was her turn to raise an eyebrow. "Sure, Jackson. Anything I can do to help."

"Great. I'll meet you at 12:30 … unless you need me to squire you in your wheelchair?"

She rolled her eyes. "I don't think 'squire' has been used in about fifty years. Thanks, though. I think I can find my way."

Two hours later she met Jackson at the hotel's signature restaurant. The hostess led her to a table that used to be their favorite, one that overlooked the sea. She sipped a glass of water that had been brought to the table and glanced outside to where the tide rolled in on this late summer day.

Jackson interrupted her musings. "Glad you made it."

His shirt was white and crisp, his suit coat black and expensive. A faraway memory came to mind … She longed to press her nose to his neck and breathe in his cologne—probably some type of mint mixed with oak. Any other situation and he may have bent down to kiss her cheek, or better yet, her lips. She would have smiled and leaned into the moment. But today he was her boss, someone she had agreed to get along with … *for better or worse.*

He draped his coat over his chair and sat opposite her. "Thank you for agreeing to meet me."

He said this like he wasn't her boss, like it wasn't expected that she would meet him. "What can I help you with, Jackson?"

"Just a moment." He motioned for their waiter to approach. "Please bring us a bottle of sparkling water."

"Yes, sir."

Jackson turned to Meg. "You still like fizzy water, right?"

She nodded, a slight smile at his recollection of an old term.

When the bottle had been delivered, Jackson poured her some in a fresh glass, his smile engaging and kind. He stared at her for a beat longer than she expected him to.

After they had ordered lunch, Meg asked, "What is it I can help you with for your meeting, Jackson?"

"As you know, I've been thinking of rebranding Sea Glass Inn as more of a destination. One part of that would be adding a spa."

She nodded. "You mentioned that quite a while ago."

"I did, but—" he seemed to shrug— "I faced some opposition for a time."

"Pepper?"

"She doesn't understand that this is an investment that could pay out in years to come." He took a sip of wine and set his glass back down onto the table. "Before we get into specifics, tell me about some of your travels—what you've seen and enjoyed."

"Do you mean, what I think might work here at the inn?"

"Not necessarily." He leaned forward, his voice low. "If you had the freedom to do anything while you were traveling, what would you choose?"

He sat back and continued to eye her, as if listening intently to whatever she had to say. She looked down at her plate and studied the pattern that mimicked the arc of a wave. Whenever Meg traveled, her mind was on her work—what the clients needed to make their events stand out, what she could do to cause them to return, and how all those efforts affected the company's bottom line.

She looked up. "Until recently, I've had the freedom to travel to our little hotels and make sure that each event provides a win-win situation for guests and our rock star employees."

He frowned. "I've no doubt that this is how you've done your job, but now I want the non-scripted version."

"Pardon me?"

"Tell me what you would have said if you weren't speaking to the boss."

Meg leaned her head to one side, considering this.

"Don't tell me that if you had time all to yourself you would stay inside and figure out how many additional rounds you could fit into a banquet hall."

She scoffed.

Jackson stared at her wide eyed. "You really would do that, wouldn't you?"

Meg rolled her eyes toward the ceiling. "Please. You make me out to be so boring. Can I help it if I like working?"

He was silent for a moment. Then quietly he asked, "Do you … really?"

For some reason, the way he asked that simple question caused a catch in her throat. Yes, of course, she liked to work. She had fixed her eyes on leaving her hometown in the middle of the state and did so before she had even reached eighteen years old. Wasn't that something to be proud of?

A server delivered their salads, but Meg had little appetite. She reached for her fork and let it hover over her Caesar. "I've done what I had to do to provide a good life for myself," she said. "If I had more time on my hands, I probably would go outside and read something other than client files."

"Or business magazines?"

He had noticed. She shrugged a shoulder. "I like magazines that help keep me spinning with new ideas—*Fortune, Inc., Fast Company,* etc."

"Like the goat yoga classes you booked out on the lawn for guests?"

"I only *wish* that had been my idea, but no. Truthfully, I don't have that many fresh ideas myself." She paused. "Maybe I should not be telling that to the boss."

"You are selling yourself short, but I do agree about reading. When I was a kid, I was too impatient to sit down and read an entire article, let alone a book. But now? Finding a terrace with a nice view, an abundance of quiet, and an unread book sounds like paradise." He reclined, leaning an elbow on the arm of his chair, exposing tan skin beneath the open collar of his shirt.

She bit her top lip just as his cell phone rang. He glanced at the screen and barely hid a frown. "I should take this."

"Of course." She set her napkin by her plate and pushed her chair back, but Jackson motioned for her to stay.

The voice on the other end of the call had become unmistakable: it was Pepper's and she was unhappy about something. *How unusual ...*

Jackson winced more than once at the screeching directed at him. *Financial improprieties! Things to get to the bottom of! Unqualified staff!* After only a minute and a half or so, he had clearly had enough. "Pepper, I've got to go. We'll talk about this later." He hung up before his sister could protest.

He sent a wary glance at Meg. "I've never asked, but do you have any siblings?"

She shook her head.

"Want mine?"

She smiled at this. "Not a chance. Did she have an issue with something in particular?"

He ran a hand through layers of wavy hair, his look now slightly disheveled. She had to force herself not to reach out and run her own fingers through that hair. She cleared her throat. "Maybe it would be a good idea to hold a staff meeting with both you and Pepper. If she could see how hard everyone worked, what a great team your dad built, maybe she would, um, relax a little."

Jackson leaned forward on his forearms now and smiled

kindly at her, like he knew that she meant well and he appreciated it, but … "Everyone knows how she is, Meg. My inclination is to ignore her." He sighed. "Now tell me about your ideas for the spa."

WHEN SHE RETURNED to her office, Meg found Liddy curled up under a blanket, a copy of *People* in her hands.

"Girl, you know I tried reading that, but it made no sense."

"You read it *one* time," Liddy protested. "It was an off week, I promise you. Give it another chance."

Meg sat on the other side of the L-shaped couch. "Not happening."

Liddy's eyes zeroed in on Meg's foot. "Hey, you got your cast off. Does this mean …?"

"No surgery."

She lunged for Meg, crushing her with a hug. "Ya-hoo!"

"My gosh, you are suffocating me!"

Liddy stood, her stomach most definitely pooching forward. She had one hand on her ample hip and a child's pout on her face. "Mean girl."

Meg cracked up.

"What's going on with you?"

"What do you mean?"

Liddy examined her closely, like a mother bear searching for crumbs. "Hmm, yes, there's a light in your eyes for the first time since the accident … since awhile, really."

"I'm feeling better."

A half-smile appeared on Liddy's face. "Is that all it is?"

"Isn't that enough? How about you—you're glowing."

"Yes, well, I've got Beau's baby growing inside of me."

Meg wrinkled her nose. "Sure, but what about the addition at your house? Isn't that a lot to deal with while pregnant?"

"Not really. Except our contractor is mighty chipper in the morning. Plays church music."

"You like church music."

"But he smiles constantly. Very weird."

"You would prefer the opposite?"

"All I'm saying is he's loud and happy at 7 a.m. Who does that?"

"Um, babies?"

Liddy groaned. "Don't remind me. I'm not exactly a morning person!"

Meg laughed. Her friend would no doubt become one very soon.

"Speaking of loud and happy," Liddy said, "the staff seems to be in a better mood these days. "

"I know what you're getting at. I was pretty upset the way Pepper swooped in and commandeered my travel schedule, but even I admit that life is much calmer around here without her." How would her friend feel, though, if she knew how much she itched to get back on the road again? This, of course, meant Pepper would have no further reason to stay away. "Jackson and I were having lunch when she called and started berating him."

"Lunch? You had lunch with Jackson? Do tell."

"Please. It was business."

Liddy gave her best mafia impression. "Nothing personal … strictly business."

"Don't you have some reservations to take or something?"

She pressed the home button on her phone until the time lit up. "Nah, I've got time."

Meg made her way to her desk. "Not me. The local chapter of the True Grit Legal Society is in tonight for their annual dinner. I've decided to stick around to see if I might be able to be of assistance."

Liddy curled up her nose. "At a legal dinner?"

Meg flashed her friend a grin. "I Googled and learned that there are TGLS chapters all over this state. Sounds to me like they might be in the market for a statewide conference. Wouldn't you think?"

"Now, see? This is why you are good at what you do. I hear that lawyers are going to be here and can't run away fast enough. You, on the other hand, see the potential for business—maybe even for years to come." Awkwardly, Liddy pushed herself up from the couch. "Excuse me while I practice my waddle on the way back to my office."

Meg watched Liddy leave, a twinge of envy needling her. With a quick chastisement, she brushed away the thought and opened the True Grit Legal Society file that waited on her desk.

THE LEGAL SOCIETY dinner turned out to be more entertaining than she had ever imagined. In little more than two hours Meg had heard terms such as "vigilante justice" and "uncoverers of truth" being bandied about. She'd learned that these were men and women who were not afraid to plow over anyone who got in their way, and more importantly to Meg, that they had been thinking about holding a statewide conference. By the time closing remarks had been delivered by the outgoing president, Meg had drafted a proposal complete with date options and delivered it to the incoming president to take back to his board.

She hustled into her house, surprised to see a light on and her mother on the couch, wrapped in her fuzzy robe, working on a crossword puzzle.

"Hey, Mom. Is Uncle Greg still incarcerated?" she asked, her mind still abuzz with legal jargon. "Is he doing okay?"

Deena put down her puzzle. She removed her readers from her nose and set them on her lap. "Well, hello to you, too."

Meg grimaced. "Sorry. I know it's late, but I've been thinking about him and wondered how he's doing."

"He's in jail, Meg, not in the hospital. He has no nurses fussing over him"—she drew out the word "fussing" until it hissed—"only guards and bars to keep him from leaving on his own."

Why did I open my big mouth? She longed to slip out of her long skirt, soak in a warm tub, and curl up in a robe herself. Did she dare try to extricate herself from further discussion and her mother's gaping stare?

"I understand. He is still not doing very well," Meg said. "I am sorry about that, and even sorrier that I brought it up."

Her mother crossed her arms. "There's a lot of stuff that shouldn't be brought up."

Meg narrowed her eyes. "What kind of stuff? Stuff about Uncle Greg?"

Silence.

"I don't know why I even try anymore …" her mother said and put her slippered feet up on the coffee table, crossing them at the ankles. A bottle of red on the table tipped. Meg lunged for it. Empty. A single "old fashioned" glass rested near one of her mother's slippers. Empty, save for a ring of burgundy in its bottom. Meg gathered both the glass and the empty bottle from the table without comment.

As she entered the kitchen, Meg heard her mother say, "Don't judge me."

Meg's mind swirled. Don't judge her for what? She put the glassware in the sink. For having a brother with addiction problems? For sipping some wine to take the edge off? Meg stood at the kitchen door, one hand on the doorjamb, a cacophony of emotions running through her. *Don't judge me.* She'd heard this often when she was young, but when? And why? Meg stood beneath the door's frame, trying to pull the memories from somewhere deep and covered over.

A bath and sleep would have to wait. She approached her mother and knelt by her side. A mixture of tears and redness marred the whites of her mother's eyes. How had she missed this when she'd walked in? "Mama, what's happening?"

Her mother took both of her cheeks in her hands. A tear trailed down her face, and she bent forward until her forehead touched Meg's.

"What happened to Uncle Greg?" Meg asked. "Why did he get so addicted to drugs?"

Her mother hugged her close, her breathing ragged in her chest. She kept her eyes closed, and her voice had become a whisper. "Meghan," she said, "some things are better left buried."

Without opening her eyes, she kissed her daughter on the forehead, then found a soft place to lay her head on the couch and went to sleep.

CHAPTER 9

In the past two weeks she had learned to wield her booted foot like a speed walker. Stepping in as conference services manager demanded that she be on the move, and though she enjoyed the fast pace of the position, she wanted to throw out a whoop at Judy's return to the hotel after having her sweet baby, Amelia.

"Here's the last of them," Meg said, handing over a thick stack of files to Judy. "You may want to lock your office door for a day to get through them all."

Judy laughed as she left the office. "Thanks so much for all your help. Appreciated!"

Meg turned to her desk, which looked more like a storeroom for unwanted paper. She could stay and tackle the outburst of files and documents that needed a proper place or go home and see what her mother was up to.

Her mother. She had hinted, then outright told her mother she was fine, but Deena had not appeared to be interested in leaving. She swallowed back the confusion that welled inside of her every time she thought about the night she'd come home to find her mother in tatters about Uncle Greg's situation. What had she meant about things untold? She hated to admit It, but her mother had always been so dramatic with no real reason behind it. Surely there was nothing earth shattering buried?

She blew out a long sigh, still considering her evening's options.

"You look like you could use some cheering up," Jackson said, entering her office wearing beat-up jeans and a tee that looked worn and soft. He had been gone all week taking potential investors from Miami on site tours.

"You're back," she said.

"I'm back."

"Good trip?" She carefully avoided letting her eyes sweep over him. When he didn't answer, she swung around to find him staring at her. "Was it?"

A slow smile spread across his face. He held her eyes with his gaze. "Sure. Good trip. Better to be home, though."

Her cheeks warmed and she looked back at her desk, but nothing came into focus. "I bet." For someone who preferred travel to home, she knew the emptiness of her response. But what was she to say with him looking at her like a slice of chocolate cake? It was wrong in a million ways for a boss to assess an employee like that, but Jackson wasn't just any boss. They had a history. A history she didn't dare repeat ... as tempting as it may be.

Jackson crossed the office and half-leaned, half-sat against the edge of her desk. Oh boy. Eyes on her desk, she kept shuffling paper, praying she didn't lose something important while at it.

"I reviewed your notes about the spa while on the flight back."

"And?"

"How many times have you been to a spa?"

"What does that have to do with anything?"

"Don't look so annoyed. You made some great observations, which made me think you must be a regular visitor to top spas."

She didn't reply.

"So. Are you? Which are your favorites?"

Head games. Whether he knew it or not—and she suspected he did—Jackson's questions played with her head. Everyone knew that one of the best ways to assess the competition was to, well, partake of their offerings, i.e., taste their food, try on their clothes … visit their spas. But Meg had gathered her information on observation alone. Whenever she worked a trade show, she would either ask for a formal site tour of the hotel, or give herself one. She kept detailed notes of these visits, listing meeting space square footage and on-site amenities, such as cafes, fitness centers, swim facilities, and of course, spa services. She rarely ever used any of the services herself—work always took precedence.

"Well, there's one in Monterey that's gorgeous. Small, but it's on the top floor and guests can use workout equipment while watching the sunrise over the bay, then have a massage right in the next room."

He moved closer to her, his voice like a balm. "I hope this is not something that is just on paper, but that you have experienced their services for yourself. Have you?"

She slid him a sideways look. "Not exactly."

He nodded once. "And the reason is …?"

"I-I'm too busy. This is no complaint, because I do love my work here at the inn, but my plate here is very full."

His brows contracted. "We should change that."

"Are you saying my notes were lacking?"

"On the contrary, your observations are well taken. I was impressed by your impassioned plea to keep the spa on guest room floors, rather than on the main floor …"

"Impassioned plea? Now you're just teasing me." She shook her head, hiding a smile. "All I meant was that no woman wants to be seen in a robe down on the main floor, especially if she's attending a conference."

"And your idea to dedicate an elevator to the spa area is a great one, too. Expensive, but good."

"Can you imagine running into a colleague after having just had a chemical peel?"

"No, not at all. My chemical peels are between me and my esthetician."

"Ha ha ha."

He was grinning at her now, which caused unexpected weakness in her knees. She reached for the back of her desk chair and sat down.

He winced. "Foot bothering you?"

"Yes, that's it." It wasn't a lie—her foot was connected to her legs, right?

"Tell you what. When you get rid of that boot, I want you to visit some spas. Have the works and we will pay for it."

Pepper showed up at the door, those thin black brows of hers attempting to assault the ceiling. "We will *what*?"

Meg's neck spasmed and she bit back a groan.

Jackson continued to lean against Meg's desk but turned his chin in response to his sister's sudden appearance. "I see that I'm not the only Riley who has returned to the roost."

"I am gone, what, two months and already we are adding spa vacations to our employees' benefits?"

Jackson's expression hardened. "We can talk about this over dinner."

"Absolutely we will. I am ready now, if you can tear yourself away from—" she waved a dismissive hand in Meg's direction —"your crush."

He pushed himself away from the desk, a grunt barely audible. Yet he stayed rooted in place. "Go on over," he said with a flick of his chin. "I'll see you when I'm finished here."

Pepper twisted her lips into an annoyed smirk. "Yes, you will."

"The time away has been restful for her, I see," Meg said when she had gone.

The scowl on his face turned to surprise. His mouth relaxed

into a grin and he leaned toward her and bumped her with his shoulder. "Want to take my place?"

She shook her head slowly, smiling. "Not a chance."

This time he groaned audibly. "You had your chance," he said as he stepped toward the door.

"Jackson?"

He stopped, a question in his eyes.

"Have the grilled cheese and tomato soup. Some of the best comfort food out there."

"Good advice," he said with a laugh. "May have to get the chef to make up a double batch."

After he left, she found herself thinking of him—the way he looked in his battered denim, the way he'd moved closer to her as if it were natural. Suddenly, she could no longer concentrate. The avalanche of paper on her desk dissolved into further chaos until she wanted to reach for a lighter and burn the whole thing down. Her mother had texted her that she wasn't feeling well and would be going to bed early. Might as well head home, too, and make it an early night.

She gathered up her belongings and was about to leave when her eyes alighted on the book Liddy had spontaneously given her a couple of weeks before. When she had not found time to browse its pages at home, she had brought it here. Maybe, she thought, she would find time during a break or lunch hour to devour it … to dream a little.

Sadly, it had stayed wedged in the corner of the coffee table where she had laid it when she had brought it to work.

On the cover, a collection of pastel-painted villas hugged mountainous terrain that burst from the sea. She exhaled, seeing the image for the first time. Though the book had been in her home and then here in her office, its beauty had not made it past her eyes and into her heart. If someone were to tell her that she was looking at paradise she would not have questioned them. She ran the pads of her fingers across the smooth and shiny cover. For the first time in a long while, she realized, she did not wonder whether any of the colorful buildings could double as an event destination.

Maybe Jackson had been right about her obsession with business and trade magazines. Had she become immune to life outside of the inn? To life in general? She flipped open the cover, another image drawing her into its iridescent playfulness.

Italy ... she will heal you.

Meg smiled at the memory of William's words.

Another's words sprang to mind. Domenic Marino, William's longtime friend and attorney, had called to console her after William's death. "You meant the world to him, *cara mia*," he had said, using the Italian term for "my beloved." "You must know this."

"Yes," she whispered into the quiet now. "I knew."

Domenic and his wife, Elena, had retired and moved to Italy more than a year ago. She glanced at the clock: 6:07 p.m. Still the wee morning hours there. She sighed and shut the book. She had not taken a vacation in years, well, other than to clean her neglected house or run errands that were past due. She determined to give William's old friend Domenic a call first thing in the morning. Who knows? Come next spring, maybe she would finally take a real vacation—to Italy.

THE KNIFE in his back twisted. His welcome home dinner consisted of listening to Pepper's conspiracy theories about why the company was steadily losing money, more than one revolving around Meg. Would her questioning of their sales director and her relationship with his—their—father never end?

"Are you aware that he co-signed for her auto loan?" Pepper had asked with a sneer.

"I am."

"And you are okay with this?"

Jackson had lifted his gaze to the ceiling, collected himself, then re-engaged. "Father took her under his wing when she was very young. She paid off that car long before he died. Can we talk about something else?"

He spent the rest of the meal listening to her rail against Meg's fierce protection of her clients, "As if they need protection from me!" She also talked nonstop about what a fabulous job she did running the booths at three trade conventions: one in the north, one in the south, and one in the middle. He'd made a mental note to ask Liddy if there had been an influx of reservations after those shows.

Despite his less-than-palatable dinner companion, his meal was delicious. He smiled thinking of Meg's recommendation. Because of her, he had ordered the three-cheese grilled sandwich and tomato-basil soup. "That is not dinner!" Pepper had said after he ordered. He'd let it ride, of course. If he couldn't have Meg sitting across from him, he would at least have something that reminded him of her.

Had he lost his mind? If she never came around, he very well might.

MEG STROLLED along the path that wound its way above the ocean. At this point, the boot seemed like overkill, as her foot did not ache at all. She waved to Rudy, who used an old-fashioned rake to clear the path of stray leaves and berries that fell from palm trees after semi-regular windstorms. A few beachcombers moseyed on the sand, dogs in tow.

So this is what early morning sea lovers did.

Admittedly, she woke up early every morning, but instead of slowly joining the world, she dove in to her to-do list—coffee in hand. The thought of calling Domenic had stayed with her through the night, even igniting a bit of insomnia. Part of her simply wanted to hear the lawyer's gentle voice. She had spoken to him often when she was William's executive assistant, and he never asked for her boss without first engaging her in small talk. He and his wife were lovely, well-traveled people who had found their forever home in Italy after a lifetime of working in America. She had missed those conversations after she became sales director and no longer screened William's calls. But the finality of saying goodbye to Domenic and Elena was never more sobering than after William's passing.

At her desk, phone in hand, Meg dialed the + sign, country code, and number for Domenic.

"Pronto?"

That voice was like comfort food for the ears. "Buon giorno, Domenic. It's Meg calling."

"*Cara mia*! It is you! How beautiful to hear your voice after these many months. I hope you are well."

She glanced at her foot, which she believed was as well as could be expected. "I am, I am. How are you? How is dear Elena?"

"We are old!" He laughed and released a string of Italian words that made no sense to her but seemed to make him happy saying them. "To what do I owe the pleasure of this happy surprise?"

His kindness brought tears to her. She blinked them away. "My friend, Liddy, gave me a book about Cinque Terre and it made me think of you. I think … I think I would like to plan a vacation to Italy, maybe for the spring. I am hoping you will advise me and maybe have dinner with me while I am there?"

"My word! What is this talk about dinner? You must come and stay with us—we will feed you!" His voice became more distant then, as if he had turned away from the phone. "Elena, Elena … she will be here in the spring! She will stay with us!"

Meg was crying now, full on happy tears. It felt heady and slightly dangerous to leave her job for weeks at a time to … play. But Domenic's reaction confirmed to her that she was making a good decision.

They spoke for a time about places they would take her on her trip, and she in turn asked about Cinque Terre and how easy it would be for her to travel there. She was just about to say her goodbye—work was calling—when Domenic said, "Tell me about the siblings."

"I'm sorry. What do you mean?"

"I am asking how Jackson and Pepper are getting along. I rarely hear from them, so I can only assume that all is well. Tell me. Are they a good team?"

A million responses came to mind, none that would calm any misgivings Domenic may be having.

He continued. "How is Pepper faring? I could never reach her after William's death—she traveled so often, you see. It broke my heart that I had to send her the news in a letter. I take it she has come to terms with the news? Would you say that she is happy there, at Sea Glass Inn?"

"Oh Domenic, I'm not sure whether I'm the right person to ask. Pepper hasn't been here very much all summer. She—"

"Excuse me?"

Meg jerked a look toward her open office door where Pepper stood decked out in a leopard pantsuit and black stilettos, her mouth ajar. "Are you speaking with Daddy's attorney?" she screeched.

Meg's mind spun. She looked from Pepper to the untouched papers on her desk, and back to the angry woman with long white hair that stood at the entrance to her office. She nodded toward Pepper, in the vain hope that she would go away.

Pepper charged into the room. "Hang up, hang up right now!"

Meg shrank back. She had done nothing wrong, but she turned toward the phone in a hurry. "I'm very sorry, Domenic, but there is a crisis at work right now and I have to run. Ciao-ciao."

"This is highly improper!" Pepper stood over her now, wagging a nail-sharp forefinger at her. "What were you and he talking about? Tell me!"

Meg rose to meet Pepper face-to-face. She had the ability to clear up any misunderstanding right now, but something about the way Pepper drew erroneous conclusions, the way she ground her jaw and her eyes flashed, brought out the rebel in Meg. "It was a private matter."

Pepper stepped closer. "There are no private matters when you are on *my* property!"

"This is my property, too." Jackson's voice cut through the tension in the room.

Pepper swiveled. "I caught her on the phone with Daddy's attorney talking about private things," she said, wagging that insidious finger. "This is an act of insubordination ... we must not allow this, Jackson."

Meg groaned and sat back down. "This has got to stop."

Pepper dug a fist into Meg's desk and bent, lunging toward her. "Yes, it does. And it begins with you and your constant meddling in private affairs. Domenic is Daddy's attorney, not yours, and I advise you to keep your distance."

Meg lifted a defiant chin. "Or what?"

"Woah, enough you two."

Pepper poked her finger at Jackson. "Tell her. Tell her what we know ... so far."

Meg leaned her head to one side.

He set his jaw. "This is not the time."

"It is precisely the time. Otherwise, she will think her prying into family affairs can continue. Okay, if you will not say it—I will!" She turned to Meg, her eyes like liquid fire. "We know you benefited greatly from our father's wealth. I have seen the notations!"

Meg glanced at Jackson. "What is she talking about?"

He hesitated, concern etched across his forehead. He glanced at her, his mouth a flat line.

"Jackson?" Meg asked.

Pepper let out a haughty laugh. "Things are not so special for you these days, are they, Meghan? Not since the money train has stopped for you."

Meg's mouth dropped open. "I-I have no idea what you mean?" She swung a look at Jackson. "I have never taken a dime from the company other than my paycheck."

One of Pepper's brows arched. A disturbing smile spread across her face, outlined in scarlet. "The evidence is to the contrary."

Meg gave Jackson a "come on" look, her eyes pleading with him to step up and tell his sister to back off. Surely, he knew the emptiness of her accusations.

"Well, I, for one, am tired of all of this." Pepper's open palms volleyed upward. She had come in with a wrecking ball, did her damage, and had, apparently, decided to flee and allow someone else to pick through the chaos. "I am going home now, but I expect you to take care of this ... mess," Pepper said, looking Meg up and down.

When she'd left, Meg took in Jackson's torn expression. "Must have been some dinner you two had last night."

"Were you really just on the phone with Domenic?"

She scrunched her eyes. "Why? Would that be a problem?"

Jackson ran his hand through his hair, then down his neck, pausing there as if willing away the tension. "Not too many twenty-somethings make it a point to call elderly men in other countries."

Meg spurted a sarcastic laugh. "You think I'm a call girl?"

"What? No!"

"Well, then what kind of comment was that?" She flailed her hands in the air, exasperated. "You obviously have questions, so go ahead, Mr. Riley, spit them out."

"Meg." He reached for her wrists, wrapped his hands around them, then pulled them gently toward his hips. "There are some things I'm trying to figure out."

"What kinds of things? About me?"

That skin between his eyes furrowed. "No. It's-it's complicated …"

"Well, I have time."

He exhaled and lowered his voice. "It would be best if you laid low for a while."

She wrenched her wrists from him. "You don't trust me?"

"It's not—no, that's not true at all. I think, though, that now would be a good time for you to take a step back. Take a few days off while this blows over—"

Meg bit her top lip, lurched backward, and took in the sight of Jackson standing there, asking her to disappear. He had acted as if calling Domenic had been seedy and untoward, something that she needed to hide from. *Why not just tell him the truth? I wanted to hear an old friend's voice again and plan a real vacation for the first time in my life!*

She looked at the boot on her foot, huffed out a sigh, then raised her chin. "If that's what you want, Jackson. Fine. I will 'lay low,' as you put it." She picked up her hot list, i.e. clients poised to sign on the dotted line, and handed it to him. "Good luck with these."

Without as much as a glance over her shoulder, Meg headed home to pack.

CHAPTER 10

Jackson's head pounded like a hangover caused by a bottle of two-buck chuck. Only this affliction had been powered by something other than alcohol. He put a palm to his temple. Sleep eluded him, as did rest, and shortly, sanity would go too.

Meg had not shown up for work the day after their tense exchange. Not thoroughly surprising—Pepper's caustic comments would make anyone want to hide. But what surprised him happened today: She had not shown up for a second day in a row. Nor had she called.

Jackson groaned into the dark night and flipped over onto his back, the ceiling fan working overtime to cool his temper. So much more he'd wanted to say that night, but he held back for his own reasons. His sister's vehemence sucker punched him. So much to consider when it came to her, and unfortunately, Meg had misunderstood his reticence as an indictment against her—as if he agreed with Pepper.

Good job, man.

With a grunt, he threw off the covers and launched his legs over the side of the bed, thinking over his options. A glance at his phone told him the time. When had he become an old man who turned in so early? He rubbed his hand down along his neck, the pressure helping to soothe his headache. With resolve, he pressed palms into his thighs and willed himself to stand, get dressed, and get out the door.

Ten minutes later he stood on Meg's stoop. Her car in the drive and lighted lamp in the window told him she was home. Would she be up? And would she talk to him? *Get a grip, man.* Jackson rapped his knuckles on her door, which swung open in a hurry.

Deena greeted him, coat on, suitcase by her side. "Jackson?"

"Yes. It's me. Are you ... Deena, it looks like you are leaving."

"I thought you were my taxi driver. I need to catch a bus ride home."

"I see. And Meg's still not driving all that much, I gather."

"Meg's not here. I thought you knew she took a vacation."

He startled. No, he had not considered she would actually leave town.

Deena's face softened, her smile, gentle. "The night air is cool. Would you like to come in ... ?" She opened the door wider.

He shook his head and almost turned away, but stopped. "It's a ten-minute drive to the bus station. Let me take you—you can cancel your ride."

Moments later they were in his Mercedes heading to the bus station that would take Deena back home after a summer at the coast. He took in her profile, illuminated by the flicker of street lights. A million thoughts were written in her expression.

"I'm surprised Meg left before you did." He wanted to fill the quiet with *something*.

"My daughter has a mind of her own." She peered at him. "I take it you already know this about her."

This brought a guffaw from him.

"I thought so." She forced a sigh and glanced at the terrain whizzing by in the night. "Meg and I talked it over. She had a sudden need for a break—no pun intended, ha!—and I have needed to get home for some time. I stayed on after she left to clean up after myself. No one will call me a sloppy house guest!"

He laughed. "I'm sure Meg would never say such a thing."

"Eh, maybe, maybe not. Besides, my husband has been lonely. I told him to come visit, but—" she gave him an assessing look —"you know how stubborn men can be."

"I hadn't realized Meg had a stepfather."

Deena shrugged. "I am not surprised."

He waited, but she added nothing more and instead continued to stare out the window. "She mentioned, years ago, that her father had passed away when she was little."

"She told you?"

"When I asked about him. She didn't have much to say more than that. I took that to mean it's not a memory she likes to revisit."

Deena nodded, her eyes far away.

He drove, silent now, trying to recall what Meg had said about her father. Remorse rose in him. He'd been a selfish kid in a man's body back then and could not recall anything significant. *What a jerk I was ...* "Tell me about him."

Deena shrank back, eyeing him. "Who?"

He kept his eyes on the road. "Meg's father."

Silence.

"If you don't mind, that is."

"He-he was a wonderful man." She paused. "Jonathan loved Meghan and me. He would have done anything for us. I guess you could say he was ... perfect."

Jackson doubted that, but didn't say so. "May I ask how he passed away?"

"No."

"I'm sorry. That was prying."

Sniffles. A hitch in her voice. More sniffling.

Now I have done it. "I apologize, Deena. I was prying into something that's none of my business."

"It was years ago, nearly twenty now. Car accident. So generous, he was—if you were cold, he would build a fire. If you were hungry, he would light the barbecue. Everybody loved him."

"Sounds like someone to be celebrated."

Jackson stopped at a light. Deena was watching him, a quizzical expression on her face. "Did I say something odd?" he asked.

"N-no. It was wonderful. Truly." She paused, her forehead bunched, her mouth frowning. "Maybe I have been stupid."

The light turned green and he continued down the narrow road. "I doubt that."

"My daughter is like a closed book. I thought I was protecting her all these years, but I don't know. Perhaps if I had been more open she would be too." She sighed, the sound of it like an ache. "Now she flies off to another country all by herself as if she wants to be alone."

Jackson whipped a look toward his passenger. "Meg left for another country?"

"I thought you knew."

He let out a sigh of his own, a long, frustrated sigh. "I almost hate to ask ... do you know where she went?"

"She took her passport from the drawer, packed her things, and flew off to Italy, of all places. I don't understand it. All that gluten—I thought she avoided that!"

He was the one who had told her to lay low for a while. Jackson gripped the steering wheel, picturing Meg limping through customs all alone. The wrench in his chest was unmistakable.

"I APOLOGIZE FOR CALLING SO LATE."

Liddy's voice sounded tired. He had awoken her. "Jackson? Is-is everything okay at the inn? I left Amanda in charge, and—"

"The inn is fine. I'm calling about Meg."

"Oh."

"I know she went to Italy."

"How—?"

"Her mother told me … it's not important how. Listen, could you tell me how to reach her? I've tried her phone and she's not answering. I suspect she has gone to see my father's … old friend."

"I mean no disrespect, but she's on vacation and I really have to honor that."

"You won't tell me?" *Even though I'm your boss?*

"I'd rather not, Jackson. Everyone deserves a break. Don't you think Meggie deserves one?"

What was he thinking, chasing after her like a lovesick kid? He sat on his cold bed, sleep far away from him. He wanted to protest, to compel his reservations manager to tell him the whereabouts of his sales director, but suddenly felt foolish. Who wakes up their pregnant employee at nearly midnight to ask about a co-worker?

"Are you still there, Jackson?"

"Good night, Liddy," he said, pulling himself together. He hoped her husband would not show up in his office tomorrow to throw a fist.

"I will see you tomorrow," she said with finality.

"Yes," he said, "tomorrow." He hung up but stayed awake, his rhythmic breaths his only company. It was nearly 8 a.m. in Italy, surely not too early to phone an old friend …

He punched in Domenic's phone number and identified himself when his father's attorney answered.

"William's boy!"

Domenic's aged voice on the line calmed him, reminding Jackson of his father. "Yes, sir, it is me."

"Please. Tell me how you are. Tell me everything."

"You are kind to ask, sir, but I did not mean to trouble you this … this morning. I am in somewhat of a hurry and I have a question for you."

"I see. Well, then, go ahead and ask me your question. But, please, call me Domenic."

"Of course. You do know Meg, correct?"

"Ah, Meg, yes. One of our favorite people, Elena's and mine. Is everything okay?"

Jackson's heart landed with a thud in his stomach. "I was hoping you could tell me. She, uh, she took a vacation, and, well, there are a few questions I needed to ask her before she left."

"I'm very sorry, son, but perhaps you have gotten your signals crossed? We spoke briefly only a few days ago and she mentioned that she would like to visit Italy in the spring—she said nothing about coming now."

Alarm gripped him. Days ago, Pepper had accused Meg of interfering in their private lives. He had not believed that, of course. Now Domenic tells him that Meg phoned recently to tell him she was planning to visit in the spring—for a vacation. More than one swear word came to mind. He should have shut Pepper down. He should have—

"Are you still there, son?"

"Yes, sir. I'm sorry to have bothered you, Domenic." He released a breath. "I promise to call again … when there is more time to talk."

"I would welcome it."

BY LATE MORNING, Jackson's countenance resembled the inn's night auditor after hours of reconciling daily statistics. Only he had nothing to show for his fatigue. He punched the button on his office phone for Room Service. "Bring me a large, dark coffee. No cream."

"Right away, Mr. Riley."

The headache that had tormented him last evening had returned today with a vengeance. Sally leaned in from her office on the other side of his. "Long night?"

"Something like that."

She nodded once and left him in peace, without jumbling those pearls of hers. Grateful, he was. Through his window, he stared into a grey-painted sky. How often had his father stared at this same sky? Did he experience the letdown of a day without sun? Or did he welcome the cooler days that so often occurred out here on the coast?

"Sir? Your coffee?" The server delivered a tray large enough for two meals that held one large mug of coffee and a carafe of cream.

"Thanks."

The coffee burned going down, a wake-me-up he needed desperately.

Several of the investors he had met with days ago had left messages, and if he expected to make headway with plans to upgrade their properties he would need to stay attentive to their questions and concerns. He took another gulp of hot coffee and buried himself in the details of the inn's profit-and-loss statement, the first in a stack to review.

An hour later, he pushed himself away from his desk, numbers filling his mind. Without much thought of direction, Jackson wandered outside at a fast clip, eager for fresh air. He rounded the first bend of the seaside path and nearly collided with Liddy, which, considering her condition, might not have ended well.

"Don't tell me, let me guess," she said with a laugh. "You didn't see me coming?"

He avoided looking at her belly. "Sorry if I scared you, Liddy."

"No worries. You look deep in thought. Lots of meetings today?"

"Thankfully, no." He leveled a look at her. "Listen, I want to apologize for calling you last night. It won't happen again."

"I'm relieved that you mentioned it first. It wasn't easy for me to say no to my boss."

"When Meg didn't show up, I grew concerned."

"That's all it was?"

Her question lingered between them. Avoiding truths came naturally, but lying? Not something he wanted to associate himself with. "Let's just say that's part of it."

She smiled. "Totally acceptable. She's a big girl and is used to taking care of herself."

"Finally realized that. I called an old friend in Italy last night and he had not heard from her, and it hit me that she does not want to be found. That's her prerogative."

Liddy's smile faltered. "Old friend? Meg knows this person?"

He shifted. "Not a shining moment for me, but yes. My father's attorney lives in Italy now. I thought Meg might have gone to see him, but he assured me that she hadn't."

Liddy's expression collapsed. She frowned and seemed to be formulating a response. "Did he say whether he had heard from her?"

"He had not—do you know Domenic?"

"I—yes, well, no, but I know *of* him." She looked away, sighing.

"What aren't you telling me?"

She swung her gaze back to him. "Nothing, really. It's just that I have been trying to reach Meg for two days and she hasn't responded. Even her locator app doesn't seem to be working."

"Locator app?"

She sighed. "A BFF thing. I live vicariously through her whenever she travels. The app tells me where she is. Right now, all it says is 'location not available.'"

Maybe that's the way she wants it.

"Anyway, it's probably just phone issues, but I'm concerned that Domenic said she hadn't been in touch because … well, she was planning to go straight to his apartment when she arrived."

"Could she be lost?"

Liddy's hand went to her stomach. "No, no. She has traveled alone many times. I'm sure … I'm sure …" She reached out and grabbed Jackson's hand. "What if something's happened to her?"

Jackson put an arm around Liddy and supported her beneath an elbow. He walked her to a bench and sat down next to her. "Let's not panic. Like you said, Meg has traveled many times on her own."

"Yeah," she said, her laugh non-convincing. "Maybe she decided to do some sightseeing first. She mentioned going to see the statue of David."

"Call me if you hear from her?"

"Of course."

"Great." Slowly, he stood. "Are you going to be okay?"

Liddy nodded. "Of course. I think I'll just sit here and pray a little."

A novel thought. There was no doubt in him that he would soon be boarding a plane for Italy. "Liddy?"

"Yes?"

"While you're at it, say one for me."

MEG AWOKE DISORIENTED and drenched in sweat. The bed she slept on creaked when she turned to check the time on her phone. Dead. She shut her eyes, remembering. Not only had she forgotten to purchase international calling, she had neglected to pack her charger. Even if she had, she realized, it would not have worked in Italian electrical outlets. She made a note to buy one tomorrow.

They did have Apple stores in Florence, right?

She had arrived in Rome and taken a short flight to Aeroporto Amerigo Vespucci in Florence. From there, she had planned to hire a car to take her to Domenic and Elena's apartment … but she lost her nerve. What would Domenic have thought if she'd shown up there today after telling him not more than three days ago that she would see him in the spring?

A short-lived breeze entered through a screen-less window that she had left open all afternoon in an attempt to shake the sweltering heat. She had arrived in the afternoon, her body clock in disarray. Logic told her to adjust by staying awake, but heavy eyes and tired limbs had won out and she collapsed onto the less-than-comfortable bed and fell into a mesmerizing sleep.

Packing in a hurry had been easy enough—she knew how to roll her clothes, always kept small toiletry bottles on hand, and thanks to a trade show in Toronto, her passport had been handy. What she had not counted on was the choke-worthy heat and that she would arrive with a sudden sense of protocol. She had lost her mind—she could fathom no other reason for hopping on an impromptu (and expensive!) flight out of the country.

She yawned and stretched, glancing around the plain, dark room. An English-speaking booking agent at the airport had called the owner of this apartment and arranged for him to meet her with a key. Not until she had paid a two-night deposit did she realize there was no air conditioning—and that a faint smell of BO lingered in the hall.

The din of revelers on the streets below brought her reality closer. She leaned out the window, taking in Florence's star-filled sky. What Northern Italy lacked in cool breezes this time of year, it more than made up for in charm and a welcome embrace. The aroma of truffle oil from a nearby restaurant called to her and her stomach grumbled. She had nothing but a free packet of pretzels with her to eat—*but this was Italy!* She pulled herself up and headed out to join the throng.

The ancient streets had worn unevenly, causing her to step with caution. The piazza heaved with life—lovers holding hands, friends eating gelato stacked precariously, and children darting through the crowds. It was like Stars Hollow—Italian style.

She continued to walk, unaccustomed to such freedom at

home where fog rolled in and businesses closed in a hurry after dark. If she had learned anything from her travels it was to eat where the locals ate. True, not many of the places she passed as she strolled were empty, but some screamed "tourist trap" to her anyway—especially those with expensive specials that skirted the edge of the piazza.

Down a narrow street, she spotted a line of people outside of a small shop and knew she had found dinner. One by one she watched people exit the shop carrying a pizza box, a bottle of red wine, and a stack of small white cups. The line moved steadily, and it wasn't until she got closer to the entrance that she realized there was little room to sit inside.

A couple of guys moved past her on their way out, each holding a pizza of their own. Her mouth watered at the aroma of sauce and cheese and garlic. She was third in line behind two girls who had been talking nonstop about their study abroad program. After they placed their order, she reached the counter.

"Una pizza margherita, per favore."

"Prego. Chianti?"

When she hesitated, the man nodded his head quickly. "Ah, you try." He grabbed a plastic cup and filled it to the brim with the dry red wine and handed it to her. "Enjoy!"

"Grazie."

She moved to the side to allow someone else to order, took a sip of wine, and relaxed her shoulders for the first time since stepping on that first flight from home. On the plane, she had relived Pepper's wild accusations, but it was Jackson's reaction that hurt more. She blinked away emotion. She and Jackson had been slowly mending what had been torn between them. But when he told her to lay low, as if she should take some responsibility for Pepper's nonsense, she felt as if he had punched another hole in their gossamer truce.

Soon her number was called, and she too stepped out into the street, pizza and wine in hand, and searched for somewhere cool to eat. About a block and a half away, she found a spot on the steps of a church next to others who had spilled out of doors to get away from the heat. Live music danced on the wind, and the crowd showed no sign of thinning.

"You look like you could use some more wine." She glanced up from her slice of pizza—aka heaven on earth—to find a man with thick blond hair and a warm smile peering down at her.

He held the bottle over her empty cup. "May I?"

"Thank you."

"I wondered if you were Italian, but with that accent, I'd say west coast."

She laughed at that. "I wasn't aware that Californians had accents."

"Absolutely we do."

"So you're saying that you are from California, too."

"I knew I was right about where you're from. Although I have to say, you could pass for an Italian too. I took my chances speaking to you in English knowing there was only a 50/50 chance you'd understand."

"Oh, I don't know. You were holding a bottle of wine over my empty cup. I think that's understandable in any language."

He threw his head back at this, laughing. "True, true. I'm Garrett, by the way."

"Meg."

"Is he bothering you, ma'am?" A teen with a goofy grin and hair that could use a solid trimming body slammed into her wine bearer.

The man shrank back, holding the bottle at bay. "Hey, watch it. I've got wine here."

The kid rolled his eyes. "Stuff's like water around here."

Garrett slapped one side of the teen's head with a palm. "What are they teaching the young uns these days?"

She tsked, tsked.

"I've been sent over here to tell you Pastor says it's time to go." The kid gave Meg a fake pout.

Garrett dipped his chin. "And just when I was getting to know the lovely Meg."

The boy threw an arm around Garrett's neck like a hook. "Sorry," he said, a teenage cackle to his voice. He shot a look at Meg. "We're with a church group—he probably didn't tell you that when he was flirting."

Garrett ignored the teen. "We will be staying in this area for the next couple of days, touring museums and hiking before sunrise. I hope to run in to you again, beautiful Meg."

She stayed put and lifted her glass in salute. "Thank you for the wine, Garrett."

When they'd gone, she finished her pizza and continued to people watch. She had no phone and no plans—only a longing to forget about the drama going on at home. Any other time, she might have felt alone, maybe even a little afraid. On the contrary, she looked around at the vibrant pocket in an ancient city and saw a glimpse into William's affection for this country. Though a sadness over what might have been lingered, at this moment, she felt right at home.

CHAPTER 11

Pepper continued to needle Jackson about Meg's part in their financial troubles, but something did not add up. He could feel it. He'd had a dozen hours to stare at the grim accounts receivable reports Pepper had shoved into his hands on his way out of the hotel this afternoon, but he'd been unable to concentrate. Of course, she had not realized that he would be stopping home only long enough to change into jeans and pick up his packed suitcase. While the odds of finding a woman who might not want to be found were not in his favor, hanging around the inn and worrying about her whereabouts weren't either. He stretched his legs in front of the first class seat he'd purchased on the fly, thankful he'd had enough frequent flyer miles to temper the sticker shock.

The plane landed on the final segment of his trip. He grabbed his bags, and with other travelers spilled out into a muggy Florence afternoon. By the curb, a man in a suit much too dark and heavy for a day like today held a sign bearing the name RILEY. He handed the man his bags and hopped inside.

The driver took him to an address off the Piazza del Duomo and left him there with his bags. A buzz and a click and he was inside the foyer of the grand apartment building. Relief from the day's heat came immediately. He eyed the narrow elevator and opted for the stairs instead, taking them quickly.

The door to the Marino's apartment swung open and a short woman with bright eyes and short-cropped white hair charged out. "Jackson!" She reached up for him, and he bent to hug her. "Why, look at you! I haven't seen you since you were a boy. Oh but I would know you anywhere."

Behind her a bent man with wire-rimmed glasses and thinning hair waited, a gentle smile on his face. "Come in, come in," he said.

Jackson entered their apartment, soaring ceilings and a blast of icy air greeting him. "You have a beautiful home," he said, impressed.

"Mi casa es su casa," Elena said. "Now, here. Give me those bags. You will stay in our side bedroom. It has a bathroom all its own—"

Something in his heart twisted. He'd hoped she'd be here, but obviously, that was not the case. "Thank you for your generosity, but I have already booked a room nearby," he said.

Elena gasped and slapped a hand to her cheek. "You will not pay for a room elsewhere!"

Domenic wagged his head. "My boy, she will never let you hear the end of this if you don't stay here."

"Grazie, grazie, Elena. But I am not paying. I have offered an acquaintance a room at one of our hotels in exchange for one in his."

"You are resourceful," Domenic said. "Just like William."

Elena hugged her body with crossed arms and shook her head, unhappy.

"While I understand your resourcefulness, son, I think you had better change your plans or Elena here might poison the *bistecca!*" The older man's merriment filled the apartment.

Jackson side hugged Elena. "Of course, of course. I am sorry if I offended you. I would love to stay here with you both."

Her smile returned. "Good!" She pointed toward the bedroom. "Now put your things in there and I will bring out the *aperitivo*."

Jackson returned to the kitchen after freshening up. The catnap he took on the plane was time well spent, though he'd had to stifle a couple of yawns since arriving in Florence. Nothing to do with Elena's constant chatter—she reminded him a lot of his grandmother who passed away when he was a child—but everything to do with the number of hours in the air or on the road.

He ate another olive and chased it down with a sip of Campari. Elena fussed about him, her cheeks flushed from the heat of her stove. "How I wish my container garden was well, then I could offer you fresh herbs." She pointed to the soaring windows opposite the kitchen that opened to a narrow balcony where thirsty, rambling plants trailed. "So hot here and I forget to water all the time."

Domenic nodded. "And I am no help, I am afraid."

Elena's mention of plants led Jackson's mind to Rudy at the inn. He'd probably have a great solution for the Marinos. Unfortunately, Jackson's foray into musings about the inn inevitably brought him back to thoughts about Meg. He forced himself to think about something else …

Domenic had hardly touched his glass of Lambrusco, opting instead to watch Jackson thoughtfully for a few moments. Finally, he spoke. "Tell me about Meg."

Jackson hesitated. "What is it you would like to know?"

"Why did you come here to find her?"

Aim. Shoot. Fire. Jackson gave the elderly man a grim smile. "Is that how it seems?"

"I would say so. It's not every day that a busy man as you travels for half a day by himself for a vacation."

He had let down his guard and determined to put it back up. Stat. "It is more than that, of course. I have potential business here. The friend I mentioned, who manages the hotel nearby …"

Domenic lifted his chin, examining Jackson through the

glasses that had slid down his nose. "You mean your acquaintance."

His smile went slack. "Yes, well, we have some ideas for Sea Glass Inn that we may be able to adopt from his property."

"I see."

Elena spoke without turning away from the stove. "But what about this Meg? Didn't you say she is on vacation?" She spun. "Is she alone, too?"

So many questions. More reason to stay elsewhere. If he wasn't careful, Domenic and Elena would figure out his actions even better than he could.

Domenic chuckled.

Elena nodded. "I see. You had a lovers' spat."

For the second time, he was questioning himself. "There are just some things that I would like to clear up with her. She is not prone to wander, so—" he shrugged—"I had hoped to find her here and talk it out."

Elena slid a plate in front of him with a *bistecca*—a steak—as large as his head. "Mangia," she said, waving tongs at him. "You don't worry. If she is in Florence, we will flush her out!"

THE LINE TO buy tickets to Galleria dell' Accademia straggled out the door and onto the street, but the line to enter the museum snaked like a triple row of braids. After buying a ticket, Meg took her place in line, right outside of the Cherubini Music Conservatory next door to the *accademia*. She had hoped to arrive earlier, but a fitful night's sleep made her morning slow. That and a unique soreness on the top of her foot.

Not that she was in any particular hurry. She'd woken up with the odd reminder that nothing pressing awaited her—no phone calls or emails or hysterical bosses. The line crept forward, and reflexively, she felt for her phone in her crossover purse. Still dead. She had mixed feelings about charging it, though she would have been able to buy her ticket in advance. The other part of her didn't care to know who might be trying to reach her.

Once inside, she wandered with the throng down the long corridor, taking her time to view Michelangelo's sculptures described as enslaved, their bodies seeming to struggle to make it to completion. Surely, the museum curators would save David for the very end of the tour, like a decadent dessert. She determined to be patient, to savor the trill of foreign voices speaking in whispers in their native tongues, to listen to the past as she took in the undulating figures lining the hall.

Then she spotted him. At the end of the first corridor, the marbleized David rose above the crowd, his head and body illuminated by nature's light. Her throat caught. She reached out involuntarily, as if to steady herself. Already? Perhaps this is what the gallery's creator had planned all along—to take one by surprise.

Those whispers around her accelerated, yet did not rise above unacceptable levels. A reverence filled the space beneath that dome where Michelangelo's David stood mighty and unashamed. Nothing was held back in his depiction. The smooth, veined stone displayed strength and valor, confidence and focus. He was about to slay a giant, and he was ... breathtaking.

Meg thought of the magnificent David and her ensuing impressions for some time as she traversed the streets of Florence. All around her history expressed itself, in the art, the architecture ... the faces of the old women sweeping the sidewalks outside of their shops. Several times she found herself voicing her observations to strangers. Affection for the abundance of beauty flowed out of her. Some would smile and nod, while others would look at her as if she had mistaken them for someone else. She continued to walk and see and smell and take in her surroundings.

After stopping at *Mercado Centrale* for a salad with *rocket,* tomato, and mozzarella, she continued on until reaching the Duomo. The hint of soreness on the top of her foot she had experienced in the morning had grown to a decided throbbing, so she found a spot on a curb outside of a busy gelateria to sit and watch the flow of tourists through the piazza. Others lounged beside her, feasting on cones of gelato. If it were not for the stifling heat, she might have stayed put all afternoon.

A pregnant woman stepped onto the curb next to her, her cotton sundress clinging and unforgiving. *Poor thing.* She swallowed back a sudden thought. Liddy! She had been so lost in her wound-licking that she had not bothered to let her best friend know she had arrived safely. She bit her lip and glanced around the piazza partially obstructed by the Duomo itself, hoping but not fully expecting to find a store where she might buy a phone charger.

Meg turned to a woman in a floppy hat next to her. "Scusa?" She held up her iPhone. "Dov'è il Apple Store?"

The woman smiled. "Allora cinque minuti." She pointed at Meg's feet. "A piedi."

A five-minute walk. Surely that would not be too difficult?

"Look," she said, her phone screen open to a map. "You see."

Meg nodded, taking in the route. "Grazie, grazie!"

Her walk took her along Via dei Calzaiuoli, down Via dei Pecori, until a Prada store on a side street caught her eye. She detoured to take in the colorful handbags dangling from arms of expression-less mannequins in one of the tall display windows. An Italian woman stopped next to her, exclaimed at the price, and shook her wrist at the lifeless models in the window before walking away.

She cracked up. *Liddy would have loved that.* Meg turned back toward her original route, suddenly concerned about how long the store would stay open. Uninjured feet would grow weary from all this walking, let alone one that had atrophied from non-use. She rounded the corner back to Via dei Pecori, taking note of the street she had just ducked down: Via Roma.

Something niggled at her about that street name. She

rethought her decision not to stay at least one night in Rome before moving on to Florence, but hindsight was 20/20, they say. Who knew she would chicken out about calling Domenic and Elena? A piece of her heart sank. She could not leave without seeing them. She determined that once her phone was back in use —and once she had found the nerve—she would give William's old friends a call.

HIS BODY HAD TAKEN all day to adjust to the time change. Near-constant yawning made him question whether he really had been successful. It was late afternoon, and while Domenic took a nap and Elena puttered, Jackson pushed off sleep and decided to go for a walk. He had worked plenty already, answering emails—and checking his texts for any sign of Meg. The narrow street in front of the apartment building teemed with tourists now. He waited as a tour group passed by, its leader holding up a flag to keep her travelers from becoming separated.

She could be anywhere. He frowned. Stepping into fresh air was meant to clear his head, not break his heart. Unfortunately, everywhere he looked, he saw her. A woman speaking to a friend near the corner ... a young woman leaning up against a wall, gesturing wildly as she spoke on her phone ... a petite woman peering into a store window a long block away. Everywhere.

Get a grip on yourself, idiot. A walk. A long walk away from here would help him shake off the reality that he had traveled across the world for a pipe dream. The more he thought about her, though, the more he longed to explain himself. *Would she even give him the chance?*

He turned the corner from the apartment on Via Roma and made his way west toward Via Pellicceria stopping to check the map on his phone once. Left turn, right turn, until he made it to the bridge overlooking the Arno River, across from Ponte Vecchio.

The river's water reflected its surroundings, windowed buildings and the bridge's archways like watercolor paintings. The bridge bulged with walkers, the current weather doing nothing to dissuade the crowds. Of course, he had been inside Domenic and Elena's fully air-conditioned apartment all day and only now realized that the temperature had probably cooled some from earlier. Despite the abundance of life in the streets, a sense of loneliness engulfed him. And fatigue. He questioned himself again, knowing that no matter how he had tried to spin this, he had no other reason for coming all the way here except to find *her*.

He snapped a look at his phone, in case a text appeared from Liddy. Though empty, he stared at the screen, a sudden roiling in his gut. Meg had not bothered to tell her mother exactly where she was going. Neither had she contacted her best friend to let her know that she had made it safely. She certainly had not been in touch with Domenic and Elena, two people who would have opened their arms and their home to her.

He inhaled a thick breath of Florence air and blew it back out again, his fist pressed into the railing of the stone bridge. Meg did not want to be found. Then why, he implored of himself, did he come all the way here?

Jackson shoved himself away from the bridge and began to walk. He walked past vendors and shops and restaurants bulging with boisterous diners. Yet hunger eluded him. He had a company to run, a company losing money by the day, and like a dolt he had flown out here on a whim, telling himself he would do "research" while here.

He couldn't very well add a spa to a business that was failing, now could he?

By the time he reached the carousel that stood in a piazza, he had made a decision. He would be back at the Marino's in time to eat the evening meal—he did not care to inspire the wrath of Elena by not showing up for dinner—and while he charged his phone, he would book himself on the first plane out of Florence tomorrow morning.

MEG STEPPED into her rented apartment, the interior stifling. She dropped her purse onto a vinyl chair and reached for a window, throwing open its sash. The familiar aroma of truffle oil wafted inside, along with the clink of dishware from the nearby restaurant kitchen. Maybe she should have left the windows open all day, but then again, how many gnats would have found their way inside? Not to mention her rental was on the first floor, which was technically above street level, but not by much.

She plugged the charger into the wall and then into her phone. While filling a glass with tap water, she made a mental note to pop outside again later to pick up bottles of water and snacks. Fortunately, she had picked up a “take away” of spaghetti on her way back to the apartment.

A buzz and several dings let her know her phone had been reactivated. It had, in fact, lit up like a Vegas slot machine. *How much were these texts costing?*

Hey, girl, let me know when you’re there

Living vicariously through you. You there yet?

Meg! Getting worried

This is NOT healthy for little Bruno (Current name pick, you know, like Bruno Mars. You like?)

p.s. Jackson is a wreck. Has it bad for you

p.p.s. Don't let that last text keep you from calling me. Seriously worried, Meggie.

OH NO. She shut her eyes, guilt pelleting her like hail. If she didn't answer soon, Liddy would kill her. She would haul her pregnant self onto a plane and hunt her down in the streets of Florence. And Meg would deserve it! It was late morning at home and Liddy should be at work. She lowered herself into the lone vinyl chair in the room, picked up her phone, and ran her thumbs over the text box.

So sorry. Phone died—no charger! Bought new one today I am fine. Stop worrying

She paused before texting again.

Florence is beautiful. Very sorry I scared you

SHE IGNORED the text about Jackson, wishing his interest in her whereabouts rang true. It was more likely that he took one look at her hit list and wished he hadn't been so harsh. She made a mental note to find Wi-Fi and check her email tomorrow so her clients wouldn't feel neglected.

She peered at her phone to see if Liddy had responded. Nothing. The aroma of spaghetti and meatballs reached out to her, so with a sense of satisfaction that she'd done her duty and alerted her BFF that all was well, she unstuck herself from the chair.

But on her way to the kitchen, her foot landed funny. *Ouch!* Knife-like pain emanated from her foot and up the front of her leg as she limped into the tiny kitchen. "Oh no." She swallowed against the sharp pain and hopped to the freezer where she found a few crusted-over ice chunks. Was ice supposed to be beige? At least she would not be consuming them.

Meg reclined, that plate of spaghetti on her lap, her rogue foot up on a small coffee table, soothed by the ice wrapped in a towel. She had made it her practice to carefully plan her trips to include weather-appropriate clothing, necessary electronics, and backup medicines. So far on this trip, though, she was zero for three.

She savored another bite of dinner, thankful for its sustenance. Her foot was another story. Not only had soreness reared its presence, but there appeared to be swelling where earlier today there had been none. Possibly a byproduct of doing more walking in one day than she had in a month—but a niggling of fear persisted. She glanced around, taking in the plain walls. The thought of being stranded in Italy held an air of romanticism, but stuck inside these four walls? Not so much.

CHAPTER 12

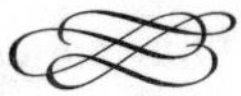

"Are you sure you must go so soon?" Domenic asked, wincing at the noise Elena was making in the kitchen behind them. Pans crashing. Silverware thrown together. He gestured toward his wife. "She is unhappy that you are not staying ... had many meals planned for you."

Jackson called out to her, "I will come back. I promise, Elena!"

She mumbled something in response and Domenic simply shrugged. "She will get over it."

Jackson stuck out a hand. "Thank you again for your hospitality. I'm sorry to have fallen asleep so early last night—and to cut my trip short, but duty calls. I'm sure you understand."

"Yes, yes, of course. I will walk you to your car."

Jackson held up a hand. "No, not necessary. I've already received a text that my car is here and cannot wait long, so I'll just run down and take off."

The driver sped off the second Jackson threw his bag in the car. "The authorities don't like it if you drive in this section of Florence, do they?"

The man shook his head. "No. But for you, I make an exception."

"Appreciated." Jackson sat back and attempted to relax. He allowed his eyes to shut. Surely, he had made the right decision. Email had been stacking up. He had only brought clothing for a week. The profit-and-loss reports in his bag painted a sad picture. Yes, yes, he assured himself, his decision was correct.

A moment of pause came over him.

What if something really had happened to Meg? What if she wasn't simply being hardheaded—but had gotten lost, like he had mentioned to Liddy?

He swallowed a groan. No sense drawing the driver's attention to this sudden onset of indecisiveness in his life. Liddy had said she would let him know if she heard from Meg, but no call had ever come.

MEG AWOKE to the buzz of passersby outside her window, warmth and light streaming through the curtains. She pictured brioche and cappuccinos. Eager for her own breakfast, she kicked off the thin cotton sheet she had slept under, rolled over—and yelped.

Her foot, tender and puffy, greeted her. With a regretful sigh, she rested her head in her hands. She had only paid for this apartment through the morning. She had no desire to stay in this low-cost sauna any longer than necessary, but if she could not continue her sightseeing, where would she go?

She glanced out the window, not caring that her bedhead might be spotted through the gauzy curtains. A world of tourists and locals mingled just beyond those windows, but she doubted she could traverse the streets with the same gusto that she'd carried on with the day before.

When she switched on her phone, a ping startled her. And again. Four times in all, the screen of her phone lit up like Christmas:

Thank the Good Lord! I was at the doctor's office when you texted, btw! Baby is growing!

Have you seen Domenic and Elena?

How about that yummy statue of David?

Oh! Jackson is AWOL. Nobody has heard from him. Probably out looking for you. Lol

SHE DOUBTED THAT LAST ONE. More likely, he was out looking for her replacement. She grunted and forced herself to stand. Her room looked like the inside of a dryer, her clothes and other belongings tumbled everywhere. No more of this! She had allowed herself to act quite out of character, but it was time to pull herself together.

She made a call on her phone.

"Pronto?"

"Domenic? Good morning—buon giorno. This is Meg calling."

"Meghan! It is you!"

She chuckled. "I am here—in Florence. I know that might come as a surprise—"

"Beautiful news. You must come to our home on Via Roma. We are so happy to see you!"

Tears pooled. *Why had she waited so long?* "Grazie. I am so sorry for not calling you sooner, but I will be there later today."

"How far could you be?"

"Not very. I am just moving slowly today after too much walking yesterday. My foot is very sore, so I will call a taxi after I am able to pack and get downstairs."

"Nonsense! I will come to meet you. Please stay put." His voice muffled, as if he had turned away. "Elena! Our Meghan has hurt her foot. We will need ice!"

She laughed out loud at this. "Grazie, grazie, Domenic. I will shower and be ready in an hour."

"Cara?"

Her heart tugged at his endearment. "Yes?"

"I am sorry to tell you this but Jackson just left here."

"Jackson … is here? In Florence?"

"He was here. But he only recently left. I believe he was looking for you."

"Did he say that?"

"Not in so many words, but I am certain that he was."

A barrage of questions crowded her thoughts. Jackson. In Florence. How did he know where to look? She shook her head tightly. Of course. Pepper had thrown a fit when she heard Meg on the phone with Domenic. Sibling pressure must have driven him to fly all the way out here to see what she was up to.

Would these people never give up with the antics? With the accusations?

With newfound energy, Meg rolled her wayward clothes and tucked them into her suitcase. She would not allow this unexplainable turn of events to ruin her vacation to one of the most beautiful places in the world. Gingerly, she stepped through the rest of the apartment, looking for belongings she might have left in a corner or under a chair. She took a shower, grateful for more than a trickle of water pressure, and towel-dried her hair, realizing that for the second time in years she would have to let it dry naturally. She was glad he had gone—thankful she had narrowly missed letting Jackson find her. The woman staring back at her in the mirror, the one with the wavy hair, looked refreshed. Hopeful, even.

Purse across her body, her bags by her side, she waited. Moments later a knock on the door signaled her ride had arrived. She flung it open.

"Jackson?"

He leaned against the doorframe, a questioning smile on his face. "I know you were expecting Domenic. Sorry to disappoint."

She reached for the wall, lightheaded. Jackson jerked forward, his hands finding her waist. "You okay?"

She did not dare meet his eyes. He smelled good—looked even better, though tired around his eyes. Why was he here? He was supposed to have gone!

"Meg?"

"I thought you left?"

"I did."

"But you're here." Obvious was all she had at the moment.

"I was on my way to the airport when I realized I had left my phone plugged in at Domenic and Elena's."

She pressed her lips together and gave him a nod. "So you went back for your phone. That makes sense."

His eyes swept over her face. She glanced away.

His voice turned husky. "See, the thing is, I reached for it in the car, hoping there would be some word about you."

"Well, you can let Pepper know that I've been found." She raised her chin and flashed a look at him square in the eyes. "And there's been absolutely nothing untoward going on regarding your father's attorney. As you apparently know, I haven't even seen him and Elena yet."

He quirked his chin to the side, eyeing her. "Pepper has nothing to do with my being here. Doesn't even know I've gone."

"But you came here, knowing I would seek out the Marinos."

"Actually, no. I'm not diabolical enough, I guess." He gave her a "come on, I'm teasing" smile. "Meg, I had no idea you had left town. I showed up at your house to apologize, and found your mother there, waiting for her ride to the bus station."

Lights went on. "My mother told you."

"Don't blame her. She figured I already knew." He paused. "May I come in?"

She took one hobbled step back. His hands stayed at her waist, the two moving together, like a dance. He kicked the door shut and pulled her into him, speaking into her hair. "I couldn't stand not knowing what had happened to you."

A rush quickened her. She wanted to believe him, but did she dare? Her head swirled from jet lag and heat and the beauty of Italy that she already experienced. She had been so angry with him for days—years, actually—could she let all that go in one moment?

"Look at me."

She lifted her chin.

"There is so much more to say. How about I get you out of this steam bath and let me convince you on the way over to the Marino's air-conditioned apartment to let me have the time to explain myself."

Her hand rested on his chest. "I'll get my things."

He shook his head. "Not a chance." One of his hands slid down along her back and the other swooped beneath her knees. He lifted her in his arms and she inhaled him as he did, her hand resting on the back of his neck.

"I hardly think this is necessary, Jackson."

"I'm not about to let you take another step on that bad foot. Give me your key to this heap."

She dangled the lone key in front of his face.

He smirked. "Tuck it into my back pocket." He paused. "If you don't mind."

"Uh, doubtful I can reach, in this position."

He moved into the hall, leaving the door ajar. "Probably better that way. Car's waiting, so I'll come back for your suitcase."

For reasons she did not bother to dissect, she allowed Jackson to carry her from her apartment to the street where a car waited. He spared a look at her more than once beneath his lashes. Had he half-expected her to bolt? Frankly, she expected it of herself.

The driver opened the door to the back seat of the car and

Jackson gently released her to stand on the uneven street. He traced her cheek with his finger and tucked a flyway strand of hair behind her ear. "I'll be right back," he said. "Wait for me?"

She nodded her agreement. As she slid in behind the passenger seat, she felt in some ways that she already had been.

CHAPTER 13

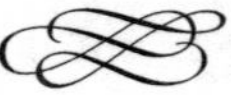

"If you could go anywhere today, where would it be?"

Meg looked out to the busy Florence day. "This place … there are so many beautiful sights I've yet to experience, but my foot." She shook her head. "What was I thinking not bringing my boot?"

Jackson reached over and rubbed the back of her hand. He had surprised her by sliding in next to her in the back seat after retrieving her luggage. "Geno," he said to the driver, "take us to Piazzale Michelangelo."

Geno laughed. "Ah, you are a romantic. Si, I will take you."

Meg cut in. "But what about Domenic and Elena?"

He lifted her hand and kissed it. "They will be fine. I'm not quite ready to share you."

Warmth breezed through her. Her mind filled with myriad protests, but she didn't care to utter a single one. Instead, she reminded herself to breathe and hoped she would not be waking up anytime soon.

Soon they arrived at the base of a winding road. She caught Geno smiling at her in the rearview mirror. "You will soon see the masterpiece that is Florence." He sounded as excited to show it to them as she was to see it.

Jackson leaned closer to her, pointing at the sky outside of the car window. "My father used to talk about this place."

She glanced at him, his face inches from hers. "He did? I don't remember hearing him mention it."

"I had forgotten about it until now. Said that when he was young he would hike up here to think, that it was magical to him."

They made their way around another bend, taking in glimpses of Florence's topography beyond a line of trees. Once they reached the top, their driver stopped and turned.

"We will stop here so you can enjoy the view without so many tourists," he said. "You should carry her outside to take a selfie."

"Great idea." Jackson hopped out and came around to Meg's side of the car. He opened the door. She stopped him with one hand when he attempted to scoop her up.

"I'm fine. Really."

He stood and offered her his hand instead, which she took to steady herself. She attempted to let his hand go, but he kept hold of hers and tucked it under his arm. "Walk with me," he said.

Together, they walked to the short wall along the edge of the road where they could take in the vista. Meg gasped. The Palazzo Vecchio, the Arno, the bell tower … the Duomo. So much to take in from one spot. "It's better than a postcard."

"C'mon," he said, turning her around. "We'd better take that selfie or else our driver will become impatient with us."

She laughed. "Wouldn't want that."

Phone in the air. Click. He looked at the screen, then showed it to her. The photo of the two of them together, smiling, with an ancient city as their backdrop sobered her. They were entering new territory, and what would become of it? Would they end up like those couples from *The Bachelor* who fell apart after the spell of faraway places had returned to the everyday?

She chased away the thought as quickly as it had come. No

sense in building castles where only moments stood. Instead, she told herself, enjoy the experience. A driver—and a friend—in Italy. She should want for nothing more.

After their whirlwind tour of Piazzale Michelango, their driver took them to Domenic and Elena's apartment. Via Roma! No wonder the name had sounded so familiar when she had heard it. Inside, Elena squeezed her with the strength of a hundred grandmas.

"So, so happy you are here! But look at you—you are too tiny. You must be starving."

Domenic chuckled. "Don't fight it, *cara mia*."

Before long, Meg sat cozied up beneath the large window that looked out onto the street below, a few straggly plants in view. If she were to lean slightly, she could see a peek of the Duomo.

Elena served her a tray with coffee she had made with her Moka pot. "No matter what anyone tells you, this is the best way to make coffee." She glanced at Domenic, who was in conversation with Jackson, and whispered, "He always tells me the French press is better, but no. It is too grainy that way. You will love this. Cream?"

"Yes. Grazie."

"I will leave the pot here. Americans sip coffee all day long, but Italians throw it down like medicine. You take your time. I will bring you some brioche to enjoy while I make your lunch."

Lunch, too?

Jackson said, "I've made arrangements to stay at Hotel Pace, so I will drop my things off there and come back for you later this afternoon."

"If I may," Domenic said, "I would like to take you both out to dinner tonight. Elena will be leaving soon for Sienna."

"I am so sorry to have to leave you," Elena cut in. "I promised my sister, Alice, I would help her shop, but I will return in two days. I will leave meals for you. Mark my words!"

Meg gave Domenic and Jackson a guilty smile, then said to Elena, "Please. Don't trouble yourself one more minute for me!"

Elena bounded back into the room, wooden spoon fanning the air. "Enough of that talk. Your visit has made me young again!"

Meg laughed at this. "Oh ... thank you! I wonder if I could trouble you for one more thing, then? May I borrow an adaptor so I can use my flat iron?"

"Si, of course, of course. I will find you one."

Jackson reached out and touched a strand of her hair. "I was going to say that I like your hair like this. You look relaxed ... and happy."

She touched his hand as it rested on her wild mane, as she had begun to think of it. "Really?"

He smiled back at her. "Yeah. Leave it."

Though her breath caught at the way he looked at her, she managed to breathe. She swung a look at Domenic, who had grown quiet. "We would love to have dinner with you. Already you have been too kind."

"Marvelous." He turned to Jackson. "Go on now and get yourself settled at your friend's hotel. I will take care of Meg here. She can watch the parade of tourists go by until you return."

Jackson's gaze brushed her. He touched her shoulder before leaving, but nothing more.

When he had gone, Elena bustled back in, winded and slightly flushed. "I have made you a panini with prosciutto, basil, robiola cheese, and cherry tomatoes."

Meg glanced at the feast, a sandwich the size of the state of Ohio. She caught Domenic peering at her, a hilarious expression on his face.

"I have faith in you."

She quirked her cheek. "Okay if I just order a salad tonight?"

He threw back his head in laughter. "I am sure that can be arranged."

THE AIR in the trattoria swam with the aroma of truffle oil and oregano, tomatoes and olive oil. Jackson felt the familiar growl of his hungry stomach.

Domenic refused the wine list and ordered a bottle of the house red for the table. He leaned forward. "Always the best choice," he said. "Remember this when you are dining out together."

Jackson slid Meg a teasing look, but she glanced away and focused on the menu in front of her.

He darted a look at the menu too, every word of it in Italian. He could struggle through it, of course. But Meg's proximity to him had already churned up another struggle.

Meg closed her menu and tapped Domenic on his wrist. "Will you order for me?"

His smile beamed at her request, so Jackson closed his menu, too.

"Yes, please. Order for us both. We trust you."

"Well, then, that I will do! I will order *bistecca,* of course, and a number of other dishes we can share."

After he had ordered, Domenic turned his attention to Jackson. "Tell us about this hotel you are staying in. How are the accommodations?"

"Not as grand as yours."

"Tell the truth, son."

Jackson laughed. "The hotel has a spa that I think we might want to emulate in California. Of course, I will need to get some feedback on their treatments, to make sure they are worth the hype." He glanced at Meg. "Care to help me out with this?"

"Sure. I can take a tour and give you my impression." She had switched into work mode—not exactly the response he had hoped for.

"Not a tour, although you can if you want to." He pulled out a slim sheet of card stock and an envelope and handed it to her.

"Here is their menu—and a gift card. Take some time for yourself this week to enjoy anything on there that you'd like."

She accepted the menu. "Well, if it's for work—"

Domenic winked at her. "I think he is trying to give you a gift. A generous man, like his father."

Meg froze.

Jackson glanced at her. He'd been able to sweep her off her feet earlier in the day, but why was giving her a gift so difficult? "You said you had never been to a spa."

She glanced at Domenic, then back at him, a tinge of red to her cheeks. "I ... could we ... maybe we should talk about this after dinner."

Domenic cut in. "I am sure if you don't want to use the gift card my Elena would gladly take a massage—she is tough, though. Hopefully the masseuse could handle her."

Meg burst out laughing at this.

The wine arrived and their waiter poured them each a glass of Sangiovese.

Domenic lifted his glass to toast. "*Cin cin.*"

They clinked their glasses and sipped, then feasted on a platter of greens and sipped some more.

More than once Domenic told them both how happy he was to see them. "At our age, we do not travel back to the States anymore. I hope this is one of many more trips to come for the both of you."

Jackson looked at Meg for some sign that she hoped so too.

A plate of pasta followed for them to all share. Domenic poured them each more wine, then sat back, resting from the meal, his expression thoughtful. "Jackson, I have not said this to you before, but I am so pleased at the man you have become. Though I have not seen you in a long while, I can say that you remind me very much of your father."

The second time he had said so this evening. Jackson could not see it, though. His father had been stubborn beyond belief, had made decisions he had not always understood. An enigma. Still, Jackson bobbed his head in hopes that this conversation would go away.

Meg said, "How so?"

"William worked hard with a singular purpose. He used to tell me that he worked hard not to think of himself."

Jackson considered this. "Are you saying he was selfish? And that I am too?"

"That is not what I mean at all. Your father knew how easy it was to become self-centered; he acknowledged that as a fact of human nature. But he aimed to look outward, and over time, I think he became quite good at it."

"I agree. He was quite good at thinking of other people first." Meg's voice sounded gentle.

This time he couldn't hide a frown. "Like Pepper."

"I'm sure you know that your father carried much guilt where Pepper was concerned. He had not known of her for many years —not until after your mother passed away. Once he learned of her, he did everything he could to find her, but her own mother had passed away." He paused. "It was a difficult experience for him."

Meg touched his sleeve. "And for you, too?"

He nodded. "I wanted to help him as much as I could but had my own challenges to deal with."

Jackson nodded, remembering the mild heart attack Domenic had experienced, the one that sent him in search of a place to retire.

"Pepper is lovely, don't you think?"

Meg had just taken a sip of wine and began to cough. Jackson patted her back, allowing his hand to linger there. He focused on Domenic. "To be straight with you, we've had our challenges with Pepper."

Domenic frowned. "I see. I *am* surprised. Perhaps she does not care to be part of the business?"

"It's the opposite. She has become quite overbearing."

Both of Domenic's brows rose. He glanced at Meg. "You have not said very much."

"I am not a fan."

Domenic took a large breath. "Well, I see. Your father had great hopes that you and she could work together. Of course, you are ultimately in charge. You understand that, don't you, Jackson?"

Meg's brown eyes grew wide, imploring him. How could he explain to her that he had the legal right to force Pepper from an active role at the company, yet had not done so? He pulled his arm back to his side. How could he explain it to himself?

Finally, he spoke. "My father chose to make Pepper an integral part of his company upon his death. I have tried to honor that."

"But you don't understand it."

"No, I don't. And there are other things my father did as well that I cannot understand."

"For example?"

"Why he banished me from the company while he was alive, for example."

"Banished you? I don't quite understand what you mean."

"Maybe too strong a word."

Meg gaped at him. Insulting her memory of his father had gone too far, he guessed.

Domenic hummed to himself as if in thought. He took up his fork and knife and cut into the steak Florentine on their table, slicing the meat into three equal pieces before dishing it up to each of them.

Meg shook her head, but Domenic coaxed her with a jut of his chin. She relented, allowing him to add the steak to her plate.

As he slid a hunk of steak onto Jackson's plate, a light of recognition went on in his eyes. "Do you mean when he sent you to work for someone else?"

"He didn't give me much choice in the matter."

"Ah, finally something I know the answer to. It is simple: He wanted you to work for someone else for a while—someone other than him. He believed that dealing with difficult people and situations on a daily basis outside of the family business would help you when you came back to work with him."

He took in the expression on Meg's face, pain and surprise housed there. She blinked rapidly and broke eye contact.

Domenic sighed. "The sad fact is he passed before that could happen. His heart was in the right place, I believe. You know, Jackson, I think your father was very much looking forward to working with you as equals."

A lump formed in his throat. He had never thought of his father's actions in this way. It surprised him when his father had left him in charge of the company—especially when he seemed to think of him as so unworthy. It occurred to him that he had spent the last year trying to show his father how wrong he'd been about him. Could his father have simply wanted him to learn from others so he could enrich the company—and their relationship?

Meg slid her warm hand over his and squeezed.

CHAPTER 14

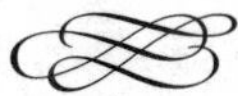

"Where are we?"

"Piazza della Signoria."

She glanced around the piazza, which glowed under the moonlight. They had dropped off Domenic at his apartment then asked the driver to bring them here. A small crowd had gathered where a quartet played in the loggia. Jackson put his arm around her, in support.

"Is your foot feeling okay?"

She nodded.

"Because I can always carry you around." He dipped as if to scoop her up again.

She pressed a palm against his chest. "Don't you dare."

He laughed, pulling her close. "Don't worry. I've got you," he whispered.

The day had been a dream like none other. Had she really woken up this morning to find Jackson Riley at her door? Didn't seem possible, but there he was. He was still here now.

They stopped for a moment, swaying to the breathtaking music drifting through the piazza. A lit castle rose to the sky on their left, a hulking art installation on their right. She relaxed into him, her head nestled beneath his chin, unwilling to question her own change of heart—or where this might lead.

"Domenic's insight played a number on me tonight."

"Hmm. Yes." She hadn't been able to forget some of what Domenic said either.

He pulled away from her slightly, peering into her eyes. "Why did you break up with me?"

She opened her mouth to answer, but only stared back at him. In the months since his return, this was the first time he brought up the subject.

"Listen, I know we were kids—or, at least, I was acting like one. A dumb one." His eyes clouded. "You blindsided me."

"I was afraid. We were going too fast—well, I think you know that." She dropped a sigh, recalling with regret the night that William found them together. "And then out of the blue you announced that you were leaving to take a job in another state. I-I broke up with you to save you the trouble."

His eyes searched her face and she shut her eyes. "That's not exactly true. I did it to protect my own heart." Her eyes flopped open, watery. "When you made the decision to leave I thought it was to get away from me."

He took her cheeks in his hands and pressed a kiss to her lips. She breathed him in.

"My father insisted that I leave, but I was too full of bravado to admit that to you. Nor did I realize, until tonight, his reasoning for insisting I go. I was young and brash and kind of a know-it-all back then." He gave her a sad smile. "But I am as into you now as I was then." He kissed her again. "More so."

Heat rose through her neck, filling her face. "I think I made—no, I *know* I made a mistake back then. In more ways than one. I'm sorry for breaking up with you so abruptly. If it helps any, I was miserable."

He chuckled. "It helps a little."

She smiled at him through her sniffles.

He kissed her again, her hair tangled in his hands, danger in his mind. He willed himself to pull back, forbidding himself to make another mistake where Meg was concerned. Gently, he lifted fingers of her hand to his mouth and kissed them.

She leaned into him and together they strolled slowly through the piazza, wandering down a narrow street with others out enjoying the balmy Italian night. Some shops had closed, while others had kept their doors wide open, light from their interiors spilling out onto the cobbled street.

"Perfect." Jackson had spotted something in a shop window and pulled her inside. He plucked a cane from a tall bucket, its handle carved into a wine bottle lying on its side. "A walking stick for you."

She giggled. "Looks more like a cane for a wino."

He shrank back, feigning hurt. "The lady does not appreciate the gifts I choose just for her."

Meg rolled her eyes. "Please."

A clerk approached and Jackson handed it to her. "We will take it."

"Jackson …" Meg shook her head, but the exchange was done. He handed the merchant euros and she quickly made change. "Fine. Let me try this thing out." She stepped outside and leaned onto the cane, the wine bottle comically smooth and comfortable in her hand. "Well, come on, Sonny. I haven't got all night."

He cocked his chin, laughing, then bent forward and scooped her into his arms, eliciting a yelp from her. "But I do."

She squealed, not caring that curiosity seekers turned their chins toward them.

"That's not much of a protest," he accused. His face beamed.

She took in his smile, the crinkle around his eyes, the intensity of his gaze. With one arm hooked around his neck and the other outstretched, cane in hand, she kissed him on impulse. "I could get used to this."

He tipped his chin, gazing at her. "Well then, I'll have to make sure you have the chance to try."

"Yeah?"

He stole another kiss that lasted longer than a beat. She opened her eyes, applause filling her ears. A woot. A whistle. Four women and a handful of men had stopped to watch their spectacle.

"We're a hit!" Jackson's hearty laugh enveloped her. While she ducked from embarrassment, he set her on the ground carefully, then took a bow.

"I've loved seeing Florence, the architecture, the art ... *you*, but this scenery is gorgeous." Meg swung a glance at him, touching his knee. "Thank you for taking me here."

"My pleasure." Jackson switched gears, the pulse of the engine beating beneath his feet. Sunroof open, it felt good to drive instead of leaving their decisions up to others. He glanced at Meg, her hair like liquid chocolate in the wind.

"There goes another one," she said, pointing to a castle among the trees. "I wonder who built it. Did he know he was building a castle? Or did he consider it just a place to live, like any other house? Did families gather there? Did they make food fit for royalty or just mounds of spaghetti? So much to learn!"

Jackson smiled at her questions. To him, the castles were interesting piles of stone, but she saw something different: life. He had never seen her so animated—and he began to understand that he could never grow tired of her enthusiasm. He rounded another bend, taking in the deep green hues of rolling vineyards. He regretted that he could only stay one more day.

Jackson pulled the car into a pebbled parking lot in front of a small winery and home on a knoll. Giovanni invited them over to a carved wooden counter where several others had gathered. "Come in, come in," he said and set out two more wine glasses. "I will pour you our best!" They sipped the wine and savored the conversation, which consisted mostly of the beautiful weather and how blessed they all were to be in Italy's wine country. They tried a few more red wines, until the final pour: Chianti Classico.

"There is none like this anywhere else. It is very dry and won't give you a headache like those other wines!" He tapped his temple and frowned. "You can get Chianti, of course, but for it to say 'Classico' on the label, it must be from this region." He waved his hand through the air, indicating the land around them, then he pointed to the neck of the bottle. "See here? This rooster on the bottle tells you that you have found the 'real' Chianti Classico."

When Giovanni had moved on to pour for a pair at the end of the bar, Jackson slipped an arm around Meg. "You like?"

She held her gaze on him. "I absolutely like."

He pulled her close, kissing her temple, when Giovanni called out, "Lorenzo will be giving tours of the vineyard, should you like to join him."

Jackson glanced at her. "Do you feel comfortable enough to walk?"

She held up that goofy cane he had bought her. He grinned. He had bought it on a whim, a fun joke, but she had reveled in taking it with her everywhere they had visited the past couple of days: the Uffizi Gallery, the Boboli Gardens—even on a late-night gelato run. He should not have been surprised that she'd insisted on cramming it into Domenic's small Citroën, a car he kept housed in a garage more than two kilometers away from the apartment.

Glasses in hand, they began to stroll outside when Meg stopped near the gift shop. She stroked her fingers over a stalk of rosemary, then breathed in its scent. "Here," she said, holding her open palm to his nose. "This smells so good, doesn't it? We should buy some for Elena—I noticed that her balcony garden could use a refresh."

He nodded. How did she do that? He'd noticed the Marino's

garden too, but then dismissed it as quickly as possible. But here she was shopping for herbs in an Italian winery to give away.

Meg tucked a pot of rosemary under one arm while reaching for a glossy-leafed plant.

"Here." He gently extracted the rosemary plant from her. "Let me." Jackson picked up one of the containers Meg had been eyeing. "This one?"

She nodded, her smile warm. "Basilico—it's basil."

For the next several minutes, they chose plants they could gift to Elena and Domenic, their arms overflowing. A robust woman brought them a woven basket and offered to hold onto their items until they were ready to leave. She then shooed them out the door toward the vineyard with a forceful sweep of her hand.

With laughter, they joined the others to follow a guide to the grounds where he explained the process of growing wine grapes. They meandered behind, half listening and half just *being*.

"It's so quiet here," she whispered. "I will miss this place when I leave Italy."

"I'm going to miss you when I leave in a couple of days."

Regret crossed her face. "Don't remind me."

"There it is."

She looked up at him, her eyes blinking in the sunlight. "What?"

"You pretty much said that you'll miss me when I'm gone from here."

"I said no such thing."

He pursed his lips. "Uh, I believe you did. Don't lie to the boss."

She took another sip of wine, peering at him over the top of the glass, those lashes-for-miles batting at him.

"You're killing me, you know," he growled.

"Okay, I wish you didn't have to go. But I understand … I will be right behind you next week."

"That's not right behind me." He slid an arm around her, taking in the countryside. "It's far too long, in my book."

"It will give you time to sink yourself back into the goings on at the inn and at the other properties, too. They will … need you."

He was quiet for a moment, and then, "You have more to add, don't you?"

"I don't want to spoil this view with my concerns."

"But I need to know them." He inched a look at her. "Are you worried about us?"

She hesitated, then shook her head. "Liddy says Pepper has been on the rampage more than usual. She threatened to fire a valet for having one of his collars flipped up or something. You really should talk to her."

She was right. He didn't care to talk about Pepper while they were enjoying their last day together in Italy. But worry etched her forehead, and though he longed to kiss those lines away with the passion he held for her, he knew it would take more than that.

He blew out a sigh, regretting how frustrated it sounded. "I will. I promise."

She kissed his cheek. "Love you."

He stared down at her.

"What?"

"I love you, too." Despite the impact those words had on him, his voice cracked.

A soberness came over her. "You do?"

"I do."

She smiled, her face fully lit. "I-I love you, too, Mr. Riley."

He turned to face her, encircled her hand in his and held it to his chest, kissing her with a ferociousness. "You don't have to call me mister, you know. At least not in private."

She paused, then laughed, the sound of it like music to his soul.

CHAPTER 15

Jackson and Meg had been working all morning weeding and replanting Elena's balcony garden, the muggy Florence day offering them an occasional breeze. Neither had spoken much, instead relying on brief brushes of their hands and their arms to communicate as they moved in sync digging, potting, clipping.

Elena joined them out on the narrow space, her hands clasped near her mouth. "My word, you are so precious to me. How beautiful my new garden is! I only hope I will not forget to water."

"You won't have to worry about that, Elena," Jackson said, a grin splitting his face. "Meg has it all figured out for you."

"No! You don't say?" Elena gave Meg's shoulder a smack. "Show me."

Meg giggled and held up a terra cotta watering spike. "We found these at one of the wineries we visited. It's a watering carrot."

Elena frowned. "But where does the water go?"

"Well … that's where your old wine bottles come in." Meg plucked one from the balcony floor. "I hope you don't mind, but I dug this out of your trash. All you have to do is fill it with water and set it upside down in the little carrot." She demonstrated by flipping the bottle, filled with water, into a spike sticking out of the dirt. "Voila!"

"Well, I'll be!"

"Just check the water level when you come out here to snip herbs, okay?"

Elena nodded and gave Meg another slap. "Oh, I will—I'll send you photos of the delicious foods I make with those herbs, too. The pictures will make you want to return for a visit."

When she'd gone back inside, Jackson nuzzled Meg and whispered, "What will they think of next?"

She shook her head, laughing. "Help me clean up our mess, you."

They had one more day together in Italy. Just one. And he intended to make it their best yet. Unfortunately, the investors he had been courting demanded a call and he could not put them off again for much longer—though he wished he could.

As they stacked up empty plastic containers, Jackson said, "Come back with me to my hotel. I have a surprise for you."

She quirked a brow at him. *One of these days he'd find out how she did that ...*

"I'm serious. Here's the thing: I have to take an important call today. It can't be helped. But I've spoken to Luca and his concierge wants to give you a tour of the spa *and* mani-pedi—on the house."

"Wait, did you just say mani-pedi?"

"I am a man of the world—I know what one is. And considering all that dirt under your fingernails, I'd say my timing is perfect."

She laughed. "But you already gave me a gift card."

He leaned forward and kissed her on the mouth, the taste of her even sweeter than before. "That's for a spa day after I leave here. Today is a freebie since I have to attend a meeting instead of spending that time with you." He reached across the table.

"Domenic and Elena told me they had some chores to do today. You in?"

She smiled. "I'm in."

ONCE INSIDE THE lobby of the historic hotel, Jackson led her to the concierge desk and introduced Meg to an international student named Izzy who worked part-time.

"Such a pleasure," Izzy said. "I will be so pleased to show you our spa."

Jackson kissed Meg's hand. "Come find me when you're done and I will take you to lunch."

When he'd gone, Izzy smiled. "He's sweet. You two are lovely together. Now. Please follow me."

Unlike the lobby, rich with tapestries and crystal chandeliers, the spa areas were simpler in design, the walls monotone and clay-like. Instead of harsh lighting, pillars of ivory candles in varying heights illuminated warmth throughout the halls and spa rooms. Soft instrumental music filled the space, encouraging quiet conversation. Even without a treatment, meg felt her body relax, her muscles unwind.

"Have you tried all the treatments here?" she asked Izzy.

"Oh no. Many, but not all. It would take many weeks to have them all."

"I am amazed at all you have to offer—wine and chocolate scrubs, aromatherapy, water therapy … and those are only a few."

"You are correct—there are many more than that!"

They wandered through an open-air garden space surrounded by four interior walls of the hotel. A courtyard created as a "space for visitors to recline" after treatment. Lizzy also showed her through interior quiet rooms where guests could rest after having a deep-tissue massage.

Meg was impressed. "Are you booked all year?"

"Yes, yes. People come from all over the world to stay here and try our spa treatments. Our staff attends classes weekly to keep educated. It is truly a remarkable place."

Thirty minutes later, Izzy led her to the chicest nail salon she had ever seen. Like the rest of the spa, the walls were monochromatic; however, this section also had pops of white and cherry in the furnishings, and chandeliers with layers of glass baubles dripped from the ceilings. The salon buzzed with women, their faces pink and glowing.

She was led to a cushy seat to wait for a manicurist. Though she'd had manicures plenty of times, usually to repair her fingernails after an aggressive dishwashing session, she generally kept up her nails herself. Her kryptonite had always been clothes, and if giving herself mani-pedis meant she could spend a little extra on her wardrobe, then she happily made the sacrifice.

The manicurist sat down and examined her nails, no doubt realizing the enormity of her task. "You have lovely nails," she said instead. "Let's get started. Shall we?"

Two hours later Meg waited for Jackson in the lobby, her body fully relaxed and ready for lunch. Both her fingernails and toenails shone in light pink, but the massage of her extremities had been the pièce de résistance of her experience. She could not wait to get back to Sea Glass Inn and revise her proposal for a day spa.

She watched Jackson stride across the lobby, straight for her. He leaned down and kissed her on the cheek. "Hey, beautiful."

She swooned a little.

"You okay?"

She stood, smiling. "I'm great. And your timing is impeccable because I'm starved."

He chuckled. "Timing is everything." He took her hand, noticing her fingernails. "These look beautiful, by the way."

They wandered to a café several blocks away and found a couple of seats near a window that looked out onto the street.

"Luca said they had great coffee here and they won't laugh at you if you order a cappuccino at lunch time." He slid a menu toward her. "He also said their avocado toast is the best in Florence."

"Then I'll take one order of each."

Food ordered, they people watched in silence.

"You've been quiet. How was your meeting?"

"Their questions were tough, but I held my own."

He seemed to have cut off his thoughts. She quirked a look at him. "Something's bothering you."

"My sister. Pepper insisted on being on the call. I would have preferred to keep her out of negotiations, but she does have more than a bird's-eye view of our expenditures, so I relented."

"And she was her regular self."

"Not really. She was almost charming. Asked about their families, told a few well-placed jokes. I almost wondered what happened to my sister."

"Be thankful for small blessings then."

He nodded. "I am. I think we are close to finalizing the deal."

"What will this mean for the inns when you take on investors?"

He took her hand in his, examining her fingers. "For one thing, it means expansion at each one, such as adding a spa at Sea Glass."

She nodded.

His eyes hooked with hers. "I want you to know that I appreciate all you did for my father."

Where had that come from all of a sudden?

"I've thought a lot about you and what you meant to him, especially over these past few months."

"He was a great man. Gave me my start. I can't imagine anyone else being so patient and kind to someone so obviously green."

"Yes, well, after you came to work for him, he seemed to mellow. At least until ..."

"We should probably talk about that."

He eyed her and it sent a chill right through her deepest parts, so much that she had to look away. Emotion pricked her and he warmed her with a touch of his hand.

"I'm sorry," he whispered.

She turned her chin back to him, her eyes meeting his. "I am too."

I never meant for things to go so far." He pushed away from her and sat back. "That's a lie."

"We were young."

"That's no excuse. I took advantage of your trust—and my father knew it." He played with her hand, which rested on the table, and quirked a look at her. "I think that's the real reason he sent me away."

"It never occurred to me that William was behind your leaving."

"You always thought that was my decision?"

She shrugged and pulled her hand away.

His eyes scrutinized her, intense. "You thought I was done with you, that I'd used you and had decided to move on."

She swung her gaze back to his, aware that the pain of those days surely shone on her face, fresh as ever. "Yes," she whispered. She had learned a lesson great and deep from that lapse in judgment and had not allowed history to repeat itself since.

"Two avocado toasts?"

Meg jerked her chin upward, startled by their server's sudden appearance.

"That's us." Jackson assisted, placing one of the plates in front of Meg and the other in front of himself.

The woman reappeared a few seconds later with two creamy cappuccinos. "Buon appetite."

Meg stared at her meal. She had not lost her appetite per se, but the honesty between them had made her want to reboot, to not ignore the things from the past that hurt and confused her, and yet she wanted to begin again fresh, with a more seasoned mind, a ripened soul. This took thought and care.

"Do you understand now that it was not my choice to leave?"

She nodded.

He sliced into his toast, but did not eat. "I'm sure what Domenic said is true, that my father wanted me to work under someone else so that I would not be the guy with the silver spoon in his mouth when it was my turn to take over." He dropped his chin and shook his head. "But taking advantage of his protégé, that was all too much for him, I think."

"He never said a word to me."

Jackson reached for her hand. "He had too much respect for you, Meg. He probably knew that for you, it was a momentary lapse. That you cared for me and got caught up in the moment. But for me? It was a character flaw. And I have to say—I believe my father was right."

"Then I'm grateful that we have been given this chance to make a U-turn."

He cradled her hand in his, tender, yet more fiercely. "Me too, Meg. Me too."

"EAT MORE brioche and your foot will heal faster, Meghan." Elena said this with a straight face.

"I think she means it," Domenic said from the side of his mouth. "In fact, I think I'll have myself another."

Elena slapped his hand. "Two is your limit!"

"Ah, but my love, I have only had one." He looked nonplussed.

"Eh! You may have one more, but that is it!"

Jackson winked at Meg over his cappuccino. She tried to smile, but melancholy at his leaving today had thrown a blanket over her mood. A glance at the time told her he was pushing it—he'd have to leave soon to make it.

"Well, son, I am sad to see you go, but I cannot say that I am unhappy that Meg will be staying on with us a few more days."

Elena cut in. "Yes, we will have her all to ourselves. We will take you to see a show, oh, and you must shop with me near Ponte Vecchio." She flipped one shoulder toward Domenic, dissing him in jest. "He does not share our taste for the finer things."

Meg giggled, thankful for the distraction.

Jackson's phone lit up on the table. She glanced at the screen. "It's Pepper. Sorry. Couldn't help myself."

He sighed. "Probably should get this since I'm going to be on a plane for a while." He punched the answer button. "Hey, Pepper."

A barrage of profanity loud enough for Meg to hear greeted him. Thankfully, Domenic had stepped into the kitchen for coffee. He and Elena were laughing together over the Moka pot.

Jackson's brows bunched, his eyes focused on the table. He sat there, listening to Pepper go on and on. Though Meg could not make out the words, she could tell by the tone that his sister was not greeting him with happy news.

He let out a breath and slid out from beneath the table. With a quick look at Meg, Jackson pointed toward the bedroom where she'd been staying. He would be taking the call in there.

She nodded, but pointed at her wrist to remind him of the time.

"So," Elena said, her hands clasped in front of her. "Today you and I will go shopping, eh? Take your mind off of Jackson leaving. And then we will stop for a sandwich as big as your head." She demonstrated this by holding her hands in front of her like two half circles facing each other.

"I would love to, Elena. Thank you for the invitation." She finished up her breakfast, casting several glances in the direction of the bedroom. She stood to bring her dishes to the sink, but Elena waved her away, taking the plate and cup from her hands.

Jackson finally emerged, his expression unreadable but decidedly less amiable than before. He hitched his briefcase over his shoulder.

Elena clamored over to him and pulled him into a hug. "Aw, you come back and see us. Don't be a stranger!"

He hugged her back and then shook Domenic's hand, pumping it with gratitude. His eyes caught Meg's. "Walk me out?"

They took the elevator this time, silence caught between them. She hoped it was the stress of goodbye, rather than something ominous happening at the hotel. Maybe she should cut her vacation early, she thought, and get back to the business of selling hotel space.

The elevator door opened, whining and grinding as it did. She stepped out and Jackson followed, but she did not spot a driver waiting for him.

She shielded her eyes from the morning sun. "Doesn't look like your car is here."

"It isn't. I wanted to talk to you alone for a minute."

She smiled up at him, but his expression was guarded. "What's wrong?"

He glanced out onto the busy street, his face a jumble of expressions. Finally, he swung a look back at her. "I know about the checks to your mother."

She blinked. "What?"

His Adams apple bobbed and he tapped his foot. "That's why Pepper was calling—to tell me about several years' worth of checks written out to Deena."

Meg shook her head, disbelieving. "I have zero idea what you're talking about."

"Look, whatever my father was doing … writing checks to your mother was his business. I'm not saying there was anything underhanded in the transactions."

"I said that I have no idea what this is about, Jackson. You do believe me, don't you?"

He shifted. His voice went quiet. "I want to."

"But?"

He swung a look away from her again, exhaling. "Your mother showing up at your home suddenly, well, that was kind of strange."

"My mother is one of the least conventional people I know."

He nodded. "Listen, I don't want to fight about this. I wanted to let you know what Pepper told me so you could ..."

"Confess to something?"

His eyes flashed.

"Because if that's what you're looking for, you have the wrong girl. My mother showed up to help me with my broken foot. There is nothing odd in that, I'd say. If, for some reason, there is any truth to Pepper's latest accusation, I will get to the bottom of it. I will buy international calling and phone my mother today." She tightened her hands into fists. "But my guess is this is just another one of Pepper's fantasies. She's never liked me and that's her prerogative."

He stood beside her, stoic. "She says the bank sent her copies of the checks."

She brushed away an angry tear with the back of her hand. "Who cares what she says? I can't figure out why you so easily believe her after professing your-your ... feelings for me."

A car pulled up in front of them. Jackson reached out for her, but she recoiled. "Meg."

She would not cry ... she would not cry ... "Go."

"Not like this."

Her body stiffened, fighting off emotion.

Jaw set, he threw his suitcase and briefcase into the back seat then leaned on the open back seat door. "We will—we'll figure all this out. I'm sure of it."

She watched his car pull away, making its way through the crowded street. Right now, she wasn't sure of anything. Or anyone.

MEG COULD NOT fathom how she managed to keep from collapsing into a puddle of emotion while shopping with Elena. All the years of standing in booths at trade shows with a smile on autopilot helped. Admittedly, Elena's antics kept her occupied, too.

After putting on red stilettos: "You think Domenic will think I'm a siren?"

In a hat with feathers: "I will wear this whenever I am on Twitter. Tweet-tweet."

They returned home worn out, their bellies full after a stop for gelato. Meg curled up on the lounge chair by the window overlooking the street while Elena took her afternoon nap. She fiddled with her phone, absentmindedly tapping the screen. Where had Pepper's outlandish accusations come from? They made no sense.

"... a lot of stuff that shouldn't be brought up."

What kind of stuff had her mother been talking about that night? Surely there could be no truth to Pepper's craziness? Her mother didn't even know William.

With a burst of frustration, she tapped her carrier app and purchased international calling, then called her mother.

"Meghan?"

"Yes, it's me. Hi."

"This call must be costing you a fortune. Is something wrong?

"Must there always be something wrong when I call you?"

"I knew it. Something *is* wrong! Is it your foot? Tell me it's not broken again."

"My foot is fine." No sense mentioning the swelling after a day of museum and piazza touring.

"A wonderful relief. Are you ready to come home? I can't imagine Italy is any nicer than where you live."

"Not quite yet. She hesitated. "Still so much to see and do here."

"That's nice, dear."

"But there is something I want to ask you about. This may seem strange, but I heard, well, I heard something about William that I have to ask you about."

"William. You mean, Mr. Riley?"

"Yes."

"You can ask away, but I'm not sure how I can help since I never met him."

She nodded. Yes, she'd never met him, which made this question all the more ridiculous.

Meg inhaled and puffed the air back out. "I've been asked to explain why William may have been sending you ... money."

"Who would ask you such a thing? Not Jackson, I hope."

She had not answered Meg's question.

"It doesn't matter who, Mama. Did, for some reason, William send you money for something? I know you didn't know him, but—"

"Absolutely not."

Her mother's answer was abrupt yet firm and she could feel her vehemence from thousands of miles away. It was enough for her. It had to be.

"Thank you. I'm so sorry to have had to call."

"Now don't you worry about this one more minute. You finish your trip of a lifetime and let that crazy thought lay buried."

Some things are better left buried ...

Meg hung up, grateful to put this issue to rest, even as questions tickled her memory in its deepest places.

CHAPTER 16

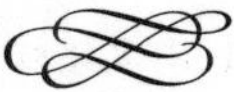

"Are you sure you want to go to Cinque Terre on this trip?" Liddy had asked her. "No cars, Meg. Did you know that? The villages are for walkers and hikers. What about your foot?"

"At this point, who cares?" She leaned against the upholstered headboard in her room. Domenic and Elena had long since gone to bed, but sleep had eluded her. "I forgot to mention, I have a cane now."

"Borrowed from your elderly landlords?"

She groaned. "A gift from Jackson. Anyway, I'll bring it with me for support. Honestly, I feel okay. The book you gave me inspired this trip in the first place and I'm not leaving here without seeing those pink and yellow houses."

She took the early train the next morning from Santa Maria Novella station in Florence, and fortunately for her foot, she found a seat. If she had joined the train at a later stop, she would likely have been doomed to stand with her belongings among a crush of tourists at one end of the train car. She arrived in Vernazza, one of the five villages, nearly three hours later, hitched her beach bag over one shoulder, and disembarked.

In some ways, she imagined this is how she would have felt if she had taken a gap year after high school and traveled the world. Of course, she neither took a gap year nor attended college—she started working instead and climbed the ladder of determination. Still, with her shorts and tee, walking stick, and solitary bag of possessions, she might as well have been a sojourner.

The platform whirled with activity, sightseers studying maps and squinting to decipher the meaning of foreign words on signs. Meg breathed in the scent of the sea, though she could not yet see it. She joined the throng that snaked its way down a narrow road and strolled past shops, open-air restaurants, and beachgoers wrapped in towels, fresh from the beach.

The road fanned out, leading to a small bay where small painted boats bobbed in a line, whimsical and inviting. Tourists splashed in the shallower waters, finding relief from the heat. She continued to stroll on a railed path to the left of the bay until the Mediterranean opened in front of her like a giant, magnificent oyster. She drew closer, mesmerized by the water, clear as glass.

"I had that same look on my face when I first saw the water here."

The woman speaking to her looked to be in her mid-forties, with burnished red hair covered by a broad-brimmed straw hat. Gold pops of color on her blue-and-white cover-up shimmered in the sunlight.

Meg answered, "It's gorgeous here. Pristine. Have you been here many times?"

The woman tilted her head. "No, I arrived only this morning. Stayed in La Spezia last night and took the first train here. I'll be staying on another night. Will be difficult to leave, but I'm trying not to think of that just yet."

"Me either." Meg smiled.

"It's almost … otherworldly." She released a lilting laugh.

Exactly what she needed—to be away from her ordinary world, to step away from those things that troubled her, to not have to think too hard about decisions she might soon have to make. She blinked back tears that attempted to disrupt her journey.

Deep breath in. "Well, enjoy your visit." Meg offered the stranger a brief wave and made her way to a curiosity of a stone building that had stood time's test. Halfway up, she stopped to take in the view that stretched farther than she could see. Her phone buzzed in her bag, but she ignored it, unable to take her eyes off water edged by Vernazza's footprint.

She did not know exactly how long she stood there contemplating, but her stomach alerted her that a substantial amount of time had passed. Meg glanced around. The restaurant in sight overflowed with people and she doubted she'd find a table there soon.

A couple of women peered into the restaurant. "Maybe there's food at the top," one of them said to the other, pointing to narrow, rough-hewn steps. They had apparently drawn the same conclusion about the wait.

After they disappeared, she too decided to take the steps, following a maze to a restaurant at the top that boasted an even wider view than the one that had captivated her earlier.

"May I seat you?" The hostess plucked a menu from her stack. "By the water?"

"Yes. Grazie."

She ordered sparkling water and took in the view. A crew of teens dove into the translucent waters from a cliff, the air punctuated with their laughter.

"We meet again!" The woman with the hat who had greeted her earlier in the day sat at the bar. She slid off her stool and approached Meg's table. "I was so surprised to see the girl with the cane all the way up here. You are gutsy."

"I'm Meg." She held out her hand.

"Priscilla." She grasped Meg's hand with both of hers, as if they were old friends. "I'm visiting from Virginia, and you?"

"California."

"Ah, we are from opposite coasts. She nodded at the empty seat across the table. "May I sit?"

"Please."

Her gaze drifted to Meg's cane, her brows arched in concern. "Was it difficult for you to climb up here?"

Meg let out an embarrassed laugh. "No, no. I broke my foot recently—it has healed now. And someone, um, a friend, gave me this as a novelty." She rested her hand on the ridiculous bottle handle.

"And it works when you need it to."

"A little unwieldy to carry around, but yes, you are right. I'm not sure I would have ventured up here if I hadn't brought it along."

"Well, then, we need to toast."

Meg reached for her water, but Priscilla gently stopped her with a wave. "I'll order us a bottle of prosecco. May I?" She gestured toward the bartender. "Giovanni! Vorrei una bottiglia di prosecco, per favore."

Meg remarked, "Even asking for a bottle of prosecco sounds beautiful in Italian."

"Except for how I say it!" Priscilla laughed and removed her hat, revealing flowing red hair that trailed along her shoulder. "Thankfully, I taught myself a few phrases before embarking on this solo trip."

"And that was one of them?"

"Why, yes, it was. No judging!"

"I wouldn't think of it."

Priscilla's lilting laughter filled the space between them as Giovanni reached their table with the bottle. He filled both of their glasses and bowed slightly before leaving.

Priscilla took a sip before asking, "So how about you? Are you here with friends, family?"

No, yes, no … how was she to answer? When she didn't reply

right away, Priscilla's smile turned sympathetic. "I see I may have poked a tender spot. You look a little like you've lost your way. I hope I haven't disturbed your lunch … if you'd like me to leave—"

"No. Please stay—I'm enjoying the company." She fiddled with the stem of her wine glass. "I was just thinking about my response, about this trip in general."

"Has it been a good one?"

Meg bit back an odd laugh. "Florence has been amazing. Beautiful. Gritty. Historic … I have enjoyed just about everything about it." She soldiered on, skipping the parts about her whirlwind tour of the city with Jackson. "And you? Have you been to Florence yet?"

"Yes. My first stop after Rome. I could have used a cane like yours after all the walking I did while I was in Florence—through the Boboli Gardens, the museums and piazzas. It was magical."

"Agreed. I'm staying with friends from the States. An older couple who live here now. But I decided to give them a break from my presence today."

"I'm sure they miss you."

She thought about Elena's antics while shopping and her love of a good home-cooked meal. "I'm the one who misses them. They are precious people, really. I'm glad I will have another couple of days with them when I return."

"They sound lovely." She glanced out to the expansive view beyond their table. "You know, I think I could sit right here all day and watch that sky change colors. Can you imagine living here centuries ago?"

"I'm amazed that people found their way here at all. Forget about my cane, that's fortitude for you."

"We have it so easy, don't we?"

"In some ways, we do. But there's a simplicity here that intrigues me somehow." She thought about the surrounding forest, the terraced hills, and imagined herself climbing them each day and taking in the view. "Maybe we don't have it so easy after all."

"Ah. The simple life. Vita semplice!"

Meg smiled at the toast and sipped her wine.

Their waiter appeared at the table, pen and pad in hand. Meg ordered the fresh fish and Priscilla asked for the pasta with pesto.

When he'd gone, Priscilla said, "This morning I climbed the watchtower. Have you seen it?" She pointed north. "The train arrived and I went there first, determined to take in a full view of the town. It was built to watch for pirates, you know."

"I didn't know, but I'm not surprised. They saw what others had and their little black hearts tried to take it away." She sighed. "I'm glad to know they failed."

Priscilla lifted her glass. "To the bad guys losing!"

"Cheaters never prosper!" Meg said.

"Off with their heads!"

Meg giggled in response to Priscilla's quote from *Alice in Wonderland* and added one of her own. "Curiouser and curiouser!" Her phone buzzed in her purse, but she ignored it.

"Thank you so much for allowing this introvert to join you for lunch."

"Uh, I would not consider you an introvert."

"Oh but it's true." She blinked rapidly and quickly dabbed her eyes with her napkin. "I'm sorry. I'm sorry. I truly am an introvert, but after days and days traveling alone, I missed the sound of my own voice. Is that nonsensical?"

"No, of course not." Meg had been in that place many times before but had never couched her unease in that way. Travel had been the one thing over the years that she could count on to displace whatever it was in her head that needed to go. When she stepped onto a plane or strode into a convention hall filled with people and activity and purpose, she left all her unfinished truths behind. She'd been proud of the fact that those she'd met on her travels knew her for her skills in filling Sea Glass Inn and their smaller properties—and nothing else.

Priscilla sighed. "I once read that keeping silent is a bigger sign of misery than if you talk about it."

"Then talk about it. I'm here and I'm safe."

"You are darling. Ah, the story is that my husband, Leo, was sick for a very long time and I've spent the last few years nursing him back to health."

"I'm so sorry. It must have been very difficult to see him suffer."

She grunted. "I only wish he suffered now."

Meg blinked. "I'm sorry? What do you mean?"

"I nursed that man back to health and once he was well again, do you know what he up and did?"

Meg wagged her head slowly.

"He left me for someone else—a neighbor who used to visit him while I worked to pay the bills. I'd come home and tend to him ... but it appears that she was tending to him during the day."

Oh no ...

The server brought over two plates, interrupting their conversation. The vibrant green of Priscilla's pasta made Meg's mouth water, but when the server set down the plate of fish in front of her, she gasped. Fish eyes stared back at her, the head of her lunch still attached.

"Oh my," said Priscilla. "It's as if they ran downstairs and plucked that beautiful *pesca* right from the sea."

"Si. Pesca ... fresca!" Their server refilled their wine glasses before leaving.

Meg bit her bottom lip and poked at the fish with her fork. "Here, kitty, kitty." She looked up. "Just making sure."

This time when Priscilla held the napkin in front of her mouth it was to hide something else—peals of laughter. "Oh honey, we're not in Kansas anymore." She cracked herself up.

With resolve, Meg carefully began the task of readying her fish to eat. "At least I didn't order the beef."

Another roar of laughter from Priscilla's side of the table.

They managed to finish their meals and wine, then pay the old woman on the way out who counted euros at a small table near the front of the restaurant. "Have some limoncello before you go," she said, pointing to a cart.

Priscilla held up her shot glass. "To new beginnings."

"Here, here." Meg nodded. "New beginnings."

They savored their liqueurs, said goodbye to the restaurant staff, and made their way down to the waterfront, making small talk like old friends. Priscilla turned to Meg. "You can't leave until you dip your toes into the Mediterranean. You just cannot!"

"I think you're right." Meg's smile bubbled from somewhere deep. "Want to join me?"

Priscilla hooked her arm under Meg's. "I'll lead the way."

CHAPTER 17

Meg and Priscilla stepped across the pebbled beach and splashed around in the Mediterranean until the bottoms of Meg's shorts had soaked through. Afterward, they each found a large rock to lounge on until the salt from the sea had baked into their skin.

"I'll show you where to shower off," Priscilla told her with a sneaky wink. "It's in plain sight, but nobody seems to know it's there."

Sure enough, a hole in the rocks hid two showers. A mother was washing her baby in one, while her toddler in a pink bathing suit danced beneath the spray of the other to her inner music. As soon as they were finished, Meg and Priscilla commandeered the showers, rinsed the sea salt from their skin, and scrambled back up to the main part of town to grab gelato—cinnamon for Meg, pistachio for Priscilla.

Meg's train arrived to take her back to Florence, her skin and hair reflecting a day spent in the sun, but it was her heart that had experienced the most change.

"I will miss you, my new friend," Priscilla told her, hugging her tight. "Promise to keep in touch."

Meg hugged her back. "I promise." Except for Liddy, she had few real friends and had wondered more than once if she was incapable of making them. A spontaneous day with her new redheaded friend changed all that and she knew she would remember this day for a long time.

With some surprise, she found an open seat near the back of the train filled with bedraggled passengers whose faces glowed much like she guessed hers did. Conversations rose in pockets around her, some in languages she could understand, and some she could not. Her eyes felt heavy and she longed to allow them to close so she could drift away on the headiness of a day well lived.

A ping reminded her that life still existed outside of this day trip to a magical village. She rummaged around in her bag and squinted at the screen.

Two texts from Liddy:

> *Was it as beautiful as the picture?*

> *Jackson's been barking around here all morning. Says it's jet lag. Right!*

And one from Jackson:

> *It's important that I speak with you. Soon. I understand that you do not have phone access, but text me your schedule so we can meet as soon as you arrive back in California.*

SHE ALLOWED her eyes to flop closed and her mind to succumb to the rocking of the train car as it made its way back to Florence. Closing her eyes was the only way she could remind herself of the beautiful day she'd spent in one of the villages of the Cinque Terre

—while also shutting out the impersonal text from a man who had said, not more than two days before, that he loved her.

JACKSON LEANED his elbows on top of his desk and rested his forehead on his fists. Something was off. Very off. He reviewed the latest figures Pepper had left for him for the third time this morning, trying to figure out how Riley Holdings could have lost this much money in such a short amount of time.

His father had always been tight-fisted where money was concerned, one reason for the wedge that often landed between them. He winced, recalling the know-it-all way he spoke to him at times. "Come on, Dad. You're the boss. Live a little!" What he really meant was, *Stop being such a cheapskate! As your son, I deserve to have all my wants taken care of!*

No wonder his father had grown concerned about his offspring's ability to run a company someday. *Could he even do so now?*

He looked up to find Rudy trimming a hedge by hand outside of his office window. The older man lifted a gloved hand when he looked up, smiling at him as if all was well. *He wished it were true.* Not only did Jackson have a mess to untangle with the company, but he had left Meg in Italy with only hurt to remember him by.

He dropped his gaze back down to his desk, lost in the memory of the way she had looked at him when he questioned her about Pepper's accusation. The confusion on her face haunted him. Couldn't he have waited until they had both returned home? Oddly, the minute he arrived back at the inn and told Pepper how he had confronted Meg, his sister seemed to lose interest. It was as if her fiery phone call across the world had never happened.

His eyes grazed his phone. No text back from Meg. He puffed up his cheeks and exhaled. He'd been so preoccupied with the way he'd left her that he had dashed off a text to her during an early morning call with the local chamber of commerce board. Though he had not re-read that text, he feared it might have sounded more professional than personal.

"Jackson." He snapped a look up to where Pepper stood in the doorway. *Speaking of the she-devil.*

"I have decided to take a trip to our property in Florida." She examined her long black fingernails, her lips pursed. "I think I will stay quite a while. I assume there are no objections."

Well, a whoop just went up from the front desk ... He leaned back in his chair, stretching his hands over his head, interlacing his fingers. "You thinking of relocating?"

"I prefer the climate and the culture out there. California weather is too finicky."

"You mean, as opposed to hurricanes, which know exactly what they are after."

She blew out a huff. "The fog is so thick here in the summer that I think I will go mad. And anyway, someone needs to be an east coast contact. Your girlfriend won't have to travel so much; it will save us money."

"My girlfriend."

Her grin grew across her face, stretching her lips like putty. He stared her down. "I had not realized you were away with your girlfriend when I called. Now that I understand the score, I will be more careful about what news I bring to you—and when."

"What's your problem with Meg, anyway? You've never actually said, but it's been obvious from the start that you have some problem with her."

She shrugged, the bones of her shoulders indenting the pale fabric of her blouse. "You exaggerate. It is only as I have said for as long as I have been here. Our sales director keeps a tight collar on our clients and that is dangerous. What if she were to up and leave us for the competition? She could take everyone with her. And then where would we be?"

He had asked himself that same question. But this was Meg they were talking about. His mind wandered back to the rolling hills of Chianti, the smile that brightened her eyes, the sunroof open and her hair billowing every which way.

He snapped out of it to find Pepper leaning close to him with that Cheshire cat grin, one stick-straight arm digging into his desk. "I asked you a question, but you are too busy daydreaming to answer. This is why we have a problem."

He glared at her and pushed his chair back away from his desk. He stood behind the desk and leaned forward until they faced each other nearly chin to chin. "I suggest you pack your bags as soon as possible."

"Or what? Don't tell me my little brother has a violent streak."

"Jackson?" Hans, the desk manager, stood at the door.

"What is it?"

"Uh, it's Liddy. She's … going to the hospital. She's not feeling well."

He broke eye contact with Pepper and strode to the door. "How is she getting there? Her husband? If not, you take her."

"Certainly."

"And Hans? You tell her if there is anything she needs us to do, just ask."

He pivoted to find Pepper leaning against his desk, her long arms crossed in front of her, her eyes narrowed. "This is your problem. You are too busy taking care of everyone else's business to run your own."

He breezed past her and sat behind his desk. "Send me fresh reports before you leave."

She dropped her arms by her side and marched toward the door.

"And Pepper?"

She spun around.

He smiled slightly at that. "You may be moving across the country, but I'll be keeping an eye on you."

"IT SOUNDS like you had a lovely time in the Cinque Terre, cara mia. We have not visited in many years—too much walking for old people, I'm afraid."

"Speak for yourself!" Elena spun around and did a soft shoe, one hand on her stomach and another in the air. "I am fit as a fiddle! Alas, my husband is an old man now."

Domenic grimaced. "You are older than me, my dear."

Elena swatted at him. "It is never proper to speak about a woman's age."

Meg laughed. "You are both forever young in my book."

Elena scurried to the kitchen to retrieve the aperitivo. Meg had arrived back late last night and had spent much of the day resting, except for an uneventful walk to the Piazza della Repubblica. Somewhat touristy and bland compared to the more spectacular areas of the city she had seen, but she'd welcomed the chance to rest cross-legged on the ground with a group of exhausted parents who watched their children on the square's merry-go-round.

"Oh! Speaking of books," Domenic said, interrupting her musings. "I have a lovely book about the *accademia* that I want to give to you. A lovely gift from a friend, but I have been there many times and have no need for it. Would you like it for your collection?"

"I would love it. Thank you, Domenic."

Elena put three glasses on the table. "There are too many books in his office. Take more!"

Domenic opened the Chianti as Elena set before them a board of charcuterie: cheese, crostini, nuts, and sliced salami. "She is always trying to thin out my office, this one."

Elena pounded a fist into her side in mock protest. "I ask you, when we die, who will take all those books? You must gift them to people who will love them, Domenic."

He nodded, pouring them each a glass of the red wine. He offered up a toast, took a sip, then looked to Meg. "Before dinner, we will go into my study so I can give you the book—and you may take any others that you like."

Meg's phone buzzed from where she had plugged it in near the kitchen table.

Elena stood. "Go ahead and look. I will go and get us more cheese."

Meg glanced at the screen. A text from Jackson.

Liddy admitted to hospital. No details. Thought you would want to know.

"Oh no!"

Domenic's forehead bunched. "What is it, cara mia?"

"It's Jackson. My friend Liddy is in the hospital." She looked up. "She's pregnant."

Elena added a chunk of parmigiano reggiano to the board. "So she is having her baby now?"

"It can't be—it's too early. Oh ... I hope everything is okay. Maybe I should call. I wonder if she can answer in the hospital."

Elena touched her hand. "Call her. We will leave you alone."

Emotion built in Meg's throat as her mind lingered on the possibilities. She hated to admit this, but she reminded herself of her mom, always thinking the worst. She caught Elena's eyes. "No. Please. Will you stay?"

"Of course. Of course." The older woman stroked her hand. "I will stay here as long as you like."

Domenic touched Meg's shoulder as he rose from his chair. "I will be in my study until you need me."

BEAU ANSWERED WHEN MEG CALLED. "She and the baby are doing fine," he assured her. "But she will have to stay on bed rest."

Meg's shoulder released. "I am so relieved, Beau. Can she do that at home?"

"I believe so. And she will have to stay there until the baby is born. No more working. The hotel will have to understand."

"I'm sure they will." *Well, everyone but Pepper will.*

"I'll be hiring someone to come in and cook and do some cleaning, though I'm sure she'll complain that she is bored."

"She'll get over it! And I promise, as soon as I get home, I'll come over and entertain her."

Beau groaned into the phone, but it came out more like a tortured laugh. "I will leave a stack of chick movies on the table for you."

"You'd better!"

He chuckled. "Be safe, Meg. I will tell Liddy you called."

She hung up and Elena smiled at her. "See?" she said. "All is well."

Meg's stiff upper lip dissolved into a messy pile of tears. She put her forehead on her arm, which rested on the table. "I was so … so worried."

Elena stroked her hair, her grandmotherly side coming out in spades. "But she is okay. The baby is okay." She lifted Meg's chin with her forefinger. "I tell you what. We will pray together for your friend. Then you will have peace."

"I would like that."

MEG WONDERED, and not for the first time, how much weight she had gained since setting her feet on Italian soil. She cleared the dishes from the table, in awe of Elena who had just begun to braise meat in a large skillet. First a spectacular array of appetizers and now dinner. Between Elena's love of cooking and the constant draw of gelato in the heat of the day, she knew to avoid the scale for a while after she returned.

"That smells delicious." Meg dried the cutting board and put it on the rack. "You spoil me."

"Eh, it is my joy!"

Meg squeezed her into a hug. "Thank you."

Domenic appeared in the kitchen. "Would you like to come take a look at my collection of books, Meg?"

"I hope you have tidied that office of yours first!"

"Yes, yes, I have."

Elena turned to Meg. "Well, then, you may go and take some books. Take a whole stack!"

Meg laughed on her way out of the kitchen. "There's a weight restriction on planes, you know."

"Ah, but you are so skinny you should get a weight credit."

Meg giggled. *Hilarious.*

The inside of Domenic's office reminded Meg of scenes from a legal thriller. Floor-to-ceiling bookcases—one that even covered a window—were filled with books, thick hardbound books, some stamped in gold as well as glossy travel books and paperbacks.

"Wow. Elena wasn't kidding."

"Elena never kids. She has been after me to give away my books for years." He looked up, a thoughtful smile on his face. "But from time to time, I enjoy revisiting the books of my career, especially. They stir up memories."

She ran her fingers along the spines of several books, reading their titles. "I know what you mean. Reading kept me sane when I was young. Classics, mostly. I have less time now, but I enjoy reading magazines that pertain to my work." She didn't mention that Jackson had teased her about this once.

The credenza near Domenic's desk held stacks of magazines and a spattering of framed photographs. Meg picked up one of a young couple in black and white. "You and Elena in your wedding?"

"Yes, indeed. She was a looker—still is."

"I'll say. You both look so happy."

She set it down and scanned the others. One of them on Highway 1 in California near Big Sur, one of several young men who looked much alike—probably family members of Domenic's, another of

Elena and a woman who resembled her. She smiled, remembering how Elena traveled to Sienna to shop with her sister, Alice. Though she had no sister of her own, Meg had Liddy—who felt like family.

"You know, Meg, I believe that William thought of you like a daughter. He always spoke so kindly of you, concerned for your welfare. He had searched for his own daughter and did not find her until nearly the end. I am happy he did, but also I think he gained peace watching out for you."

Meg nodded. "I've thought about him often. He was like my … protector." Her voice hitched and she gave Domenic an apologetic smile. "Sometimes I still become weepy thinking about him."

"Truth be told, I do too."

Meg smiled and continued taking in the magnificent office full of books and photos and mementos of a life lived well. Her eyes landed on another photo on the credenza, this one of Domenic and a young woman with striking green eyes. The way the woman smiled, almost shyly, reminded her of someone, but she could not nail down who. She picked up the frame.

"Is this a family member?" she asked Domenic. She did not think that he and Elena had ever had children of their own.

Domenic frowned. "That is Pepper, of course. You don't recognize her?"

Meg swung a curious look back at the photo. "Pepper?" She inspected the photo more closely. Green eyes, petite nose, slight parentheses around her smile, and full lips—though unlike the Pepper she knew, these looked real. She peered again, realization enlightening her like a day after rain. The young woman in the photo had a deep cleft chin—like Jackson's.

Her mind spun and her chest began to pound from the harsh beating of her heart. "Domenic?" she said. "We have a problem."

CHAPTER 18

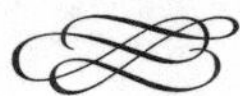

Thomas stared at Jackson, his expression one of suspicion, distrust. The valet sat in a chair opposite Jackson's desk, his chin resolute.

"I understand that you and Pepper had a difficult discussion recently."

"Yes, sir. She called me out about my uniform."

It still felt odd having a contemporary call him "sir." He and Thomas would have gone to high school together if they'd grown up in the same town. He wasn't sure he would allow such formalities to continue at the inn. Still, the sight of the valet squirming in discomfort across from him reminded him of the position he was in—and he determined not to take it lightly.

"What about your uniform?"

"My collar was up. On one side."

"And you folded it down, I take it?"

"Yes, sir."

Jackson felt a scowl cross his face. "Did she have any other issues with your ... uniform?"

He shifted, a confused look on his face.

"What I mean is, did Pepper talk to you about anything else?

Because, frankly, having an upturned collar is hardly a good reason to write up someone for their file." Maybe he should not be this forthcoming with an employee, but he was starting to think that he—and Pepper—may not be able to extract the best from their staff if they continually felt unfairly targeted.

"Not really. I mean, she gave me a hard time about talking about—well, you know."

"Talking about what?"

Thomas did not meet his eyes. "About Meg's accident on the beach, when you were, uh, behind her."

Jackson pressed his lips together, the uncomfortable sensation of warmth spreading up his neck and cheeks. "You saw that."

"Yes, sir."

Jackson waved his hand in front of him and leaned forward. "Stop calling me sir. You've worked here longer than I have. It's Jackson."

Thomas squinted, that suspicious expression back again.

"Okay, so you saw me chasing after Meg and you saw her fall. And you've had your fun talking about it."

"And the drone."

"Drone?"

"Yeah, well, that's the funny part. I'd never make fun of Meg—she's great. Everybody loves her."

"Wait. I have no idea what you're talking about. Can you enlighten me?"

"I mean, that drone dive-bombing you guys was crazy. It seemed to come out of nowhere, and then it was gone in a hurry." He shrugged. "It's just a great story. Sorry if I was being rude, though."

A low buzz. Something catching his eye. He shut his eyes, remembering the brutal way she had fallen after he'd called out to her. He had been so focused on her—*on them*—that he'd hardly noticed anything in the sky. Could it have been as Thomas said? Why would someone dive-bomb them with a drone?

Or had Meg been the target?

He snapped a look at Thomas, who sat in an uncomfortable silence, as if he was about to be handed a pink slip. Jackson stood and stuck out his hand. "Consider this matter dropped," he said, shaking Thomas's hand. "I'll make sure your HR file is clear."

When he'd gone, Jackson shut his office door. Breathe, Riley, he told himself. He turned toward the window, taking in the expanse of sky and water. Unhappy staff. Upside-down financial statements. Now a strange report of a drone following them. "Dad," he whispered, "what would you do if you were faced with all of this?"

He turned back to his desk and unfolded the latest P&L report Pepper had given him, the one she'd left with him before saying she would be relocating. He had not heard from her since. He buzzed Sally. "I'll need you to hold my calls indefinitely." He turned off his phone and stuck it in his desk drawer to avoid distraction. With his head in his hands, Jackson took a closer look, intent on going through each line of the report, one by one.

"HE'S NOT ANSWERING. I think he may have turned off his phone." Meg turned to Domenic and Elena, who both looked stunned. "What should I do?"

Elena bounced from the table. "I will serve you both a plate of my meatballs. You need nourishment to think."

The last thing Meg could do was think about food. If she could fly back home this minute, she would. She could not call Liddy to get information, not in her current state.

Domenic gave her a steady gaze. "I think you should, perhaps, call Sally at the hotel and make some inquiries about Jackson. She could tell you where he is."

"You're right. Of course." She paused. "I'm just so confused by all this, Domenic. How could this be true? I don't understand how someone could get away with impersonating someone else. And for this long."

Domenic gave her a pained expression. "I blame myself. If only I had been able to reach Sophia myself after William passed. I tried many times."

Meg reached across the table, stilling his shaking hand with a touch. "You are not to blame for this."

"You know, I originally found Sophia living in Italy. Sophia is Pepper's real name. William had looked for her for years and had come up empty. He believed that she would be in New York, or possibly New Jersey; he had never thought to try to find her living abroad."

"Where in Italy?"

"She lived in the north, outside of Milan. Her mother had dual citizenship, something William had not recalled. After Sophia was born, Rebecca married a man named Agli, I believe it was. I learned this when I found her. Sophia was shy. Quiet." He smiled, as if remembering. "She told me that she prefers her fabrics over people—she sews quite well. She did not say this in an unloving way. I believe it is her shyness that draws her to create her clothing."

Meg shook her head. She could not imagine the woman posing as Jackson's sister had ever threaded a needle. "Isn't there some way we could go see her? Jackson deserves to learn the truth. That ... that the woman he believes is his sister is ... an imposter."

Domenic frowned. "The last I heard she had moved to upstate New York, but I could not find any information other than her last known address, which I gave to Jackson. I am sorry to ask you once again, but is it possible that she has changed her hair, perhaps her makeup? Perhaps the woman you know as Pepper is the same as in the photo, but she has changed her looks."

"The thought had occurred to me. There is a slight resemblance around the mouth, but," Meg shook her head, "there is no other resemblance to the woman I know. She is also not the least bit shy or reserved. Oh Domenic, what are we going to do?"

"Now would be a good time to phone the hotel and see if you can speak with Jackson's assistant."

"Right." She punched in the hotel's phone number, her fingers shaky. She said, "Sally Myers, please."

The operator patched her through. "This is Sally. How may I help you?"

Meg settled her breathing before answering. "Good morning, Sally," she said, noting the time in California.

"Meg, is that you? I certainly hope you are not working on your vacation."

"No, no. Nothing like that. I'm wondering, though, if I could speak to Jackson? I have a … a question for him."

"I'm sorry, dear, but he is unavailable right now. Strict orders. Is there anything I can help you with?"

She bit her lip. Was he unavailable just to her—or to everyone? Daring to ask would give her away, so instead she asked, "I don't suppose Pepper is available. Is she?" She had no idea what she would say to her if she were to reach her. *Hope you look good in stripes, maybe?*

"I'm afraid not. Since you are on vacation, you have not heard the news."

"News?"

"Pepper has decided to relocate to Florida. She will be working out of the Sea Castle." She paused. "The staff is delighted."

"Which one? Not the Florida staff, I take it."

"Now, Meg. That is not appropriate," Sally said, her tone chastising.

"Of course not. You're right."

"Would you like to leave Jackson a message? I could connect you to his voicemail."

"Yes, please. Thank you."

You have reached the voicemail of Jackson Riley. Leave a message at the tone and I will return your call. Thank you.

The soothing sound of his voice, so familiar to her, caused an ache in her chest. A million thoughts and emotions traversed her mind. She had to warn him about Pepper's deception, yet she had to keep her feelings toward him separate. This call was not about them, but about Riley Holdings. If she could only keep her personal feelings out of it . . .

Beep

"Jackson." Hesitation. "It's Meg. I-I need to speak with you as soon as possible. Call me. Please."

She let out some of the breath that she'd been holding. Tears pooled in her eyes.

"You are trying your very best," Domenic said. "Do not worry. He will call and we will get to the bottom of this."

Meg nodded, fear rising in her. Why would Pepper suddenly up and move to Florida? What if Jackson refused to call her back? If she waited until returning to California to tell him the news, what other havoc might Pepper have time to wreak?

"If you don't mind," she said, "I'd like to call my sales manager in Florida. Sally says that Pepper is relocating there and I think it would be good to stay one step ahead of her until this is all over."

"Not until you have eaten your dinner!" Elena placed a platter of rigatoni and meatballs on the table, steam rising from it.

"Elena is right. We will all need our strength to help Jackson with this problem."

Meg blinked. They meant well, and though hunger eluded her, the aroma of tomatoes and spices wrapped her in an embrace. "Thank you. I will try."

After they had finished their meal, Elena stood. "Now, I will clean while you go and make your phone calls." She stopped and put a hand on Meg's wrist. "I am so sorry about what is happening."

Domenic, too, stood. "I will find the information that I have on file and send it home with you. I suspect it won't be too useful, though."

"I had no idea that Pepper was her nickname, although I always suspected."

"Of course, Sophia is the 'real' Pepper. When I met her, I told her that her nickname did not suit her, in my opinion. She said that her mother gave her that nickname because she enjoyed spicy foods."

"I can't believe this," Meg whispered. She picked up her phone and called the sales office at the Sea Castle Inn.

SALLY CRACKED OPEN the door to his office. "I'm leaving now, Jackson. Is there anything you need from me before I lock up for the night?"

Jackson peered up at her, unaware of the time. "Before you go, could you find Alex's cell phone number? I may need to call him after hours."

"Absolutely."

He had been poring over the reports for hours, creating a list of questions. He'd tried Alex in IT a few minutes before, but had missed him. A turn in his gut told him he would have more questions soon and would not want to wait until daybreak for answers.

Sally entered the room and set a 3 x 5 card in front of him. "I took the liberty of phoning Alex to let him know you may be calling him this evening. He says to tell you he will be available all night. Good night, Jackson."

He kept his eyes trained on his list of questions. Thousands of dollars had been paid to their bank, ostensibly for company credit cards. But why so much? Meg had not traveled for months and Jackson surely had not spent that kind of money on his card. He tapped the desk with a pen. Are there other expenses that were being put on those cards, items he had not known about or authorized?

What he needed to see were the accounts themselves. He silently cursed himself for not taking greater care where money was concerned. "Son, you have this notion that money appears on the ground every time an onshore wind blows through the trees." His father's admonishment reverberated in his brain.

He reached for the card Sally had left on his desk and dialed up Alex, who answered on the first ring.

"Yes, sir!"

Again with the sir. "Good evening, Alex. Jackson Riley here. I wonder if you could help me with a project."

"I'm at your service."

"I'd like to have access to Pepper's email account."

"You would like to break into Ms. Riley's email?"

"It is not breaking in if I ask my IT manager to grant access." He bit back a stronger rebuke, frustration rising in him. "Ms. Riley is traveling and I have some important projects to complete —tonight."

"Absolutely. Sorry, sir. I will get that information and send it to you A-SAP!"

"And if I need more information, you will be available tonight, correct?"

"Yessir."

As promised, Jackson received an email with Pepper's user name and password. He held his breath, the seriousness of what he was doing—accessing his sister's email account without authorization—boxing him in. Nothing felt right about this, and yet, enough felt wrong about Pepper's numbers to compel him to investigate.

He signed in, scrolling through her email, careful not to mark anything new as read. He stopped on one that confirmed plane reservations and opened it up. She'd made a plane reservation for Tampa, Florida, leaving this morning. Nothing startling there. He scrutinized the ticket, his fingers hovering above the mouse. He froze. The name on the ticket: Gia Agli.

Jackson frowned. It wasn't his sister's ticket after all. Why would Pepper purchase plane fare for someone else with company funds? He closed the email and scrolled, landing on another one for the same airline. Click. Scroll. Same name on the ticket, although this one was for Tampa to Miami. He wracked his brain, trying to recall if he had ever met a Gia Agli, but nothing rose to mind.

He collapsed against his chair back and groaned. The sun had gone down leaving his eyes to deal with unnatural light. He rubbed them, but they burned anyway, hours staring at pages and pages of finite numbers taking their toll.

Gia Agli. Italian surname. Could she be someone Domenic knew of in Italy? Someone who he should know, but in his inattentiveness, had missed? He glanced outside at the darkness. Probably too late to call Domenic, though Meg's presence there made calling Italy all the more appealing. His eyes darted a look for his phone to check the time. He remembered then that he had hidden it in a drawer to avoid distraction.

It worked, apparently.

He retrieved his phone and switched it on, waiting for it to power up. When it did, he noted that not only was it too late to call Italy, but worse, not one call from Meg waited for him. Not one.

MEG LAY in bed that night, insomnia her companion. Over and over she shut her eyes, begging sleep to come, but over and over again worry pried her eyes back open. She stared at the ceiling, the only light in the room coming from the Florence sky.

Jackson had not returned her call. She should have left him a more detailed message, something that, despite this low point in their relationship would have compelled him to pick up the phone and call her.

After dinner, she made a call to Lucky, her sales manager at Sea Castle, keeping the rising drama to herself.

"Hey, Lucky. It's Meg. I'll be returning home soon from Italy and wanted to check in to see how you're faring out there. Anything new?"

Lucky's sigh resembled a grumble. "Other than 'that' woman moving out here, you mean? Wish I could go off to Italy right now!"

"Sorry, kiddo. I heard a rumor that Pepper was thinking of relocating."

"It's no rumor. She showed up with no warning, wanted our best suite—which meant booting a long-time guest—and has been nothing but ornery. How are we supposed to get anything done with that jaguar sniffing around here all the time?"

Meg stilled her breathing, the desire to expose Pepper for the imposter she believed her to be churning through her chest. *In due time ... in due time ...* "Other than commandeering a suite, has she made any other requests?"

A whoosh of air—Lucky exhaling—filled her earpiece. "Well, for one, she came in here and immediately said she was in charge. That did not go over very well with Janet at the desk, especially since she did so in front of a family checking in." She exhaled again. "Oh, and she demanded the night auditor turn over all of his reports to her before our bookkeeper has a chance to review them and make adjustments. Messes with our whole routine!"

She could make no sense of this. Why would Pepper up and leave California for their smallest property in the east? What did she have to gain by throwing her weight around out there?

"Speaking of Macy—our bookkeeper—she was wringing her hands in my office today." She groaned. "Said Pepper's lavish taste might just bankrupt this place."

Meg frowned. What had Macy meant by that? Pepper had

been nothing but chintzy at Sea Glass Inn. Not only with the staff, but regarding hotel upgrades. She'd overheard her arguing with Jackson more than once about improvements he wanted to make. Always said they couldn't afford it, and considering Jackson was regularly meeting with potential investors, Meg had come to believe that the company was beginning to flounder.

The only one who seemed to have any real money … was Pepper. She sat up, a gasp escaping her. Everything about Pepper, all the way to those fat-dissolving injections in her chin, were lavish—her wardrobe, nails, hair, her car. She had assumed that William had left them with plenty, but what if she had blown through her share and was now on the hunt for more?

Meg grabbed her phone from her nightstand, opened her airline app, and booked a plane—to Florida's gulf coast.

CHAPTER 19

He missed her. Jackson flopped onto his back, his bed cold and lonely. He wanted to reach out and stroke her back, to pull her close. He put a fist to his forehead, trying to still his thoughts. Why had he sent that impersonal text, the one that told her to send him her schedule when she got back to the States? He wanted to talk to her *now*. She had probably taken that as an insult, a slap against the intimate relationship they had been building. Well, the new one they had been building. The old one had been long buried. At least, he hoped so.

Jackson turned back over and punched his ice-cold pillow before sinking into it. This relationship seesaw had gone on too long and he wanted to jump off—and pull Meg off with him.

He took his phone from his nightstand and punched in her number, not caring that he would no doubt wake her up. With each ring of her line, his breathing quickened and his heart stirred a little more. He swallowed and licked his lips, waiting, waiting, waiting, until her voicemail answered:

You have reached Meg of Riley Holdings. I'm sorry to have missed your call, but please do leave me your name and number and I will return your call. Please note that I am traveling out of the country and there may be a delay. Thank you.

"Meg, it's me. I-I miss you." He paused, not sure what else to add, though there was still so much to say. "I can't wait for you to return home. Bye."

With a grunt that shook the walls of his bedroom, Jackson pitched his phone across the room with the force of a bereft man, quite sure he heard glass breaking.

SHE WOULD MISS THIS PLACE. In the dark of morning, Meg packed her bags. She took a shower and put on her most comfortable clothes—yoga pants, a cotton tee, and sneakers—knowing she would be wearing them for hours. She glanced about the room, regret filling her that she could not stay longer in this beautiful home and city. She shut her eyes, remembering the sound of Jackson's voice in this place and wishing he were still here beside her.

She unplugged her phone from the wall and stopped. A voicemail. Jackson had called her and left a message. She gulped, staring at his name on her screen. He probably was answering that phone message that she had left at the office. Could she survive another impersonal call from Jackson? To hear his voice in monotone? She shook her head in the dark, certain his call was anything but personal.

No matter. She had good friends to say goodbye to and a plane to catch. If she were to call him back, she would no doubt wake him. No sense continuing with this volley of phone calls. She would call him when she reached Florida—and ask him what in the world he would have her do.

HE AWOKE, checked his phone, and frowned. Nothing. Meg had ignored his middle-of-the-night call, the one where he'd rolled up his sleeves and shown her a piece of his heart. Had he expected anything else? Wounded, he picked up the phone to call Domenic.

"Jackson, I am so glad you called."

Domenic's voice sounded serious. Not the expected greeting. "Hello, Domenic. Before I go on, please don't mention to Meg that I am calling." He did not want her pity.

"I'm afraid I could not do that even if I wanted to. Meg has already left Italy."

Jackson glanced at the calendar. She left four days early? "I don't understand. Her flight isn't until a few days from now."

"We will get to that, son. First, tell me why you are calling."

If he weren't so desperate to hear Meg's voice, to know her whereabouts and be assured of her well-being, he might have laughed at Domenic's sidestep.

"Okay, sure. I have been doing some research regarding some of our expenditures and a name has surfaced. I was wondering if you could tell me if you know a person named Gia Agli?"

"Gia? No, no, son. I don't know anyone by that name."

He tried. It was a hunch, a long shot certainly, but he would have to find some other way to pinpoint why Riley Holdings had paid for this Gia Agli to travel to Florida. He rolled his eyes. Pepper constantly complained about company expenditures and here she was booking a flight for a friend—or someone.

"However," Domenic continued, "I know a Sophia Agli. Are you sure that is not the name you are trying to find?"

"You do? No, the name is definitely Gia, but may I ask how you know Sophia Agli? I wonder if she is related to the woman I am trying to locate."

"This is something that I am trying to determine, too. Son, we have a suspicion that you need to be aware of. It is quite serious."

"I'm listening."

"It's about Pepper. The woman who has been working with you at the inn, the Pepper you know, Meg does not believe that is your sister."

"What do you mean *not* my sister?" He paused, his mind overwhelmed by the thought. "Father spoke about her—said he met her in New York, and that she was his long-lost daughter." The term "love child" stuck in his mind, but he bit back his tongue, unwilling to say it. "Are you saying my father was mistaken?"

"Jackson, your father most definitely met his daughter, Sophia. She was also known as Pepper. But dear Meg spotted a photograph of Sophia in my study and inquired as to who she was. She stated that the woman in the photograph, and the woman you know as Pepper, are not the same." He paused, allowing the news to sink in. "I am very sorry to have to deliver this suspicion to you, son."

His thoughts exploded. Not his sister? Then who was she?

"I don't understand this, Domenic." Who was the woman who claimed to be his sister? And if this were true, how had she gotten away with it?

"I am stunned." A thought pricked him to his core. "If Pepper is not my sister, where is the real Sophia?"

"Sadly, I do not have information on her whereabouts. You might recall that we could not initially locate Pepper."

Though he had been filled with grief at the time, Jackson remembered this. "I remember now. You suggested hiring an investigator."

"And all he could provide us with was her last known address, an apartment that appeared to be abandoned."

"So I sent her a registered letter."

"You did."

"My hope was that she would ignore it."

"I suspected as much. It appears that the mail may have been intercepted. Perhaps this Pepper who you know is a relative of Sophia's."

"Domenic, I need your help. Help me find out where Gia Agli came from—and what happened to Sophia. Will you do that for me?"

"I will do everything in my power to help you—my Elena is already on her knees in prayer."

Jackson sighed. He would need all the prayers he could get. "What time was Meg's flight? I would like to know when to expect her."

"She left about four hours ago, but son, you should not expect to see her. She was bound for Florida."

SHE ARRIVED at Tampa International Airport rumpled, sore, and far less sure of herself than when she had boarded. Who knew that traveling from Italy to Florida could take as much time as if she were to fly all the way home? She texted Lucky that she'd be heading to the inn shortly and to save her a room, then she went in search of coffee, the strongest she could find.

"Double cap for Meg!"

She reached through the throng of caffeine-starved travelers and downed her cup before she'd left the airport. In the cab, she scowled. Three missed calls from Jackson. Her heart flipped, conflicted. She'd missed him, but after the way they had ended things in Italy, she did not dare admit it. Still, she ached over the thought that the inns—and his life—had been invaded by an imposter. She couldn't put him off any longer and punched in his number.

"Meg."

"Hi. It's me."

"Where are you?"

She glanced out the window. Uncharacteristic grey sky. "About thirty minutes from Sea Castle Inn."

His voice sounded like a growl. "Why do you always have to run ahead?"

"Excuse me?" The grumpy tone to his voice had startled her.

"You can't fix this, Meg. Come home."

Fix what? Their relationship and all their rocky starts? "Jackson, we can talk about us later. I have something important to tell you … to talk to you about. It's the reason I'm in Florida now."

"I know."

"You … do?"

"I spoke with Domenic." A rushing sound filled her ears, as if he had just exhaled a thousand sighs.

"I'm so sorry," she whispered.

"You should not be there, Meg. Get out of Florida today. I'll handle this."

She sucked in a harsh breath. The force of his tone unnerved her. "She lied about my mother. Put a wedge between you and me by saying William was sending checks to her. That alone is reason for me to confront her."

He whistled. "You are stubborn."

"I know this isn't just about me." She sensed her guard crumbling. Why did he not seem to understand? "I-I just hate that she's done this to you."

"What she said about the checks … that was accurate. Over the course of several years, my father wrote checks to your mother, often in amounts in the thousands."

"That can't be true! I would have known about it."

"Meg."

She laid her head against the seat of the cab, despite the sickening reality that this car had probably not been cleaned in, well, forever. "Why would you believe this?"

"Look, I'm sure my father had a good reason for writing those checks. I don't question that—although I do think your mother owes you some kind of explanation so you can put this to rest."

She glanced out the window, a familiar change in the sky as they moved closer to the gulf. "I'm on my way there now. Just tell me what to look for and I'm all over it."

"No."

"What do you mean no? I'm here. I can help."

"I mean no. Absolutely not. This is my battle—not yours. I will deal with this."

"Now who's being stubborn? I'm here now and you're not. Why not just let me help?"

A long pause fell between them until he said, "Because I will fire you if you do. If you set foot on the Sea Castle property, you will no longer be employed at Riley Holdings." More silence. "And I won't speak to you again."

Her bottom lip trembled. She had heard him loud and clear, but where had this venom come from? Her stomach turned. She had fallen for this man not once, but twice. How had she been so terribly wrong about him?

"Did you hear me?"

Meg stared into the cab's grimy ceiling and harnessed her colliding thoughts. "You don't need to say another thing about this, Jackson. Now or ever again." Meg puffed out a harsh breath. "I will go back to California and I will work hard to honor your father until I can find another suitable position somewhere. But unless it's work related, I don't ever want to hear from you again either."

WHEN SHE WAS LITTLE, Meg often sat on top of her quilted bedspread and stared out the window, book in lap. This moment felt a little like that, although as a child her heartbreak came from the sudden loss of her father and the lack of explanation of where he had gone. Though this heartbreak came about in a far different way, it did not hurt any less.

After Jackson threatened to fire her, she'd tried to book a flight out of Tampa, but nothing was available. She couldn't go to Sea Castle Inn, so she came here, to this resort nearby. Rooms were at a premium this time of year, but the front desk clerk had taken pity on her tear-streaked face and upgraded her to a room with a peek-a-boo of the gulf.

Her phone rang. Liddy. She barely had time to answer it when

Liddy said, "Where are you? I thought you were coming home to watch chick flicks with me and eat ice cream."

She pictured her friend prone on her couch, bored, maybe even fearful. Guilt washed over her. "I'm sorry, Lid. Still traveling." How often had she said that to her best friend?

"I'm only teasing! Baby and I are fine and we do NOT expect you to leave Italy for us."

"If only I were still there."

"Wait … where are you?"

Her resolve to keep it together dissolved into a shake in her voice. "Oh Liddy. I'm in Florida. There's so much to tell you. I-I just can't believe all that has happened since I left California."

"Honey, what is going on?"

Meg sniffled, suddenly hyper-aware of her friend's recent trip to the hospital. The last thing she wanted to do was cause her any stress. "Actually, I'm fine. I came here to look into some things at Sea Castle, but they, uh, have everything under control. I'm going to leave in the morning."

"Hold it. You can't brush me off that fast—it's me. Remember?"

Meg's attempt at a stiff upper lip crashed like a rogue tide. Tears so hot and fast she could barely eke out a word of explanation. "Jackson came to Italy to see me … but it's over now." She gave her friend the highlights from their time in Italy ending with, "He doesn't want me, Lid. He never did."

"I will kill him."

Meg pictured her much-pregnant friend chasing down Jackson and smacking him over the head with her giant reservation book. She sniffled. "There's more."

"Great. I can't wait."

"It's Pepper. She's not—at least I think she's not—Jackson's sister."

"Come again?"

"I saw a photo in Domenic's office of the real Pepper. Her name is Sophia—Pepper's just a nickname—and nobody seems to know where she is. We believe that, somehow, this Pepper that we've all come to know and *love* is an imposter."

"I can't ... no way. Is there any chance that the real Sophia just doesn't want to be found? That she sent this ... this *crazy* woman in her place?"

"Hadn't thought of that angle." She sighed, her breath ripply from tears. "I'll mention that to Domenic since I'm, well, I almost quit my job today."

"What?!"

"Shush. Oh no, don't get stressed, Lid. Please. You need to keep calm for the baby's sake." She paused. "Jackson threatened to fire me. You know how hard I've tried to honor my promise to William to stay on, but I can't do it ...." She couldn't finish, her words garbled by a fresh onslaught of tears.

"It's okay, Meggy. You tried your hardest, but there's been so much drama there over the past year. Plus, your rocky relationship with Jackson—and now the shocking news about Pepper... still can't believe that! Oh I love you so much, girl. Give yourself a break for once."

Her voice turned raw, raspy. "Thank you. I'm tired now. Going to grab a nap. I'll see you tomorrow, 'kay?"

"I'll have all my wallowing supplies at the ready. Godspeed, my friend."

After they'd hung up, Meg closed her eyes, but sleep would not come. She had not told anyone but Liddy, and Jackson, of course, that she would not be working for Riley Holdings much longer. Tears sprang again to her eyes, surprising her with their relentlessness. She had believed that she would always be a part of the company. In a deeply painful way, she realized that saying goodbye to the inns would be like saying goodbye to William all over again.

Her phone rang and she dropped a gaze to the screen. Janet from the Sea Castle. She inhaled sharply and answered on the third ring. "Hey, Janet. What's up?"

"Hello, Meg. Lucky mentioned that you would be coming in soon. We have a suite set up for you—do you still need it?"

Jackson had not informed them of her departure, apparently. And she had not had the heart to say goodbye to the staff.

Her spirit wavered. She wanted to duck out and pretend that her fight with Jackson had not happened, that he hadn't treated her so poorly. She certainly did not want to tell anyone at the little inn on the gulf about her predicament. "Change of plans. I made it to Tampa but got called back to California." It wasn't that much of a lie—she did live there, right? "I won't be making it to the inn, so you can go ahead and release the room."

She braced herself for a barrage of questions.

"Uh, okay. Lovely."

Apparently, she'd sounded believable. But something about Janet's response bothered her. She sensed timidity. Janet did not intimidate easily, one reason she was the best desk manager on the planet. Kind, but firm. "I understand that Pepper is at the property now."

"She is."

"Is she … is everything okay?"

"Funny you should ask." She lowered her voice. "I'm actually in the back office right now. There are two gentlemen out front who have been quite forceful about their request for a suite with a view. Even Pepper seemed openly unnerved by them—she is the one who told me I had to give him the suite."

"And the only one with a view left was mine."

"Yes, we are booked solid."

She found her reason for Janet's tone. Pepper was in-house—enough to scare even those with a strong backbone. "Well," Meg said, "I'm glad I could help, then."

"Mm-hm. Yes. I have to go now. Thank you, Meg."

She clicked off the line, her eyelids heavy, her body pressed into the bed. Sleep had come.

CHAPTER 20

Jackson's jaw clenched as he stared out the window into the abyss of clouds, rehashing the words he had spoken to Meg, and the tone in which he had delivered them. He had done what he had to do. No second guessing. No regrets.

Alex, it turned out, had been an even better resource than Jackson had expected. With his help, he had begun piecing together a picture based on a number of questionable transactions. When added together, the answers to those questions raised one massive red flag over the company. When this was all over, he would have to find a way to give their IT man a raise.

Once he was in Pepper's email account, Alex helped him log in to her credit card accounts. Jackson winced at the recollection of finding four credit cards in the company's name that he knew nothing about. "They're all from the same bank," Alex told him. "Since that's the company bank, those cards didn't stand out to you on the reports. My guess, anyway."

Even digging into the accounts did not immediately raise concerns. Many of the charges were inn related, such as payments to their laundry service and gift shop suppliers. But as he dug deeper, Jackson noticed the cash advances: some in the hundreds, but most in the thousands of dollars. What would Pepper need cash for in relation to the inns?

Jackson fidgeted in his seat. More aware of the company's dire financial situation than ever, he had opted for a window seat in coach. The seats, he'd decided, had been created with children in mind, not adults. He shifted, trying to get comfortable, his mind cramped with myriad dark thoughts.

The first came late last night, when he printed out Pepper's plane tickets. If he were going to build a case of fraud, he would need evidence, so he scanned the documents for clues and stuck them in a file. He pulled one of the tickets back out and scrutinized it. Miami. For a cruise? He suspected that, now that she had charged up all the accounts associated with Sea Glass Inn, Pepper had plans to similarly drain Sea Castle Inn's resources.

He stuck the document back in the file, mulling his options. There were few.

With two thick files of evidence in his briefcase, Jackson stalked across the inn's parking lot and headed home. He had almost arrived when his phone rang. The number on his screen, though not Domenic's, indicated a caller from Italy. "Yes?" he answered.

"Jackson."

The woman said his name with a familiarity that tugged at his insides, but caution dictated.

"This is Jackson."

"It is Sophia. Your sister."

Pepper would not announce herself this way. This woman did not screech. She did not attempt to dominate the conversation. Her voice was soft, almost timid. "Sophia?"

"Yes, it is I. Domenic found me."

"Wait ... You say that *you* are my sister?"

"I am."

"I hardly know where to begin." The inky black night surrounded him. "How much has Domenic told you?"

"Ah, I believe he has told me all that he knows. I am so sorry, Jackson. I had no information about any of this." Her voice tremored. "I learned about William. My heart is broken. This explains why my last letter was returned."

He willed himself not to fall prey to another scheme. He would not cut her off, however. Instead, Jackson would listen to her story, gather information that might help him figure out this chaos, and stay emotionally detached. It was the only way he could function after nights of no sleep and sudden, unwelcome information.

"Sophia, where have you been?" A simple, open-ended question—simple if she had an answer to it.

"I am in Italy. Domenic said you had come to visit him and I am grieved not to have met you while you were here."

"I was not aware that you lived abroad."

"Neither was Domenic. When my mother died, I did not see any reason to stay in New York. She taught me to sew and I have been able to find work near Milan, not too far from where we lived for a little while when I was young."

Her story yanked on him. She was beginning to sound authentic. "If you are who you say you are, who is Gia?"

"Oh Jackson—she is my half-sister. Always in trouble, from the day she was born. My mother married her father when I was a baby. When Gia was born they gave us both the same last name." She paused. "All my life I did not know I had another father."

"Sophia, you must know the trouble Gia has caused."

"You need to be careful, Jackson. That is why I called you right away after Domenic reached me. My sister … my sister is too smart for her own good. I don't trust her."

"We believe she intercepted the letter I sent to you regarding our father's death."

"She will do more than steal mail, I am afraid."

"Like money?"

"Yes, Gia stole from my mother and from me. She has the ability to work hard and earn her own living, but she still takes what is not hers. Worse, she dances with devils."

"Meaning?"

"She associates with bad people. That is why I was hiding from her all this time. When I heard from Domenic what she had done now, I knew I had to come out of hiding."

Jackson peered through the window next to his seat, his eyes unable to focus. *She associates with bad people.* Last night, the words Sophia had spoken to him played over in his mind until the floating slivers of information joined together to form a vivid, tortured picture. Before Sophia's phone call, Jackson had come to realize that Pepper had been stealing from the inn. She had taken out cash advances then paid the credit cards with the inn's funds. No wonder their expenditures had skyrocketed.

He booked his own flight to Florida last night, determined not only to confront Pepper with his findings—but to get her confession.

But as he had begun to deconstruct the web of deceit he had lived with for so long, a more sinister thought weighed on him: Pepper could be dangerous. He already suspected she was behind the drone that dive-bombed Meg and caused her broken foot. If it were true, she probably had help—from the "bad people" Sophia warned him about.

He couldn't—he wouldn't—let anything happen to Meg.

Fear ground through him like blades to the gut. Pepper complained about Meg nearly non-stop, blaming her for improprieties, for being too controlling, all of it fabricated, of course. Why? It struck him that Pepper was afraid—of Meg. If anyone could eventually have sniffed out a liar, it was the woman who had helped her father build Sea Glass Inn into a warm and welcome destination.

The woman he loved.

I'm on my way there now ...

When Meg said those words to him, he knew. He had to stop her. *Had to*. If Pepper had taken things this far—far enough to potentially chase her down with a drone—who knew what she could accomplish? Meg could be in real danger. He could not allow her to show up—and he'd done what he had to do to make that clear.

The only thing worse than losing everything would be losing *her*.

MEG SQUINTED at the watery image in her mind. His top half came into focus. A man, tall and wide, his face cloaked except for his eyes. He pointed at her, his gloved hand unyielding. "Can't stop the money train," he said. "Can't stop the money train." His eyes burned with evil. She gasped, waking herself up. For a few moments, she lay there listening to the scrape of her own breath as it accelerated through her chest. She could not recall the last time she'd had a nightmare, nor one so palpable.

She rose, slid the door open to her small balcony, and stepped out. The balmy weather of the Florida gulf had cooled some, enough for her to lean against the railing, though the sky continued to morph into layers of darkness. The image of a dangerous man had been too real for her to completely shake. Despite the weather, goosebumps alighted on her skin and she rubbed them away with her hands.

Two gentlemen ... quite forceful ... even Pepper seemed unnerved.

She had not been able to get the tone of Janet's voice nor what she said about the strangers in search of a suite out of her mind. What had the image in her nightmare said? Something about a ... money train. She sighed, the sound of waves crashing filling the night air. The inns were no longer her problem. She had to remind herself that she had left her job, though technically,

Jackson had forced her out. The reminder brought a sharp blow to her windpipe.

Still, Pepper becoming unnerved in front of guests? Not typical. Angry and confrontational with staff, yes, but guests were her bread and butter, so to speak. She shook it off. Pepper likely learned that the only thing between collecting the nightly rate for that suite or not was Meg's impending arrival. And her dislike for Meg ran deep.

She would never forget the memory of Pepper shouting at her, inches from her face, those black fingernails like claws. "Hang up, hang up!" Meg had only called Domenic to say hello, and when she figured this out, Pepper had not been happy. She almost laughed at the absurdity of the moment. A grown woman squawking like a lunatic.

Then again, she was not who she claimed to be. Meg was as sure of this as she was of her own breath. Why, if she were not who she claimed to be, would Pepper have such a dislike for a lowly sales director? If she did not have a true stake in the company, why would she care about some supposed long-ago money to Meg's mother?

Meg frowned. She stepped back inside her room, noting the need for more air conditioning. After adjusting the dial, she took a seat at the wicker desk and called her mother.

"Buona sera, Meghan."

"Good evening to you, Mom."

"You must be back home."

"Not yet. I arrived in Florida this morning on business. I plan to fly out tomorrow, though."

"Florida during hurricane season? Are you trying to give me a heart attack?"

So dramatic. "Actually, I am calling to talk to you about something serious."

"What could be more serious than a heart attack?"

"It's about William."

"William … ?"

"You remember—my boss." She paused. The idea that William, who had never met her mother, had been secretly sending her checks sounded so bizarre. Though she had asked her mother a form of this question before, the issue continued to fester and she had to put it to rest. "I'm sorry to have to ask you this question again, but I must: Did William ever send you money … for *anything*?"

"Wow. You travel to Italy and the only thing you have to say when you get home is that your boss gave me money?"

"I'm sorry if I've disappointed you, but this is what I've been told—more than once. Do you have any idea why someone would make this claim?"

"I do not."

Meg waited for more, but her mother had clammed up. As usual. It occurred to her as well that though Meg did not put a lot of stock in the allegations, her mother had not yet answered her question.

She swallowed rising concern. "Mom, did you know William? I mean, had you ever spoken to him?"

Silence.

Meg flopped back and rubbed a palm over her eyes and cheek. "You knew him, didn't you." It was not a question.

"I did not know William Riley!"

"But you had some sort of connection to him, right? I can hear it in your voice."

"I am only going to say this one more time, Meghan. Some things are better left buried."

"Even if it means the loss of my job?"

A sad sound, like a cry, came through the phone line. "Please stop this. You haven't lost your job—you wouldn't. They love you there at that hotel."

Meg's gaze dropped to the woven pattern of her blouse. She still had a hard time believing she would not be going back to the inn. "I was forced out, Mama," she said, her voice barely above a whisper.

"But William promised you'd be—"

"What? Mom? How can he promise you anything if you don't *know* him?"

"I promised him I'd never say a word!" She let out a harsh cry. "It was our special bond. No, I did not know him in person—but he promised me that you would have a job at the inns as long as you wanted it!"

Meg's eyes closed at this news, so unexpected. "You rarely visited me. When would you have had the chance to speak with William?"

"It was years ago, when you first started working there. You were a baby when you left home—*a baby*."

"Seventeen is hardly a baby."

"I should not have let you leave, but you were headstrong and you had the money, so I did not fight you. After you got that job at the inn, I was happy for you. I was also very scared, so I called him."

"You called William?"

"Yes. I read an article on the Internet about how he had bought that old hotel and was trying to revitalize it. He had a nice face so I called him and thanked him for hiring you."

"You're kidding."

"No. I am not kidding. Why do you think I'm kidding?"

"But this doesn't explain the money."

"I know, I know. You see, William doted on you. He asked me all kinds of questions—I did not expect so many questions! He asked about your father, and when he learned how he'd died, he expressed such sympathy for you. What a nice man. He said he sometimes caught you looking sad and that this explained it."

Meg's mind turned this news over. Everything about this call, about what her mother was saying, made no sense. If William and her mother had talked like this, why wouldn't she have known about it?

"So … he gave you money because you, what, birthed me?"

"Don't be vulgar, Meghan." She huffed a heavy sigh. "Fine. I will tell you why William sent me checks back then, but only because you are hysterical right now."

Meg snapped a "why me" look to the ceiling.

"When he learned that your Uncle Greg had become addicted to drugs after he … he caused that awful accident and that he had no money to pay for his rehabilitation, he offered to help. William was a soft-hearted man."

Her mother had been the big sister, always rallying around her little brother and his needs. She had no extra money of her own, at least not until she remarried years later, so Meg had been sending what she could. Suddenly one day, her mother, without explanation, told her to stop. "So, this is how you were able to pay for his rehab?"

"Yes. He said that he would send me the amount you were giving me each month, but I had to promise never, ever to tell you about it. He gave far beyond what you had been sending me."

"Dear William," she said aloud. "And then he encouraged me to go to night school."

"And I was always so proud of you for using your extra money in that way." She paused, as if reflecting. "William told me that he wanted to take you under his wing, that you were like a daughter to him. Said you were the daughter he never had."

Or had not yet found? Her nose prickled with rising emotion. She remembered walking into Sea Glass Inn her first day on the coast. She had worn her favorite skirt—black, A-line, just above the knees. Her hands shook as she handed her resume to the receptionist in the Human Resources office. When she was told Mr. Riley wanted to meet her right then and there, her mouth went dry, her hands perspired. If she'd had time to think about applying for the Executive Assistant position, she might not have showed. The idea was a bold one, even to her thinking. He interviewed her and hired her all in one day.

What she had always considered a random first stop, suddenly felt anything but accidental.

She exhaled. "I never knew that Uncle Greg caused the accident he was in," she said. "What happened? Is this the one that started his addiction?"

"You were a young child, Meg. You did not understand what was going on around you." Her mother's voice sounded small, like a child's. "I would prefer we not relive that terrible time."

Relive this terrible time … like all that has occurred in the last twenty-four hours? Add to that, now her mother had essentially confirmed a financial arrangement with William that she never knew about. Could a brain handle such tumult in so short of time?

Her mind spun with bits of memory. Relive this terrible time … relive ...

Her mother's tears.

A house full of tall people. Adults everywhere.

Her own cries for her father ...

A welling reached her eyes. "Mother, I have to ask you something. And I need you to tell me the truth. Please, no more hedging." She didn't wait for her mother to respond. "Was Uncle Greg alone when he had his accident?"

Her mother's voice shrank to a whisper. "No."

Oh no. Tears dropped one by one from Meg's eyes and dripped down her cheeks. "Who was with him?"

Quiet.

"Mother, *who?*"

Her mother's sobs filled the line. "Your father."

CHAPTER 21

"Mr. Riley, were we expecting you?" Janet's fingers clicked across her computer keyboard, her eyes scanning for his reservation.

"You won't find me in the system. I decided to come in on the spur of the moment."

One of the desk manager's eyebrows rose. "A surprise inspection?"

"Don't worry. You've passed."

The relief he thought he'd see on her face never materialized. "You are fortunate to have made it in ahead of the storm."

He glanced out a lobby window, taking in the growing buildup of greys—battleship to charcoal. "Dark, but calm."

"It always is ahead of the storm. Now, we are completely booked." She tapped a few more keys on her keyboard. "But I'm checking to see if any of our unguaranteed reservations have missed the six-o'clock deadline."

"What are you doing here?" Pepper's unmistakable screech invaded the reception area.

He turned. "Good evening to you too, Ms. Riley."

She reached across the desk to still Janet's furious typing. "There is no room at the inn."

Jackson leaned against the counter and scrutinized her. "Even for your brother?"

"Sorry. You are not Jesus."

"As you may recall, there was no room for him either. Or perhaps you are suggesting I stay in the hotel's barn?"

He detected hidden laughter from Janet, who for her part kept her head down and her fingers clacking away.

"What is it you want, Jackson?" Pepper drilled those black nails of hers on the front desk. "As you can see, we are very busy."

I can see that Janet is very busy ... He nodded once. "I thought we could do a site tour together. I would like to assess the condition of Sea Castle. Perhaps the financial team I am working with would be willing to increase their investment if we presented them with a solid proposal for improvement."

The harsh lines of her face softened, her eyes less narrowed. No doubt about it. He had her the moment he suggested more money could be forthcoming.

He continued, "I will need you to provide the financial data for the proposal. And for you to do whatever you need to do to make us look solid, of course."

"Of course," she snapped.

Janet's hands stopped moving. She looked up, her expression showing relief. "I found one." She typed a few more strokes, opened a draw, and slid a key to him.

He picked up the key, tossed it in the air, and caught it again. "Thank you much, Janet. You're a miracle worker."

Pepper's glower returned. "You are lucky this time."

Janet cleared her throat, clearly unsure whether to interrupt their tête-à-tête. "Shall I have Robert take your things to your room for you?"

"Not this time, but thank you." He turned to Pepper. "I'll run upstairs to freshen up and meet you back here in thirty for dinner."

She crossed her arms. "How do you know if I am free?"

He shrugged. "You moved here, what, a day or two ago? Who could you possibly know in town yet?" He swung a look at Janet. "Other than Janet, that is. Were you two planning to have dinner?"

Pepper's flat line of a mouth smirked. "You have lost your mind."

He picked up his bag and pointed at her. "Thirty minutes."

IN HIS ROOM, he washed up, hung his clothes, and changed his rumpled shirt. He'd been stalling. Domenic had promised to hunt down a certified copy of Sophia's birth certificate. There should have been one found among William's things, but to his knowledge, none had ever been seen.

His phone rang. Sophia's number. "Hello. This is Jackson."

"It is me."

His countenance lifted. He was beginning to recognize her voice, the sound of it like family. "It is the middle of the night there. What are you doing up?" If he were being lied to again, he could not bear it.

"I could not sleep. I wanted to tell you that I signed an affidavit swearing who I am. It will help you with the authorities when you confront my sister. I will email it to you, but is that safe to do?"

Breaking into Pepper's account had been as easy as making a phone call. To the right person, that is. Alex would not betray him. He felt sure of it. Of course, he had been sure of Pepper's identity too ...

"Send it to my personal account." He gave her the address. "Any word from Domenic?"

"I spoke to him, yes. He helped me find out where I could obtain the certificate. It has been ordered and expedited. You should have it shortly."

"Beautiful." He glanced at his phone screen. "I have to go. Pepper—I mean, Gia—is sending me angry texts and I am late for dinner."

"You are confronting her now?"

"Not exactly. I am trying to keep her here until I have enough evidence gathered to confront her."

"Ah, but you have already said you have proof she is stealing from you, yes? Is it not enough?"

"It is complicated, Sophia. We are not in California where the fraud occurred."

She sighed. "This is all such terrible news. Gia has made such chaos of your life. Of mine too."

Her sorrow twisted something inside him. "This will be all over soon, Sophia. I promise."

He stepped out the door, the promise he had just made to his sister still lingering on his lips.

MEG HAD SLEPT in her clothes. She awoke, expecting to see daylight spilling through her window. Instead, the sky had opened during the night and unleashed itself on the beach. In unison, a row of palms bent in an arc, as if pointing the way out. Her phone dinged and she let go of the heavy drape.

Alert: Flight cancelled. Contact airline.

She glanced again at the window, her mind not far away from her mother's hurricane comment. Would a little rain cancel her flight? She ran her thumb over her touch screen. The airline's website gave her little more to go on. Her flight had been cancelled, as well as all others for that day. The next day's flights were temporarily suspended as well. She clicked over to weather news: TROPICAL STORM BUILDING.

Could this "vacation" get any worse?

Her thumb hovered over the voicemail icon. She swallowed. She had never listened to Jackson's message from a few nights back. No real reason to keep it now. She began to swipe it away, intent on deleting it before hearing his voice would cause her further heartbreak, when she noticed the time he had called. Middle of the night?

She played the message. *Meg, I miss you.* His voice had broken when he said it. *I can't wait for you to get back.*

Confused, she played it again. How could this be? She spoke to him a few hours later and the tone of his voice had changed. He'd sounded annoyed at first, then downright tired of her. It was as if he wanted her out of the way.

Was his middle-of-the night call just a momentary lapse? Just another swing of the pendulum that too often characterized their relationship?

"I miss you too, Jackson." A tear slid from her eye. "But I'm so, so angry with you right now."

She wiped her eyes with the back of a hand, fighting the urge to fully grieve. Last night's call with her mom unraveled the mystery of the checks from William. Up until then, she believed that Pepper had been trying to pry Jackson and her apart with a lie. A bitter laugh escaped her. Pepper had known more about William's interaction with her mother than she had.

But even though her assertions were true, why had Pepper—an imposter—bothered to accuse Meg at all? Wouldn't it have been easier for her to keep her cover if she were to lay low and not make any waves at all?

An ominous cloud darkened her thoughts. Could it be that Pepper had been trying to throw Jackson—and maybe Meg herself—off another trail? But what?

She had intimated that Meg had somehow been involved with financial improprieties—Meg had heard her screaming on the other end of Jackson's calls. She'd uncovered and blasted information about William writing checks to Meg's mother. Tension tiptoed up Meg's spine. She straightened. The day Pepper had noticed her on the phone with Domenic, she shrieked something about "the money train stopping" for her.

Was Riley Holdings in trouble financially? Maybe this was Jackson's reason for not implementing Meg's proposals for the spa and other upgrades. He had been meeting with investors, and though she had thought this to be a fairly straightforward business move, she realized with a sinking in her gut that the company must be in trouble.

Pepper would certainly know that Meg had nothing to do with a financial shortfall. Jackson had told her once that Pepper had a "bird's-eye view" of the company's expenditures. So if she knew that Meg had no part in the company's financial problems, then it stood to reason that she also knew who—or what—had caused them.

JACKSON MANAGED to keep his tone cordial and to fight his uncanny desire to lunge across the table and throttle the woman who sat across from him, lying. Her talent far surpassed his imagination. For the past twenty minutes, she had told him tale after tale, each one less believable than the one before it. Tales of loneliness as an only child, of missing the father she never knew, and now, of her talents as a seamstress.

"The clothes I made by my own hand were more beautiful than the rags that the stores sell. They were of marketable quality," she bragged.

"I suppose you still sew in your spare time," he said.

"To ever pick up a needle again would be to bruise my own soul." Her voice dripped with melodrama. "Oh no, no, no. I would feel like a pauper, like when I was a child. I could not do it."

He stilled his eyes so in a knee-jerk reaction they wouldn't roll. A couple of men walked in and took a seat at the table next to theirs. He worked to hide a wince. This café was long overdue for a rehab. Just one of the many projects that had gone dormant as Pepper had played her games with their finances.

"Let's talk about the new proposal that I told you about."

Pepper nodded, her eyes unsettled.

"Did you hear what I said?"

She zeroed in on him. "I am not deaf."

He looked away rather than let her see the disgust in his eyes, his gaze falling on the men one table over. A couple of surfer dudes, one of them more like an aging wrestler. They both wore long sleeves over their board shorts, which made him want to turn down the a/c temperature.

"What did you want to propose?"

He dragged his gaze back to her. "For one, we need to upgrade this café. I would also like to add full food service to the poolside bar, in season."

She shifted. "We will need to ask for more money then."

He nodded, his lips pursed before speaking. "Exactly."

Double doors burst open and Lucky approached their table. "I just heard Meg's not coming."

Jackson's chest constricted. "She had something to attend to in California."

Pepper shrank back. "Your girlfriend was coming here? Today? We have no room for her—unless, of course, she will be sharing your bed."

Jackson seethed.

Lucky glanced from Pepper to Jackson, her skin tinged pink. "Didn't know you were seeing each other." She shrugged. "None of my business but she had asked for her own room."

Pepper's laugh sounded like gravel ground into earth.

Jackson wagged his head. "Don't believe everything you hear, Lucky."

"Well, shoot." Lucky flopped into a chair across from them. "I wanted to tell her all about a tour coming through the hotel next month. Oh well. Can't believe she came all the way here and then decided to leave. Hope she was able to get a plane out okay. My brother's a pilot and he said that most of them are grounded due to the storm."

He hadn't thought of that and a prickle of concern seized him.

Lucky continued, "Plus, I was kinda hoping to hear about her trip to Italy, too. I've always wanted to go there and meet some Italian hunk who'd feed me olives and wine." She giggled.

Pepper's wretched grin slipped from her face. "Italy?"

Jackson tipped his head, observing the imposter. Her hostile countenance was changing before him. She twisted her hands in her lap and those eyes began to flit around again, as if she were searching for an exit.

Lucky turned to Jackson. "Yeah, I didn't even know she had gone. You probably did, though. Right? Where'd she go in Italy? She didn't say and now I can't ask her myself."

His mind went to that morning at the awful apartment that she'd rented in Florence. He had scooped her up in his arms, her body fitted against his, her eyes large and welcoming. He snapped a benign look at Lucky. "Can't say that I know. She was due a vacation, so hopefully she was able to get the rest she needed."

Lucky sighed like a romance reader. "Sounds divine. All I know is Florida, from coast to coast." She pushed her chair back. "Maybe I'll give her a call and get inspired."

He nodded. "Sounds like a good plan." He almost wanted to add, "Tell me if she is okay," though he knew the truth. He had broken her heart—again. Even if she were to forgive him for their latest argument, when you added up all the other confrontations they'd had, he feared there would be no chance left for repair.

Pepper licked her lips, her brows low. He'd never known her to be a worrier, unless you counted that fake worry over the company's expenditures.

He prodded her. "Doing okay, Pepper?"

"Yes, yes. Of course." She exhaled a staccato breath. "If Meg wanted a room here, I am sure we could have worked something out. Is it possible she is still in town?"

The possibility existed that Meg was still somewhere in the state, especially if she had not been able to book a flight home. But he knew she would not come anywhere near Sea Castle—he had seen to that.

Pepper's about-face where Meg was concerned intrigued him. "Kind of you to be concerned about our Sales Director."

"I am concerned for the welfare of all of our employees," she said. "Especially poor Meg. It must have been difficult for her to walk around Italy with that broken foot. Do you happen to know how she managed?"

Jackson folded his cloth napkin and left it on the table. "Meg is resourceful. I'm sure she found a way to see the sights." He stood up. "It's getting late and I'm going to have to get some sleep. Let's meet here at 8 a.m. for coffee and then we'll begin our site tour. Sound good?

Those eyes of hers steeled again. "I have very little time tomorrow, but I will try to work you in to my schedule."

"Really? What do you have planned for tomorrow?"

Her eyes would not connect with his. He could tell by her inability to raise that smug smile of hers that she struggled. "I have an … appointment to look at a condominium with my Realtor."

"Skip it. The weather might not be conducive to home buying tomorrow anyway."

She slapped her hand on the table. "I will decide what I do or do not have time for. My Realtor is a very busy man. I cannot just make changes on your whims."

He stuck a tongue into his cheek and watched her for several seconds. "I plan to return to California as soon as possible. If you want to see an influx of investment dollars, as I do, then make time to meet with me tomorrow."

He had dangled a carrot in front of the horse, and by the

resolve on her face, he knew he had won. Hopefully by tomorrow he would have the proof he needed to convince authorities that Pepper had assumed his sister's identity. Until that time, he would keep her busy.

"Fine." She threw her napkin onto the table but did not stand. "I will meet you here in the morning and we will have that proposal done by afternoon."

Perfect.

CHAPTER 22

"Hey there, where are you?"

Lucky's unmistakable voice greeted Meg. She glanced out at the rain-soaked sky. "I'm still in Florida. My flight was grounded but I'm in line for another. Depends on the weather."

"If you're so close, why didn't you come to the inn?"

The million-dollar question. "Ton of work to do. I decided to stay close to the airport and work."

She hated lying. But could she confess to her that not only had Jackson forced her out of the company, but that his sister was an imposter, and oh, she finally learned last night how her father had died so many years ago? Her mind had numbed overnight and a part of her wanted it to stay that way—immune to more trouble.

"Okay, fine. Bummer. I have news about a tour coming in, but first I want to talk to you about Italy. Was it everything I've ever heard?"

Meg exhaled, her laughter shaky. Lucky had asked the question with a dreamy air to her voice, but she teased her anyway. "Depends on what you've heard."

"Oh come on! That there's art everywhere, you cannot get a

bad cup of coffee, and the men are beyond beautiful." She paused. "Is it all true?"

A memory of Jackson's grin rose in her mind. Beyond beautiful. She swallowed, glad Lucky could not see her inability to smile. "Pretty much." She spoke as lightly as she could. "Especially the art. It was everywhere—in the museums, in the churches, even in some of the streets."

Lucky's sigh rippled through the phone. "I'm so jealous."

"You should go. It's a lot closer for you than for me. So, go."

"I will, I will. You've convinced me!" She giggled. "I'll have to talk the dragon lady into letting me go on vacation, though. She looked kinda shocked that you went all the way to Italy. I think she was real jealous."

"Really? What did she say when she heard?"

"Not much. But you know that face of hers. She got all bug eyed, like she couldn't believe you'd gone to such an amazing place. Hey, maybe she was jealous."

Not by a long shot. "Maybe."

"By the way, Pepper said something about you and Jackson being together, but I didn't respond. I'm guessing there's nothing to that, what with you being in Tampa and all. But I thought I should mention that she's spreading stories."

"Pepper is full of stories, that's for sure."

"Yeah, well, I would have stayed and talked more to them but there were these two creepy guys watching me. They checked in yesterday—I think they're the ones that got your reservation. Anyway, they've been hanging around in their flip flops and board shorts, staring at the women around here. They look kinda like surfers but never actually, uh, surf."

"Has anyone pointed them toward the surf line?"

Lucky's giggles filled the line. "Who knows? They look the part but only seem to sulk about the halls. Can you imagine coming to a resort and hardly venturing outside?"

Meg peeked again through the curtain at the drizzly day. "It's not exactly beach weather."

"Yeah, but you know how it is around here. It clears and everyone runs outside. Ya gotta be ready for it when it breaks."

It sounded to her like the men Lucky described were used to being couch potatoes. Or maybe they'd never been to a resort—small as theirs may be. She shook her head. Whatever. "You had something you wanted to tell me?"

"Oh my gosh, yes! So that tour operator you connected me to said she'd bring a group through here. Wanted to let you know!"

Meg's nose got that familiar tickle, like tears congregating near her sinuses. Lucky had scored a big one, based on her guidance, and wanted to celebrate with her. She would miss milestones like this. "I am so proud of you, Lucky. This was all you." Tears started to fall, but she wiped them aside and forced a laugh. "You-you landed a really big fish, hon!"

"I owe it all to you. Just hope they're happy here. I've asked Housekeeping to shine things up as much as possible—wish there was money in the budget for some sprucing, but Dragon Lady about chomped my head off when I suggested a few upgrades."

How long would Jackson allow Pepper to hang around there and bother the staff? Surely the news would be out soon. She turned this terrible situation over in her mind. Maybe he was waiting for those investors to infuse the company with cash before he let the word out. They could cancel the deal if they knew about the company's turmoil…

Her mind tumbled back to the nightmare she'd had, the one with the imposing man, his posture accusing. A fissure of fear ran up Meg's back. What if Pepper's sudden interest in moving had nothing to do with fixing what ailed the inn, and everything to do with getting to Jackson's investment team first?

My sister … insisted on being on the call.

Pepper had already been infiltrating Jackson's business dealings. If she found out that Jackson was on to her … what would keep her from taking everything he owned?

"You still there, Meg?"

"Yes, sorry. I'm here."

"I should let you go. Oh shoot!"

"You okay?"

"I completely forgot that Dragon Lady wants me to get her a free room in Miami. Ugh. It's getting late—hope I can get ahold of one of my contacts."

"What's in Miami?"

"Who knows? A meeting, I think. She told me to call one of my contacts and offer a free room swap. Completely forgot until now. Guess I'd better go."

She hung up and dialed Sea Glass Inn. If Jackson had not announced to the staff at Sea Castle that she had quit, she might still be able to garner the information she needed now.

"Hello, this is Sally. How may I help you?"

"Sally, it's Meg."

"You sound rested. How was your vacation?"

No sign that Sally knew she would not be back. "It was nearly perfect." A true statement.

"Wonderful. What can I help you with?"

"Jackson's been meeting with a firm in Miami and the name of their company has slipped my mind. Can you help?"

"Certainly. One moment." She clicked off the line. About a minute later, she was back. "I've found it. Knowing you, you'll try to book them for a three-day meeting or something." She laughed.

Meg laughed with her. "What was that name?"

"Oh yes. They are Power Financial. I have spoken with Sarah when I've called. Would you like her number?"

"That would be lovely."

She took down the number, thanked Sally for her help, then clicked off the line. If she were going to warn Jackson, she would need all the evidence she could get. She glanced at the number she had written on the hotel's pad of paper. It would be her final act of honor for William.

CHAPTER 23

Jackson had all the evidence he needed. He ran his fingers over the birth certificate of his sister, Sophia. He had received it by email after Domenic found an old friend with a scanner. The document on the desk next to it was a signed affidavit from Sophia admitting to her real name, along with a photograph. The woman with the vibrant green eyes looked so much like his father that he could hardly pull his gaze away.

Meg had seen it too. He reached for the phone, as if to call and talk to her about what he now had in his possession, but stopped. He wanted to keep her out of harm's way, and in doing so, he had put another wedge between them. He longed to do something about that ... if it weren't too late.

Speaking of late, if he were going to make his meeting with Pepper, he needed to get a move on. He tucked the birth certificate back into its file and hurried downstairs.

"Let's get this over with." Pepper had overdressed. Her fitted, houndstooth suit shimmered with silver and black and she wore enough onyx shark teeth to consume an overweight sea lion.

In contrast, he'd thrown on shorts and a T-shirt, his iPhone in his pocket. When he was ready to start recording, he would simply pretend he was checking his messages and open a recording app that he had downloaded last night.

"You planning on walking the beach path in those?" He pointed to her two-toned pumps.

"The weather has cleared so I have kept my appointment with the … Realtor. Let's make this a quick meeting."

He shrugged, giving her a wan smile. "Suit yourself. No pun intended."

They walked through the lobby, taking note of areas that needed rehabilitation. "What do you think, Pepper? Paint? New carpet?"

She shrugged. "Whatever you want."

He jotted a note in his journal. He should not be dragging this out—this he knew. But he was looking for just the right spot to drop the hammer, someplace quiet so the recording would be crystal clear. Besides, he enjoyed seeing her uncomfortable.

They passed the pool bar, which was busy now that the weather had cleared some. He turned to her. "Did you work up some numbers for adding food service to the bar?"

"What?"

His eyes narrowed. "The bar. I told you we should open it for food service in season."

She nodded. "Right. You mentioned that." She made a note on her own notepad.

The men he had noticed in the café last evening walked behind them on the path. They had donned shorts, though their shirts were long sleeved. He made a note to ask reservations to include information about the weather in the inn's confirmation emails.

At the end of the path stood a tired gazebo, one they had used in the past for weddings, though it would need some updating to become photo worthy again. Its platform sagged, its color had dulled. "What do you think about the gazebo?"

A sheen of perspiration made Pepper's face glow—and not in a good way. She scowled. "Tear it down."

"C'mon, Pep. Where's your sense of romance?" He slapped a post, its paint peeling. Was all that damage from wood rot or termites? "This gazebo alone could put Sea Castle on the map."

She shrugged. "All right. I would agree to fix this."

He pushed away from the post, vaguely aware of the wood shuddering beneath his hands. "Wonderful. Let's keep going."

She held up one hand, her nails poking the air. "Stop. I have to leave soon."

"Hold on a sec, will you?" He glanced at her, noting her unease. "I'm getting a text." He fiddled with his phone, opened the recording app, and hit "on." He looked up. "We've only started. Where are you going again?"

She sighed, agitated. "To see my real estate agent. She will be showing me a condo."

"I'll go with you. Another set of eyes is always a good idea when purchasing real estate."

She crossed her arms. "That's not necessary. I-I know what I like. My agent ... she knows too."

He tilted his head to one side. "I thought your agent was a man."

For the first time that he could remember, Pepper went mute. She rolled her eyes and sighed like a child. Pepper then tapped her pointy-toed shoe, her arms crossed. "I really must go, Jackson. I will talk to you about all this—" she waved one of her hands toward the small inn—"after I return."

He squinted in the sun. "When will that be, exactly?"

She frowned and dropped one arm by her side but left the other across her middle, as if protecting herself. "I will let you know."

He would not let her leave. Not until he had a chance to confront her with the evidence, with all he knew about her ... lies. She had pretended to be his *family*. For the past week, he had nearly been in denial. As difficult as she had been to work with, it had become just as difficult for him to believe that he had been taken in by her lies.

He turned to follow her and she stopped him. "I must use the restroom. Are you planning to follow me in there, too?"

I'm not letting you get away until I get what I want: your confession. "I will walk you back to the inn. Nothing more."

"I do not need an escort."

Testy. "There's only one path, you know, and we happen to be walking in the same direction."

"Right."

They walked in silence, her in her heels and suit and he in his casual wear. He had planned to confront her in the gazebo, but she had managed to weasel out of further conversation. No doubt there would be airspace on his recording.

Perhaps he had been too hasty in barring Meg from the inn. He'd been concerned for her safety, worried about what a lying thief like Pepper would do. She had been her obstinate self since he got here, but dangerous? She was a thief, but he doubted she was capable of anything worse.

They reached the door to the lobby and she reached for it.

"Pepper?"

She turned. "What is it?"

"We still have a few things to discuss before you leave for your appointment. I have to grab something from my room, but I'll meet you back here in about ten minutes."

She rolled her eyes. "Sure. Now, I will excuse myself."

He watched her walk down the inner hallway toward the restroom, then he quickly turned toward to path outside that led to his room.

"NICE TO SEE YOU AGAIN, MEG."

"You as well," Meg said. Gracie had only been with the inn

since the beginning of the year, but they had met on one of Meg's earlier trips out.

"I'll be with you in just a moment, okay?" Two men hovered near the desk, apparently checking out.

"No problem. I won't actually be staying, but I'd like to leave my luggage with you."

"Absolutely."

She slid her things behind the desk. "I'm looking for Lucky. Have you seen her on the property today?" Meg didn't mention the score she had to settle with Pepper—that would come soon enough.

Gracie thought for a few seconds. "I've been busy here at the desk, but I did see her a little while ago. I think she may have gone back to the sales office, but I'm not sure. Would you like me to call her for you?"

"Not necessary. I'll find her on my own."

She wandered around the corner and down the hall, her mind still overcome with the news that Pepper had a meeting with the investment team at Power Financial in Miami at four-thirty this afternoon. Sarah had been all too happy to fill Meg in on the details.

"We're so excited to be a part of Riley Holdings," she had gushed. "My boss says he can probably swing me some discounts—I've never been to California!"

"And we would love to host you at Sea Glass Inn. I'm just thrilled that funding appears to be imminent," Meg had said, hoping for confirmation.

"Oh yes. As soon as Ms. Riley arrives tomorrow, I believe the team will meet with her to sign docs and hand her a check. Again, we are excited to be a part of your team!"

She poked her head into the sales office expecting to find Lucky. Nothing. Her heart began to pound. She had no reason now not to seek out Pepper for answers. Why did she have an appointment alone at Power Financial? Why did she hate Meg so much? *And what possessed her to lie about her identity?*

That last question felt very much like stepping over some invisible line, but despite her argument with Jackson, she had to know. This woman—whoever she was—had infiltrated a family and desecrated a memory. Or tried to.

Her lungs contracted and she forced herself to take steady breaths. Breathe in. Breathe out. Steady. Steady. If she still entertained any thought about keeping her job with Riley Holdings, her presence here—not to mention her pending confrontation with Pepper—had annihilated that hope. Jackson had told her not to come, yet here she was. She had promised herself on the way to the inn that she would call Jackson to tell him what she'd learned —after she had managed to confront Pepper and to keep her from heading to Miami.

With a deep inhale, Meg pushed open the door to the outside path that led to another set of offices. She had dressed simply in black leggings, a long cotton tee, and Converse. In this heat, she probably should have worn sandals, but she wanted to be quick on her feet—especially if she had to chase Pepper down. Meg bit back a laugh, a tiny one, at the spectacle that would make. The gulf winds had stilled some, leaving a slight breeze to cool the air. She scanned the distance, hoping to find Pepper in her crosshairs. As much as she wanted answers and closure, she also desired to get this over with.

JACKSON RETURNED to the lobby and took a seat on a wicker couch that had once been nice. The front desk was in view, and the desk clerk moved quickly answering phones and checking in guests. He marveled. This place held so much potential. Great bones. And the parking lot went on for miles leaving plenty of room for expansion. No wonder his father snapped it up. He stole a glance down the hall. No more delays—no more games. He had to get her confession recorded—then kick her out of here.

Pepper was taking her sweet time. When a few more minutes passed and she failed to appear, Jackson stood and darted a look through the entry and into the lobby. Empty. Agitated, he walked out to the front desk. Something caught his eye. A purple ribbon tied to the handle of a black carry-on bag just beyond the desk.

Gracie, the desk clerk, glanced up and leaned her head to one side, her gaze questioning.

Jackson moved closer toward the desk, his eyes still on that bag. "Meg isn't here, is she?"

"Our sales director?"

He flipped a look her way. "Yes." He pointed at the bags behind the desk. "That looks like her luggage."

"She popped in for a few minutes. She's out looking for Lucky. Something about the travel group coming in next week."

He peered down the hall, craning his neck. "Really?" *Was she serious?* He caught Gracie's eye again. "Listen, I'm going to go find her. When Pepper gets back, I'd like you to tell her to wait here. Will you do that for me?"

"Absolutely. I'm on it."

"Thanks." Jackson hurried down the hall toward the sales office. He pictured her, a light against the day's grey sky, and longing knit its way through him. He had told her not to come. Said he would fire her. He bit back a groan. When he did find her, he didn't know whether he would chew her out or pull her into a long, deep kiss.

He reached the sales office and ducked inside. Empty. Maybe she and Lucky were walking the small inn's meeting space, which was in the building across the path. He stood in the sales office a few seconds, debating. He was about to give up and head back to the lobby to continue his discussion with Pepper when Lucky turned the corner.

She startled. "Hey, Jackson. You scared me. Why are you in the dark?"

"Isn't Meg with you?"

She frowned. "No. Is she supposed to be?"

He glanced around, trying to keep his expression neutral. "Gracie said something about Meg being here and looking for you."

Lucky brightened. "Well, halleluiah! I didn't think she would be here today, but I could really use her help with the tour coming in next week. I have a million and one questions for her—not to mention seating and space charts to slice and dice."

He nodded, his mind far away. "Great."

She set a stack of files on one of the desks. "She probably went over to check out who's using our pool view space—you know how she is about that! When you see her, will you let her know I'll be over after I email a signed contract to a client?"

"Yeah," he said, his heart beginning to thump noticeably. "Sure. See you later."

He headed back down the hall and through the door leading outside. Despite the muggy gulf weather, Jackson walked as quickly as he could toward the pool area. No Meg there either. He flicked a look at his phone, noting the time, and bit back a curse.

He hustled back to the lobby area. When he returned, Gracie was beginning to check in a guest.

When the new arrival had gone to her room, Jackson asked, "Where's Pepper?"

Gracie frowned. "Still haven't seen her."

Jackson stepped closer. "And Meg? Did she return?"

"No. Strange. I was thinking, though, that maybe she'd like to stay? Two guys checked out of her usual suite." She leaned forward, her voice low. "And not a second too soon, if you ask me."

Uncomfortable heat crept up his neck, like illness. "Gracie, I need you to do me a favor and pop your head into the women's restroom to remind Pepper that I'm waiting for her."

She blanched. He'd made her uncomfortable.

"I'll watch the desk," he said. "Please go now." He tapped his fingers on the desk. Meg was here somewhere—but where? And why had she come even though he'd warned her not to? He scowled. Pepper was obviously avoiding him, but he had no time for games. He pulled out his phone, punched in Meg's number, and listened to it go to voicemail.

Gracie strode back to the desk, breathless. "Sorry, no Pepper in there."

He straightened. "What? Are you sure?"

She nodded vigorously. "Yes, Jackson. I checked everywhere. She's not inside."

That heat in his neck spread through his face, his head. Thoughts in his mind tripped over each other. Pepper had disappeared. Meg was nowhere to be found.

He clenched a fist and his mind searched for explanations. He snapped a look up at Gracie. "What did you say about those two guys?"

"Two guys?"

He made a rolling gesture with his finger. "The two guys ... the ones who checked out. When did they leave?"

"Oh them. Let's see. I think it was when you and Pepper were on your tour. They were in here when Meg dropped off her things."

His fist collided with the desk, his mind wild. "Give me the key to the suite they were staying in."

"Yes, of course." She nodded her head vigorously, ran a key through the reader, and handed it to him.

He raced to the upstairs suite, the one on the top floor with a view of the gulf. His heart clenched in his chest as he slid the key into the lock. He threw open the door and lunged inside. "Meg!"

No response. He searched every corner of the space, but no

one was inside. His breaths rattled his chest, fear ricocheting in his gut. He wracked his brain. Had Pepper simply gone to her meeting with her real estate agent? A daunting fear resurfaced, the one that had clung to him ever since Thomas told him about seeing that drone dive-bombing Meg on the beach.

Jackson sped down the hall to his room. With building dread, he fired up his computer and drummed his fingers on the guest room desk. "Come on, come on." He signed in and went to Pepper's email, then clicked on her sent file. Why had he not thought to look there before? He scrolled and scrolled, looking for anything that could help him figure out if Pepper had been communicating with Meg. He stopped. An email with an attachment had been sent to Power Financial. With one click, he opened the attachment and groaned.

Pepper had sent them his Power of Attorney—and had forged his signature.

He spun around and pulled the file of evidence he had been compiling against Pepper and found the ticket in her name to Miami. He could not imagine anyone boarding a cruise ship on a day like today. If not a cruise, why go there? His only connection with Miami was ... Power Financial.

With an aggressive groan, Jackson tore back downstairs until a text popped up on his phone that stopped him cold.

MEG SPOTTED Pepper in a group at the far end of the massive parking lot of the Sea Castle. She jogged after them. "I want to talk to you!"

Pepper stopped. She swiveled around, two jagged fists slicing into her waistline, and glowered at Meg. "Look what trouble you have caused."

Pepper had picked up an entourage somewhere. The two men at her sides, one with a dirty blond goatee and the other with unwashed bleached locks, might have passed for surfers if not for the scowls they wore. Meg ignored them. "Where are you headed?"

"That is none of your concern." Pepper spun back around and the three of them continued toward the far end of the lot.

"I know about your meeting today."

All three stopped. Pepper pivoted, her white-blonde hair fanning around her like a shawl. "Excuse me?"

"I know you're planning to meet with Jackson's financial advisors."

She narrowed her eyes at Meg. "You mean *our* financial advisors."

"Well, if you were Jackson's real sister, then that would make sense. How did you pull it off, Sophia—or whatever your real name is?"

One of the men stepped forward but Pepper shot an arm out to stop him. "Well. I always knew that you might figure it out. Though it took much longer than even I had imagined."

"Why? Why did you do it?"

Pepper scoffed. "My life is none of your concern."

"It is when you hurt the people I care about."

One of Pepper's brows jutted toward the sky. "Like Jackson?"

Meg looked away. She'd walked right into that one. She swung a look back. "So it's true then? All this time you were pretending to be William's daughter. What an awful thing to do. He was a good man and all he ever wanted was to do right by his children."

Pepper swore. She crossed her arms in front of her torso. The men beside her shifted, yet said nothing. "This is one of the reasons I wanted you out of the way—you are too much of a busybody. If not for you and your little trip to Italy, this would all be over."

Meg searched her mind. How in the world could this be her fault? People unwilling to own up to their crimes always seem to blame others.

"I had *everything* under control, you know. Although you did not make it easy for me." Pepper glanced toward the taller of the two men at her side, the one with the grim mouth and unblinking eyes, as if speaking with a cohort. "This one kept me on my toes. I had to work hard to chip away at her Mother Teresa image in the company."

"Like blaming my mother and me for the company's mysterious lack of funds?"

Pepper let out a bitter laugh. "What a fortuitous find, that was. My sister's brother was so heartbroken to find out about your lie."

Sister's brother? The woman in the photo was *this* Pepper's sister? "So … you're the half-sister of the real Sophia?"

Pepper dipped her chin, her mouth curled into a sarcastic smirk. "Don't play dumb with me, Meg. I know that you know—that is why you sought Sophia's birth certificate when you were in Italy, is it not? We have friends who keep us informed of such things."

Meg kept her expression noncommittal. Something told her Domenic and Jackson must have been looking for proof. Unfortunately, she'd been taken out of that loop. "What have you done with the real Sophia?"

She scoffed again and unhooked her arms, brushing at the air with a dismissive hand. "I did not have to do anything with her. She's a quiet mouse, that one, always doing her fashion." She paused. "Of course, now that she's making some kind of name for herself I could not continue with my …"

"Impersonation?"

Pepper pierced her with a stare. "Call it what you will."

"I see. So, the real Sophia is an up-and-coming fashion designer. And that made you nervous."

"All she's ever wanted to do was sew clothes in her hovel. But now her clothes show up in New York, of all places! I was surprised to see her name talked about there—obviously, there is no accounting for taste these days."

The chin quiver, the unease in her jaw line. Though Pepper's words were filled with bravado, her world had sprung a leak that could not be fixed with needle and thread.

Meg shifted forward and the goateed guy stepped forward in warning. She slid an uneasy look at the men who stood next to Pepper like bodyguards and said, "You got greedy."

"Not greed," she hissed. "Preservation."

Silence.

Pepper's eyes twitched. *Preservation.* Had she been in trouble before all of this? Realization rolled through Meg, like a hundred light bulbs going on all around her. The "money train" had dried up at Riley Holdings. They'd all felt it. When Pepper laid into her one day about the money train ending, it was more about her own troubles—not Meg's manufactured part in it all.

Hence, the reason for Pepper's sudden desire to be involved with Jackson's negotiations with the investment team.

"So help me to understand all this ... taking on your sister's persona was a way to pay a debt?"

Pepper gave Meg a haughty look. "Such a genius you are. If not for so many delays, I would have already been on an airplane. Now, we drive."

"No way. You're not going anywhere." Meg felt for the phone in her pocket and immediately regretted it.

The goateed guy lurched forward. "Give me the phone."

She pivoted as if to leave, but he grabbed her forearm. When she tried to twist away, he tightened his grip until the pounding of her heart reached the base of her throat.

The other bodyguard stepped forward, his head the shape of a block. His tiny eyes speared her.

She looked at Pepper, incredulous.

"Give him the phone or he will take it from you."

Meg handed it to the goateed guy.

"Open it," he said, holding it up for her to see.

She typed the unlock code onto the screen. He ran his filthy fingers all over it, his blotchy cheeks pulled into a smile. Pepper watched over his shoulder. He was texting someone, and she dared to guess who. Meg's stomach roiled. She realized, with sickening regret, that Jackson had been right to warn her to stay away. How had he known about Pepper's dangerous side?

He twirled her phone in his hand, then turned and pitched it into a distant, murky field. She winced. If she were at home in California, she might have gone in search for it once they had left. But this was Florida and she didn't care to be an alligator's lunch.

"Jackson would never consent to you accepting money on his behalf."

"I don't need his approval, not with the Power of Attorney I obtained."

No. Had Jackson given her one when he had been traveling in Italy? She couldn't imagine why he would … "But Jackson's not in Italy anymore," she blurted. "He's back home, in California. No way would it be accepted."

"In California?" Pepper's smile held something sinister in it. Had she not realized Jackson had returned to the States? "Well," she said, "Power Financial certainly doesn't know that—or need to. And if you want your boyfriend to stay safe, you will keep it to yourself as well."

The goateed guy seized Meg by the arm. She jerked backward, unable to wrench free.

Pepper held up a warning hand in his direction. "She'll only be in our way." She focused her steely eyes on Meg now. "We are going to leave now and you are not going to say a thing to anyone about this. Are we clear?"

Meg pulled her arm free. "I've no one to tell." Her phone was gone and Jackson was across the country. She would try to reach him, but would he even take her call?

Pepper smirked. "That's what I thought." With nothing more, she and the two surfer "thugs" jumped into a black SUV and took off in a hurry.

Meg watched them go. If Power Financial believed that

Jackson had consented to release thousands of dollars to Pepper, who would then turn it over to those thugs, he would lose everything. Her insides crushed at the thought. Meg's eyes zeroed in on the empty field knowing she had to warn Jackson somehow. He couldn't lose everything because of her.

CHAPTER 24

Jackson paced the lobby of the inn, his phone stuck to his ear, Lucky watching him with concern on her face. "No, I don't believe she went willingly," he was saying to the officer on the other end of the line.

"Is it possible, sir, that your girlfriend does not want to be found?"

What kind of question was that? If he clutched his phone any tighter it very well might shatter in his hands. Meg had been here —but now she was nowhere to be found. Neither was Pepper or the nefarious characters that had been lurking around. He and Lucky had searched the buildings and the paths in between. His gut squeezed. *What did her text mean?*

"Jackson?"

His chin jerked toward the entrance to the inn. Meg stood in the lobby, her face flushed, that beautiful head of hair in disarray. He dropped his phone and ran to her, wrapping his arms around her in a frenzied hug.

"I-I can't believe you're here," she kept saying into his ear.

He pulled back, searching her face where splotches of dirt marred her cheeks. "What happened to you?"

She licked her lips. "I-I confronted Pepper ... she's stealing from you." She wrenched away and headed toward the door. "You have to go after her."

"Wait. Hold on. What do you mean you confronted Pepper?" He wagged his head, realization flowing over him. Meg had taken things into her own hands, and by the looks of things, had narrowly escaped trouble. "I told you not to come here."

"I had to come. She's headed to Miami … to see your investors. I wanted to stop her—I had no idea you were here." She paused. "When did you get here?"

Jackson searched her face, confused. "Then why the text telling me to come home? That you had something important to show me?"

She placed both palms on either side of her face and shut her eyes. "That wasn't me. He … the guy took my phone."

Gently, Jackson pulled one of her hands from where she pressed it against the side of her face. He lowered his voice. "Meg, did someone hurt you?"

She refused to meet his eyes. "No. I'm confused. Overwhelmed." She lifted her chin. "You and I aren't speaking, remember?"

He watched her. "Meg, what happened?"

Lucky approached them, quietly.

Meg's eyes darted around the room. She swallowed before looking levelly at him. "Pepper and two guys are on their way to Power Financial. They have an appointment at 4:30 p.m." She lowered her voice to a whisper. "Almost took me with them."

Jackson swung a look at Lucky. "What's the fastest way to get to Miami?"

Lucky's face lit up. "I have an idea."

LUCKY SCREECHED to a stop near the hangar. She pointed to a small plane in the distance. "There. That's my brother's plane. Let's go."

Jackson put his hand out to stop her. "No, Lucky. Stay behind. I don't want to put you in danger too."

But Lucky was already out of the car, a bag slung over her shoulder. "You guys need me. I know people all over this state."

He shook his head.

She set her jaw. "Are you a praying man?"

"Not like I should be."

"Well, you'd better start. C'mon. I'm all prayed up and it's decided—I'm not staying here."

He swiveled a look at Meg who had also hopped out, her own jaw set, a fire in her eyes. "What is it with all these stubborn women in my life?"

"We need to stop her, Jackson."

Lucky climbed into the plane first, followed by Meg, and then Jackson.

Lucky's brother, Brian, nodded. "Ready to go?"

Jackson gave him a thumbs-up and they were off.

Lucky leaned toward him, speaking loud enough for both Jackson and Meg to hear. "I called my friend at the hotel where Pepper's supposedly staying. She hasn't checked in."

"I doubt she has plans to do that now," Meg said. "She seemed pretty resolute about carrying out her plan."

"About that. I'm not sure that Pepper went willingly. Those guys gave us all the willies—even her."

Jackson said, "You think she was afraid of them?"

"Maybe. Kicking myself for not paying better attention to those turds. Hang on—I got a text." She glanced down at her phone. "Yes! The police have agreed to send officers to investigate."

Meg spoke up. "I saw it too."

Jackson frowned. "Saw what?"

Her face darkened. "Fear. She spoke to me with a lot of bravado, cocky as usual. But … I don't know. Sometimes she wouldn't meet my eyes and I wondered if it was all put on."

Lucky tilted her head to the side. "You think she had gotten herself into some kind of trouble?"

Meg stayed quiet a moment and peered at Jackson.

He eyed her. "What is it?"

"Do you know who she is?"

He pressed his lips together and nodded.

She let out a breath of relief. "Oh thank goodness. She told me she was Sophia's half-sister. I'm so sorry, Jackson."

Lucky frowned, looking from Meg to Jackson and back again. "She's … who?"

Jackson exhaled. "Pepper's an imposter. She's been pretending to be my sister, when she's actually the half-sister of the real Sophia. How's that for a twist? Pepper's just a nickname."

Lucky whistled, her forehead wrinkled like a Shar Pei.

"I spoke to Sophia the other night." Jackson remembered the concern in his sister's voice, the way she had warned him. "I think you are both right. Sophia told me that Pepper—her real name is Gia—had always associated with pretty bad people. So much so that she'd been hiding from her for years."

"That must be how she got away with this ruse for so long," Meg said.

Jackson nodded, his mouth a grim line. "My guess is that she owes those guys, or their network, money. A lot of it."

Lucky smirked. "And she figured out you would be the perfect source to pay them back. Wow. Good thing we're on our way to stop that now."

Jackson glanced out the window. His calls to authorities at home had told him he would need proof—which he had been working on. But he had received an even worse response when he had called the finance company.

"I'm sorry, Mr. Riley," Sarah had said, "but there's nothing I can do. Mr. Ulrick is traveling in Europe and has already authorized release of the funds."

He kept this information from Meg, though relief at the possibility that help was on its way helped to steady him. He only hoped they wouldn't be too late.

Brian dropped them off at the airport. As his sister leapt onto the tarmac, he called out, "Steer clear of trouble. I'm serious."

She saluted him. "Don't worry! The police are on their way. I'm just here for moral support."

Jackson shouted his thanks again and squeezed Meg's hand. "I'll go rent us a car." A short while later he drove as Lucky navigated through the busy streets of Miami.

The office building housing Power Financial sat on a corner shrouded by trees and hedges shaped into rectangles. The parking lot surrounded the building on three sides, with the entrance on one side and the exit on the other. He pulled into a space at the end of the parking lot, close enough to see the front door, but far enough away not to be noticed. No sign of the police.

"It's almost 4:30, boss," Lucky said. "I don't see a squad car … I'll text my contact at the station."

He nodded, his eyes laser focused on the front drive.

"Maybe we should just go inside and wait for them to show up," Meg whispered.

Jackson turned to her. "Not you. You're not going anywhere."

"Jackson, I can help you! You said yourself that the authorities will need proof of who you are. Let me be your proof."

He brushed his eyes over her. He wanted nothing more than for her to be by his side. But not today. Not now. He'd relented in allowing her to join him here, and part of that was selfishness on his part—he had wanted to keep an eye on her, to protect her. Too much had happened already to tear them apart and he wasn't about to allow anything worse to come between them.

A dark Cadillac Escalade turned into the driveway and double parked near the exit. Heavily tinted windows made it almost impossible to see inside. An unmarked police car, perhaps?

Meg sucked in a breath. "We're too late."

The passenger-side door swung open and stayed that way. A heeled foot hit the ground, then the other. Pepper.

"It's them, boss!" Lucky said.

Jackson cracked open his door and slipped out, watching the vehicle. The back door of the SUV opened and a slim man with a goatee jumped out and sidled up next to Pepper.

"The driver's still behind the wheel," Meg said, her voice tinged with fear.

"Where are the police?" he growled. "Lucky, text your contact again."

He glanced around the other side of the building where the street met the driveway. If he could walk around that way unnoticed, he would be able to reach the front door from behind the SUV, hopefully without the driver seeing him. Then he'd wait there for the police to show.

He threw a look over his shoulder. "Stay safe. I'm going to walk around the building and wait."

"I'm going with you," Meg said.

He whipped her a dangerous look. "Don't fight me on this."

She leveled her gaze at him. "You need me. If the police don't show or don't believe you, you'll need me to help convince Sarah who you are. I spoke with her on the phone. Trust me when I say I can sweet talk her out of doing anything stupid."

She had a point. Meg had always been the one for the sales team to call on when client issues arose. Even the angriest or most annoying clients didn't seem to faze her.

"Fine," he growled. "But stay behind me."

"Yes, Mr. Riley."

He quirked a half-smile at her then ducked behind the hedges with her following close behind. He held her hand as they made their way out onto the sidewalk. They rounded the corner, then crept slowly toward the front section of the building where Pepper no doubt waited for her afternoon meeting with his financial investors. *Where were the police?*

Steps from the front of the building now, they heard Pepper's whine. "The door won't open—why won't the door open?"

"Try it again," their companion snarled.

Jackson scanned the street for any sign of the police. Nothing.

Meg squeezed his hand. "Maybe your call made Sarah wary. Did she mention anything about closing early?"

He shook his head tightly. Had they come here for no reason? A stream of relief began to fill him.

"This is bull," their companion said. He pounded his fist on the door. "Hey, open up!"

A compact car pulled into the lot and parked in front. A young woman with flyaway blonde hair dashed out of the car, a to-go coffee and a set of keys in her hand. "Sorry, everyone. I just ran out for a break."

Jackson pushed Meg toward the street. "Let's go back."

"Jackson!" Pepper's shriek split the air. She had caught sight of him and jabbed a fist into her waist. "What are you doing here?"

The goateed guy came around the corner, his expression menacing.

Jackson pushed Meg farther behind him. "Stay put," he whispered. He strolled toward them, as if his presence was expected, hoping the sweat under his arms did not leak through his shirt. He kept his expression benign. "It's over, Gia."

The woman with the coffee and keys stopped, her mouth open as if in surprise. Her eyes shifted from person to person and she made no move to open the door.

"What're you waiting for?" Pepper's companion said. "Open the door."

Her eyebrows pulled together. "I-I'm sorry. But are you all with Riley Holdings?"

"Yes, we are," Pepper said. "Are you Sarah?"

"Yes, ma'am."

"We are short on time, Sarah. If you would be so kind as to

complete our transaction now, then we'll be out of your hair shortly."

He'd never heard Pepper sound so … so decent, making him all the more aware of her many talents.

Sarah held her keys like a weapon now and kept her voice steady. "I'm sorry, but I'm going to need more information from all parties before completing the paperwork."

"What do you mean?"

Sarah's eyes met Jackson's. "I, well, I understand there's some concern—"

"There's no concern, honey," the guy with the goatee said. He reached for her keys. "May I?"

Jackson stepped toward the door, eyeing the guy. "She said there would be no meeting today."

As the guy narrowed his eyes at Jackson, he detected a movement in his peripheral. Pepper had spun around and headed for the waiting SUV. Probably realized her plan had been foiled. Another movement caught his attention. Meg was heading for Pepper …

He spun around. "Wait!"

He wasn't fast enough. The driver of the car reached across the seat and yanked Meg into the SUV with one arm and pulled the door shut.

Jackson body slammed the vehicle, the sound of Meg's screams penetrating his marrow. The driver gunned the SUV and pulled it into gear. Someone hooked him from behind, pulling him back, but he twisted free. The SUV was getting away!

The driver rounded the corner of the building, then stopped. Blocked. Jackson tore after him. That's when he spotted Lucky, who had pulled the rental car out of its parking space and blocked the exit. He doubled his speed, vaguely aware of sirens. The SUV backed up, cranked a U-turn, and barreled for him.

He waved his hands in front of the speeding vehicle, then gestured to Meg to grab the steering wheel. *You can do it, Meg,* he implored. He would not allow him to get away with Meg inside—he could not! The sirens grew louder. The driver slowed at first, then accelerated. Jackson rushed the vehicle with one goal in mind, concern for his bodily welfare thoroughly suspended. A scream. The sickening crush of bones.

All fear taken from him in one mighty force.

MEG WATCHED in horror as the SUV she was trapped in barreled toward Jackson. *No! Get out of the way!* She rattled the door handle again, but the driver kept locking her in.

"Knock it off," he said. "Sit back and watch me run over your idiot boyfriend."

He smelled of bacon and cigarettes, causing her stomach to clench. Being kidnapped could cause that too. "Jackson, stop!"

Sirens swam in the air around them. The driver slowed, squinting through the windshield. "What the—"

"Just stop," she begged. "The police will be easier on you if you surrender now."

He peeled a sideways glance at her, one lip curled in disgust. "So they're going to be easy on me, huh? And you know all about this, huh?"

She shrank back. What she had mistaken for fear in his eyes over the sirens was something else: adrenaline. The presence of police had done nothing to dissuade this man's criminal intent. He snorted in defiance, revving the engine as proof, taking pleasure in taunting her.

Jackson, too, showed no sign of slowing down. He waved his hands in front of the SUV, even as it barreled toward him. "Jackson, no," she whimpered, petrified for his life.

The driver hooted with laughter. Jackson continued to run toward them. Arms in the air, he rolled his hands into fists, then bent forward like a ram, intent on stopping them at all costs. The driver accelerated.

Meg gasped. "Lord, please help us." She threw herself at the steering wheel, yanking it hard. The vehicle shuddered after a thud.

The driver swore at her and with one strong arm threw Meg against the passenger door. She struggled to breathe, but whipped a look out the window and froze. Jackson was on the ground, unmoving. Fresh emotion escalated within her. The driver wore a satisfied look on his face, as if he'd done what he came to do.

She rose up on her knees, unwilling to let him conquer and win. With newfound strength, Meg clocked the driver on the chin, wounding her fist. As he swore and struggled to recover control of the vehicle, Meg swung her door open and rolled out onto the pavement, landing with enough force to make even the smallest breath impossible.

CHAPTER 25

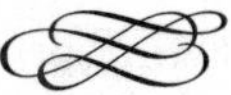

She awoke to the cacophony of hushed voices and footsteps followed by silence. Meg opened her eyes and tried to sit up. "Oh …." Pain pulsed throughout her head.

"After that Wonder Woman move of yours, I can't believe you only have a shoulder injury." Lucky moved closer to the hospital bed. "How are you feeling?"

The inside of her mouth felt web-like, as if draped in cotton. "Jaah … son." She tried again to ask about him. "Where is … Jack-son?"

Lucky frowned. "You sound funny. Let me get you some water."

Meg's arm shot out to grab Lucky's wrist. "Where … is … he?"

"Jackson?" Lucky chuckled. "A couple of rooms down. They're just keeping you guys here to make sure you don't have concussions." She brought a cup over and pointed the bent straw toward Meg. "Sip."

He's alive! Relief cascaded over. She drank the water, then pulled herself up to a sitting position. "I want to see him."

"Speaking of super heroes, first he tries to stop a moving vehicle, gets clipped by it, then bounces back up and throws himself on top of you."

"He did?"

"Yeah. After you landed on the ground." Lucky's face turned serious. "After you escaped, the driver lost control. Jackson took advantage of that! I've never seen an injured man move so fast in my life. He threw himself on top of you, then rolled you out of the way—straight out of a movie." She nodded to her shoulder. "Probably got an extra bruise or two, but heck, it's better than the alternative, right?"

"He saved me from being hit?"

Lucky nodded. "Somebody was protecting you, all right."

"And Pepper?"

"Arrested. Along with those two losers who kidnapped you. Turns out you guys were right: Pepper owed them a lot of money." She paused. "Is it really true that she's not even Jackson's sister?"

Meg exhaled. She'd woken up to the best news she could have possibly received. She nodded at Lucky.

"She is definitely *not* my sister." Jackson appeared in the doorway, seated in a wheelchair. "By the way, I've already called Trace and asked her to scrounge up a matched set of wheels for us at the inn."

One look at the battered man, his arm in a sling, dried blood still on his face, and she melted. A sense of déjà vu passed over her as his eyes bored into hers. Lucky stepped away so he could roll closer to her bed. He reached out and took her hand in his, those green eyes stroking her like a caress.

"It's over, Meg."

She nodded.

A sheen dropped across his eyes. "This entire mess—Pepper's deception, the stealing ... the dangerous people—they are all gone. The authorities will deal with them now."

She blurted a sob and covered her mouth with one hand as Jackson cradled her other in his.

Lucky cleared her throat, catching Meg's attention—barely. The sales manager from Sea Castle mouthed, "I'll be outside," then disappeared from the room.

"Hey," he said, calming her. "Never again will we let someone get between us. Pepper instigated much of the friction between you and me and we fell for it." He leaned his elbows on her bed and left his chair behind, his beautifully battered face close enough for her to taste his breath on her lips. "I promise you. Never again."

That sense of déjà vu rose in her again. She closed her eyes, remembering. "You were whispering to me, weren't you? When we were on the ground?"

He inhaled roughly. "I was … had to keep you awake, my love." He hung his head. "I don't know what I would have done if I'd lost you."

She touched his grizzled face with her hands then leaned her forehead onto his. "I'm crazy about you."

"I know."

She laughed, tears rolling down her face as she pulled back. "What do you mean, you know?"

Jackson's laughter sprang to life, followed by deep wincing.

"Oh no. I'm sorry." She dipped her chin, frowning. "It's not a cliché, is it? It really does hurt to laugh."

He chortled. "Stop. You're killing me."

"Don't ever say that."

His smile evaporated. He took her fingers in his hands and pressed them to his lips one by one, the scrape of fresh whiskers comforting her with each and every kiss.

CHAPTER 26

Two months later

MEG PACED the hospital's linoleum-lined hall, tears still fresh in her eyes.

Jackson's husky voice interrupted her thoughts as he jogged down the corridor toward her, his hands full. "Is she okay? Is … everyone okay?"

Meg threw her arms around him and held on tight. "Yes! Liddy's great—and Beau Jr. is absolutely gorgeous!" She pulled away, sniffling, and glanced at the stuffed animal with the floppy ears in Jackson's hand. "Who's this?"

He gave her a sheepish grin. "A bunny … for the baby."

She laughed now and threw her arms around his neck, staring up at him. "You are the sweetest."

He grinned. "I bet you say that to all the bunny-toting men you meet."

Behind them, someone cleared their throat.

They both swung around to find Beau standing there with a

smile as wide as the sea. Jackson stuck out his hand. "Congratulations, Dad!"

Beau shook his hand heartily. "Thanks! Best day of my life. I'm just out here trying to find a signal for my phone. Time to call the grandparents."

"Here," Jackson said, and handed Beau a box. "For later."

Meg groaned. "Cigars? Really?" She shook her head, cracking up. "Will Ricky and Fred be showing up soon, too?"

Beau reached for the box and gave Meg a sympathetic smile. "Sorry. It's tradition." He turned back to Jackson. "Thanks for these. I'll share one with you later. I have to run now, but the nurse will be bringing the baby back to Liddy soon. Sticking around?"

Jackson slid an arm around Meg. "Wouldn't miss it."

After he'd gone, they walked down the hall, stopping at the nursery viewing area where two babies slept in their bassinets. They watched the tiny peaceful faces in silence until Jackson finally said, "I have more good news to give you today."

"Tell me."

"Well, it's nothing as spectacular as new life," he said. "But … since fraud has been proven and Pepper's in jail, the credit card company has agreed to refund all the money she stole from us."

Meg gasped, squealed, and turned toward him, pressing two fists together. "This … this is a miracle! I can't believe it."

He nodded. "This will give us time to start over in so many ways. I can't wait to call Sophia with this news. Her heart was so broken over all that transpired."

"I am so happy for you both."

"For us, you mean."

"Well, yes. For you and Sophia and the staff at the inns. So much to look forward to."

He moved closer to her, his grin slightly devilish.

She quirked a smile at him. "What?"

He reached for her, cradling her face in his hands until their eyes were inches apart. "I said 'for us' and I meant it. Care to cap this great day off by making me the happiest man to walk the planet?"

A rush of fresh tears filled her eyes, and her voice teased. "Whatever do you mean?"

He kissed her forehead, then rested his face against hers, their noses touching. "Marry me," he whispered.

She smiled, closed her eyes, and gave him her answer.

EPILOGUE

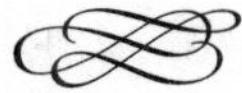

"I'm so happy that you decided not to get married in a suit." Deena fussed with wavy strands of hair that cascaded down Meg's collarbones. "This gown is lovely."

Liddy leaned her head onto Deena's shoulder and smiled at her best friend, a vision of silk and beaded pearls. "You make a beautiful bride, Meggy. Sorry I'll be so fat in your photos."

"Would you both please stop? Liddy, you've lost your baby weight already!" The light in Meg's eyes belied her scolding tone. She jiggled her perspiring hands in the air to cool them off. "I'm so nervous."

"You should be," Trace said, a blue garter dangling from her forefinger. "Talk about catching a big fish. Jackson's man-o-licious, if you ask me. You'll want to work out just to keep up with all that gorgeousness. And learn about facial peels, too. Good thing the spa is in the works."

Deena cocked her head at Trace, her eyes squinting. She made a sweeping motion with her hand.

"Oh please. Jackson can't take his eyes off you, Meg—and he never will." Liddy's usually teasing voice caught, and her voice lowered to a cracked whisper. "I've never seen a man more in love." She smiled wide, but her eyes glimmered. "Well, other than my Beau."

At a knock on the door, all four women looked up. Lucky peered in. "Okay if I join your party?"

Meg's chest squeezed, lingering thankfulness for the woman who'd proven she was much more than her name. She held out her hands. "Get in here, my friend."

Lucky rushed in and took both of Meg's hands in hers, standing back to assess. "Woo! You clean up well! Makes me almost want to get married someday."

Peels of giggles and laughter filled the bridal suite at Sea Glass Inn. How often had she spent the night as manager-on-duty in a suite like this, one hand on her phone in case an emergency occurred in the middle of the night? That kind of stress had been replaced with a joy unfolding. She gazed at the treasured sea through imposing windows, sparkle and light reflecting on the tide. She'd always been too practical for fairy-tales—until she took a starring role in this one.

Liddy turned to Lucky. "Is everyone here?"

"That's what I came to say. Yes, everyone."

One of Meg's brows rose.

"Yes! Sophia is here!" Lucky gushed. "I know that's what you were wondering."

Meg clasped her hands beneath her chin and turned to Liddy, smiling. "I'm ready now. You?"

Her best friend and matron of honor pulled her in close and kissed her on the cheek. "Are you kidding? I've been praying for this day for years." She fanned herself with her hand. "Oh my gosh. Now let's get out there before all of my makeup's gone and my milk lets down."

On their way to find their seats, Lucky and Trace ushered Liddy to her place at the back of the small chapel, the first of many upgrades to Sea Glass Inn. As the first notes of piano music played, Deena turned to her daughter. Her mother's expression resonated with love and warmth, like she had never seen. "Before we go, I'd like you to carry this," her mother said, a vibrant purple hanky in her hand. "It was your father's."

Meg's eyes filled for the umpteenth time and her hands reached out. "Daddy's?"

"Yes. He wore it at our wedding and I've held onto it all these years. It's your 'something borrowed,' but you can keep it."

Meg was overcome. She took the silk handkerchief and rubbed it between her thumb and forefinger, memorizing its softness. She tucked it into her sleeve, wanting to keep this reminder of her father close. In the months since returning to the inn, Meg had gained years' worth of memories about her father. He'd been a kind and giving man, unlike the impression her mother's lack of photos and mention of him all those years had given her.

"His passing was always too difficult for me to talk about," her mother had explained. "I had no idea, though, that my silence had shaped your memories of the man he was."

The first few notes of *Pachelbel's Canon* played. Meg dried her tears and touched her sleeve, the one holding a piece of her father, to her heart. She offered her arm to her mother, who gently slipped her hand through it.

"Ready?" Deena asked.

Meg answered, "More than ever."

JACKSON CLOSED his hand tighter around Meg's, a part of him confirming the reality of this magical night. Meg had married him —Jackson Riley—and not a thing existed that could wipe the goofy smile from his face.

He led her around the dance floor, thankful for more than his mind could fathom, beginning with a father who had longed to prepare him for life and love. Jackson had been young and impetuous, unready to lead. His father had known this, and in his own gentle, prodding love for his son, had sent him away to save him from his own destruction. Now, he knew, he was ready.

He brought their entwined hands to his mouth and kissed her fingers. "I suppose we'll have to dance with others now." He longed to stay in this embrace, surrounded by a melody.

Her dark eyes captivated him. "Only for tonight. After this, every dance is mine. Promise?"

"I promise."

The music changed and he felt a tap on his shoulder. "May I cut in?"

Sophia.

Jackson kissed his bride, who turned to dance with Liddy's husband, Beau. Then he took Sophia's hand and whirled her around.

She threw back her chin and laughed, and in her eyes he saw their father smiling back at him. For a moment, regret traversed through him, but he refused to let it linger. She was here now, on the most important day of his life. They were family. How could he have regrets?

"She is lovely," Sophia said with a nod in his bride's direction. "You have been blessed."

"Yes. Very blessed. And also to have you here. Thank you for coming all this way, Sophia."

"I would not have missed it for the world." She began to blink, those meadow-colored eyes pooling with tears. "Thank you for finding me … for not giving up."

"I, too, am grateful to have found you—and for all the catching up we will do for the rest of our lives."

She smiled at him, his big sister who seemed barely so. She was delicate, almost fragile, and Jackson became infused with the desire to protect her from further harm.

"I've been thinking," she said. "I have never spent much time on the west coast."

"Are you thinking of relocating? You know ... as I've told you, the door is always open for you here."

She nodded once, in that graceful way of hers. "And I have taken that to heart."

In a rush of brotherly love, he pulled her close and squeezed her in a hug. As the song ended, Meg joined them. She embraced Sophia, who was about to dance away with a new partner. "I am so excited to finally have a sister," Meg whispered.

Sophia hugged her back. "You do not know how deeply I have longed to hear that."

Seconds later, Meg was back in Jackson's arms. He cinched her close, possessively, and breathed her in. He spoke into her ear, "I love you, Mrs. Riley."

Her laughter, like bubbles, tickled his earlobe. "And I love you back, Mr. Riley."

He twirled her around, thankful to those who had gone before them and for all that was yet to be.

ACKNOWLEDGMENTS

Thank you very much, Readers, for picking up this second book in the Sea Glass Inn novel series. I hope you enjoyed this story (and a bit of travel as you read!). I would like to offer you a free story to read either on your computer or e-reader. You can download the story here: www.juliecarobini.com/free-book

And if you have a minute, please consider leaving a review of *Runaway Tide* at your favorite online bookstore.

Many thanks also to:

My beta readers Diana Lesire Brandmeyer, Carrie Padgett, and Jennifer Vander Klipp for your insightful, kind, and honest feedback; Lauren Upshaw for graciously sharing your foot injury details with me; and Denise Harmer for your thoughtful editing.

Dan Carobini, for everything you do to encourage and love me through the writing process. Love you back. Thank you for taking me to Italy!

My kids, Matt, Angie, Emma; and my parents, Dan and Elaine—for your constant cheerleading. Angie, special thanks to you for helping me with Italian.

Tracy Higley at Stonewater Books for your support of this novel, and Brandilyn Collins for your tireless efforts toward helping readers and authors find each other.

And the Lord, for lifting my head and inspiring me to write every time I became overwhelmed.